COZY

COZY

PARNELL HALL

An Otto Penzler Book

ORION

First published in Great Britain in 2002
by Orion,
an imprint of the Orion Publishing Group Ltd.
Published by arrangement with
Carrol & Graf Publishers, Inc., New York.

A CIP catalogue record for this book
is available from the British Library.

ISBN 0 75285 303 1 (trade paperback)
0 75285 302 3 (hardback)

Printed in Great Britain by
Clays Ltd, St Ives plc

The Orion Publishing Group Ltd
Orion House
5 Upper Saint Martin's Lane
London, WC2H 9EA

FOR JIM AND FRANNY

ONE

"I MISS HIM already."

Oh, dear.

It was not five minutes since we'd dropped Tommie off at sleep-away camp, and Alice missed him already.

Which is not surprising. This marked the first time Tommie'd been away from home. Oh, he'd been to camp before, but that was day camp in Riverdale, not ten minutes out of New York City. Camp Keewaydin was a good six-hour drive, and he was staying eight full weeks.

The camp was located on Lake Dunmore in Vermont, and a more idyllic setting would be hard to find. Tommie's platform tent, in which he would be living with a counselor and three other campers, was just behind the backstop of a baseball diamond. Right across the lawn were the clay tennis courts and all-dirt basketball court, which would become mud holes the first time it rained, doubtlessly to the delight of all; the outdoor boxing ring, which I hoped Tommie would have the good sense not to enter; the wooden footbridge over the road to the riflery and archery ranges, which we had been assured were supervised with great caution; and of course the dock with swimming raft, canoes, kayaks, and windsurfing. By all rights, Tommie was going to have a wonderful time.

We weren't.

Or at least, that was Alice's judgment. Alice felt sending Tommie off to camp was going to make the two of us suddenly feel old and useless. This hadn't occurred to me until Alice pointed it out. The minute she did, I began to feel old and useless. Only I wasn't sure if I really felt that way, or was just very suggestible.

I don't mean to sound cynical. I know Alice is totally sincere. As soon as she began sewing name tags in Tommie's socks, she got a misty look in her eye. Old and useless was just around the corner.

A further extension of Alice's theory was that we should not go home—returning to an empty apartment would only make us depressed. Instead, Alice had planned a vacation for us, hiking in the mountains of New Hampshire. She had done so on her own. It is not exactly the vacation I would have planned. Hiking is not a sport I recognize. Neither is jogging. Basically, for me to move in one direction or another, there has to be a ball involved. Either that or water. I am very happy at the seashore. I can ride the waves all day.

Inland, I do not prosper.

But Alice had her theories, and Alice had her plans. And as they stemmed from an emotional need, I didn't feel it was my place to argue with them.

At any rate, the long and the short of it was, Alice and I were off on an elaborate adventure to make sure that we didn't miss Tommie too much.

Only Alice missed him already.

So did I.

TWO

"WHERE ARE WE?"

I hate it when she does that. There it is, the simplest of questions, but it drives me nuts. Where are we? Well, how should I know? I've never driven these roads either. And I've seen the same road signs she has. So, basically, "Where are we?" is a euphemism for "Look at the map."

And I hate looking at the map. I mean, are we driving through the country to see the country or to see the map? I could have stayed at home in New York and looked at the map. If we're in the car, I would like to look out the window and see the scenery. But, oh no, Alice says, Where are we?, and there I am, fumbling with the map, trying to locate the last recognizable landmark that we'd passed.

And knowing that when I'd found it, the job isn't done. Because Alice will say, What's it near? And then I have to get out the guidebook and look up the nearest point of interest. And read the description so Alice can make a value judgment as to whether it's worth us stopping to see it.

As if that weren't bad enough, we have two guidebooks.

Anyway, we were on our way to the inn, and Alice wanted to know where we were.

The short answer was on Route 112.

I gave Alice the short answer.

She gave me a withering look. Hard to do without taking one's eyes off the road, but she managed. "I *know* we're on Route 112," Alice said. "Where on Route 112 are we?"

We passed a sign for Greely Ponds.

"Greely Ponds," I said.

This did not win her heart.

"Where is Greely Ponds?"

I whipped out my guidebook, located Greely Ponds, and was about to triumphantly impart the information to Alice when I discovered the map had no scale.

"Come on," Alice said impatiently. "Where are we?"

"Well," I said. "We're somewhere between Lincoln and Bear Notch Road."

"What?"

"And it looks like we're a little closer to Lincoln."

"Where is Lincoln?"

"Didn't we go through Lincoln a few miles back?"

"I don't recall."

"Neither do I."

"Then why do you think we did?"

"Because 112 appears to go through Lincoln on the map."

"Appears?"

"This is a hike location map. It doesn't have dots for the towns."

"You're looking at the map in the guidebook?"

4

"Sure."

"That's the wrong map."

"It's the one that shows Greely Ponds."

"You've gotta look at the other map."

I didn't want to look at the other map. It was hard enough dealing with the guidebook. "Wait a minute," I said. "Let me look up Greely Ponds."

"I don't care about Greely Ponds."

"You wanna know where it is. Hang on. Greely Ponds, page 121. Greely Ponds, Greely Ponds. Here we go. Greely Ponds. The parking lot for Greely Ponds is on the south side of Route 112, nine miles east of Lincoln. There you are," I said triumphantly. "We're nine miles east of Lincoln."

"Where is that?"

"Huh?"

"What are we near?"

"Greely Ponds."

"No, damn it," Alice said. "What's next?"

See what I mean?

We were driving along what the other guidebook had described as the state's most popular road for viewing foliage. And it was indeed a gorgeous little mountain road. Only I wasn't seeing any of it. I was reading guidebooks and maps.

"Next up is Champney Falls," I said.

"What's that?"

"I don't know. I have to look it up."

"Well, hurry up before we get there, in case we wanna stop."

I sighed, flipped through the book.

"Champney Falls," I said. "A three-point-five-mile round-trip with a six-hundred-foot elevation gain. It has a wooden foot-bridge over the brook and rocks to scramble on at the falls."

"So how far is it?" Alice said.

"I told you. Three-point-five miles."

"No. On the map."

"Oh. About a half an inch."

"Stanley."

"Let's see. It's just past Bear Notch Road."

"We just passed that road."

"Then we should be there."

We were. Around a bend a sign announced Champney Falls. We pulled into a parking lot with about a dozen other cars. Alice popped the trunk, took out a backpack.

I shouldered the backpack. Considered what conceivable subterfuge could save me from schlepping it three-point-five miles. Failing to find one, I smiled stoically and followed Alice down the path.

In the beginning it wasn't that bad. The path was relatively wide, and while there was a slight incline, it wasn't steep enough to slow us down. At least to slow Alice down, which, if I may say so, is my main problem hiking with Alice. Though shorter than me, she takes longer strides. Either that or quicker ones. At any rate, wherever we're walking, it's all I can do to keep up with Alice. Throw in a backpack, and I'm really in trouble. So, even though the going was easy, I found myself lagging behind.

We stopped to rest shortly after that, sitting on a tree trunk that was lying beside the path.

"Want some water?" Alice said.

"Just a minute. I want to see where we are."

"Where we are?" Alice said. "We just got started."

"Yeah, but there's a map," I said. I looked in the guidebook. "Did we pass a big boulder with a tree on it?"

"Huh?"

"A great big rock with a tree growing off the top of it. You recall seeing anything like that?"

"No."

"Damn."

"What's the matter."

"It's near the beginning. If we haven't passed that, we haven't gotten anywhere."

"I told you we're just getting started."

"We've been hiking fifteen minutes. We should have passed that."

"We'll pass it soon. What other landmarks are there?"

"Just that. Till we get to the top."

"We're nowhere near there."

"My point exactly."

"So, let's go," Alice said.

And with that she was up and off, with me tagging along behind.

A little farther along we passed another couple coming down. That was fine. But five minutes later another couple passed us going up. Which was okay by me—we were sitting having another rest. I was drinking water this time, having exhausted the information in the guidebook, and Alice was sitting there doing her best impression of a person who didn't mind stopping again so soon.

She did okay until the couple went by. I don't think that pleased her at all.

"Are you ready?" she asked.

I took a breath. "They're younger than we are."

"What?"

"And they've probably hiked before. This is my first time."

"How are we going to hike if we don't ever hike."

"Just a few more minutes."

I got my few minutes. Unfortunately, another couple went by. And this time there was no need to point out they were younger than we were. They were, in fact, straight out of some hiking brochure designed to give the illusion that all participants in the sport were young, tan, and healthy.

Not to mention blonde. This couple could have come from a

Swedish hiking brochure. The boy looked lean and athletic. The girl looked lean and athletic. And fresh. And supple. And limber. And smooth. And soft. And—

But I digress.

The point is, this was an attractive young couple. I say boy and girl but I shouldn't, they were probably in their early twenties, and I'm sure they considered themselves quite mature, despite how adolescent they seemed to me.

At any rate, they breezed right on by us, underlining the fact that I was still sitting down.

So I stood up.

And Alice said, "Who you trying to impress now?"

It took me a moment to figure out what she meant. When I did, it seemed totally unfair.

Yes, indeed, the woman's blond pageboy cut did bob in a casually fetching way along the high cheekbones of a most attractive face. But that was not why I got up. I had not sprung to my feet to chase after my unobtainable lost youth. I had got up so as not to suffer any more of Alice's abuse.

Unlucky there.

There was nothing for me to say that wouldn't make things worse, and sitting back down again wasn't an option, so I gritted my teeth, shouldered my backpack, and set off down the path.

Did I say down the path? I should say up the path, because the incline had just gotten steeper. Of course this didn't bother Alice, she breezed right by me, forging on ahead. I trudged along behind, looking for landmarks and wondering how soon it would be safe to suggest stopping again.

We never found a big rock with a tree on it, but after a while I noticed we were traveling alongside a stream. Which seemed an awfully good sign on the one hand, and a reason for stopping and getting out the guidebook on the other. I did, and discovered the stream was called Champney Brook, and did indeed come from the falls.

And, unless we'd been walking parallel to it for some time without knowing it, we still had an awful long way to go.

I also found out we needed to take a left turn when the path forked. Which stood us in good stead more than an hour later when it finally did. By then we had ascended most of our six hundred feet, and it was just a short scramble over the trail to the base of Champney Falls.

I must admit, it was quite a sight. Water cascading over a series of ledges down to a pool below. There were children wading in the pool, a boy and a girl. Their parents sat on a rock nearby. The older couple that had passed us were there, too, sitting on a rock eating a picnic lunch. There was also a woman with a large dog of indeterminate breed, which was lying in the shade and looking hopefully at the people eating lunch.

The young couple was not there. Not that I looked for them, you understand, but one would have expected them to be. But they were nowhere to be seen.

Alice and I had lunch, which I hadn't even noticed she'd packed, but somehow turkey sandwiches miraculously appeared in a brown paper bag, purchased no doubt the night before while I was watching a ball game in the motel. Their appearance not only startled me, but also attracted the large floppy dog. It came galumphing over, plopped down in front of me, and proceeded to drool.

The woman followed him over. "I'm sorry," she said. "Prince has no manners. I'll put him on a leash if you mind."

"We don't mind," Alice said. "He's a sweetheart."

Easy for her to say. It wasn't her sandwich the sweetheart had his eyes on. Prince was a large, shaggy, golden-brown, floppy-eared beggar, who seemed to have perfected the art of making people feel guilty about whatever it was they were eating.

"What kind of dog is he?" Alice said.

"Oh, the best kind. Golden retriever, labrador, German shepherd, a dash of cocker spaniel, and maybe just a little St. Bernard."

It seemed to me that while she'd been saying this, Prince had somehow inched closer to my sandwich. I don't know how, I hadn't seen him move, but his paws appeared closer, and I could feel hot dog breath on my knee.

"Can I give him some?" I said.

The owner was a chunky woman who seemed to smile a lot. She did so now. "You can if you want to. I have to warn you, though, you'll make a friend for life."

"I'll risk it," I said.

I tore off a crust of bread, tossed it in front of the dog. He scooped it up, held it in his mouth on long teeth, as if reprimanding me for throwing it in the dirt. Then with one sudden huge gulp it was gone, and Prince was back in his begging position, down on all fours, saliva dripping, eyes turned up at me. And this time I actually saw him move, subtly, surreptitiously, scrunching first one and then the other paw forward, very much like a soldier with a rifle creeping forward on his elbows in the tall grass. Before I knew it, he was drooling on my hiking boots.

"I warned you," the woman said.

"Stanley's a sucker," Alice said.

I tore off another piece of sandwich, held it up, and said, "Sit."

His eyes never left the sandwich, but his expression said, "Are you kidding?" He continued to drool on the spot from which I had moved my foot.

I don't know how long the dog and I might have kept it up had there not come a loud snapping sound, like the crack of a whip. It cut right through the background noise of the waterfall, and echoed in the mountain air.

A sharp, slapping sound.

And a scream.

Not a long scream. Just a short, high-pitched cry of surprise and pain.

All heads turned at once.

Saw nothing.

The sound had come from somewhere off in the woods.

"What was that?" the woman said.

"I don't know."

"It sounded like someone got slapped," Alice said.

"Yeah, maybe," I said. "Should we go see?"

Alice looked at me. "Don't be silly. It's nothing. You hear anything now?"

No, I didn't. But whatever it was was not nothing. Someone had certainly screamed. I craned my neck, continued to look around.

For a second I thought I saw something through the trees. A flash of color, like someone's clothes. But I couldn't even say what color it was. Is that strange, to see it and not know? Because that's all it was, just the impression of someone moving through the leaves. I squinted my eyes, trying to pick it up again, and—

I was shocked back to earth by a warm, wet sensation on my cheek, and the sound of laughter.

Alice and the woman were laughing at the sight of me being slobbered on as I got my face licked by the large, sandwich-eating dog.

THREE

IT WAS MUCH easier going down. Which nearly restored my faith in hiking. Going up was an ordeal, but going down, hey, you had gravity in your corner. Just point your feet in the right direction, and let nature take its course. I found myself not only keeping up with Alice, but actually skipping on ahead.

"Take it easy," Alice said. "It's not a race."

Unbelievable, after the way she'd gone pelting up this same path.

"What's the matter?" I said. "Can't you keep up?"

"You're gonna twist your ankle. If you twist your ankle, there goes the whole vacation."

"I'm not gonna twist my ankle."

"You are if you don't look where you're going."

"I'm looking where I'm going."

"No, you're not. You're looking back at me."

"Only because you're talking to me," I said.

But, as usual, with Alice, I knew better than to argue. I stopped, let her catch up.

"Take it easy," she said. "He's not chasing you."

I blinked. "I am not running away from the dog."

Alice smiled. "You looked just adorable."

"I know, I know. I made your day."

"He was a very sweet dog."

"Wonderful. I'm sorry he couldn't have licked your face too."

"I didn't give him my sandwich."

"Right. He knew a sucker when he saw one. Well, I'm pushing off. Would you like a head start, or do you think you can keep up?"

"Don't be a jerk," Alice said. "Just watch where you're going and don't get hurt. I don't want to spend the whole vacation with you laid up in bed."

We continued down the path at what was a moderate pace compared to what I'd been doing, but was greased lightning compared to our pace coming up.

Speaking of which, we passed a number of people who were on their way up, and I could not help feeling smugly superior. After all, I had survived the climb, and was on my way down. And, whether it's psychological or not, I have to tell you, on the way up the people who passed us coming down looked happy, whereas on the way down, the people who passed us going up did not look pleased at all.

I had one other observation I was somewhat amused to find true. In whatever group of people it was that passed us, the grumpiest person was always the adult male. The father, the husband, the boyfriend, whatever. In a family, it was always dear old dad. Unless, of course, Grandpa was there to outgrump him.

But by far, the grumpiest of all was a man who came up alone. He was overweight, and clearly out of shape, huffing and puffing at every step. His bald head glistened with sweat. His shirt was soaked clean through. His shorts had slipped well below his waist, and appeared to be just on the verge of tripping him. He looked angry enough to bite someone's head off.

"See," I said, after he went by, "I am not the world's worst hiker. I am actually pretty damn good."

Alice shook her head. "Sorry," she said. "You score no points at all."

I blinked. "What?"

"That man is alone. No one made him go up the mountain. He's doing it on his own. You, on the other hand, had to be dragged. That man can bitch and moan all he wants about how terrible it is, but the fact remains he's a volunteer."

"Just because no one's with him doesn't mean no one made him do it," I said.

Alice cocked her head. "Are you saying I made you do it?"

And there I was again. *She* was the one saying nobody made him do it. It was *her* premise, not mine. I was an innocent by-stander, just trying to hold up my end of the conversation. And suddenly there I was on the hook again.

"Well, for whatever reason he's going up the mountain," I said, "he certainly seemed unhappy."

Before Alice could point out that I'd deflected the question, I said, "Hey, look there."

"What is it?"

"Down there on the path."

"I don't see anything on the path. What are you talking about?"

"I don't mean on the path. Beside it."

"Stanley."

"It's the rock."

"What?"

"The big rock with the tree growing on top of it."

"Where?"

"Right there. That's the one in the guidebook."

It certainly was. I whipped out the guidebook, read the description again to make sure.

"That's it, all right," I said. "That's great."

"What's great about it?"

"Are you kidding. Look at this map. If that's this rock, we're almost back to the road. We made it down in no time."

"I told you you were going too fast."

"Come on. Let's see if it is."

We made our way down the path to what had to be the big rock with the tree growing out of it mentioned in the guidebook. When we got closer, I saw how we'd missed it on the way up. From nearby, you don't see the tree. You have to be farther away, and you have to be looking for it. We had already passed by before I noticed it in the guidebook.

I stood next to it, admiring its beauty, and congratulating myself on how quickly we'd gotten down the mountain.

There came a muffled sound from the other side of the rock. Sort of a stifled, half sob.

Alice and I both heard it. We looked at each other, shrugged. I gave a shall-we-walk-by-the-rock gesture, which Alice and I proceeded to do.

Standing in the trees at the far end of the rock was the girl. The blond girl with the backpack from the Swedish brochure who'd passed us on the way up. Somehow or other she'd managed to pass us again and get back down. She'd also lost her blond boyfriend along the way.

Which might have accounted for her mood. Her face was caked with tears, and it was obviously her sob we had heard.

She saw us, and immediately turned her head and took a few steps away.

I looked inquisitively at Alice.

She murmured, "Leave her alone," took me by the arm, and

led me away, as if I'd been about to intervene. Which isn't in my nature—a stranger's private business is their own.

Alice, on the other hand, might have jumped in, had it been anyone less attractive. That's not fair. I'm sure Alice would have offered aid, had it been appropriate.

Anyway, we went on by as if we didn't see her, and continued on down the path.

I felt bad.

No, not that we didn't help her—my personal opinion is the most help you can be to someone who's upset is to leave them alone. I felt bad for how I felt. I mean the moment I saw her. Saw her crying, that is.

Because I felt good. A sudden flash of elation. It was momentarily, fleeting, immediately gone. But there it was. The least admirable of all emotions, yet one's own.

It's hard to explain. You had to be there. You also had to be me. A middle-aged married man, incapable of winning an argument with his wife, climbing a mountain he didn't really want to climb, and being slapped in the face with the realization of just how old and out of shape he actually was.

And watching the young, perfect couple go scampering up the slope without a care in the world.

It reminded me of the scene in Kurt Vonnegut's *Sirens of Titan* where Rumfoord shows Malachi Constant a painting of his wife as a little girl, dressed entirely in white, the cleanest, most frozen little girl Malachi had ever seen, and Rumfoord says, "Wouldn't it be too bad if she fell into a mud puddle?" which startles Malachi who had just been thinking she looked as if she were afraid of getting dirty.

I realize the example isn't as great as I thought it was. The two young backpackers didn't look like they were afraid of anything. What I'm getting at is, they were so clean, fresh, young, carefree, that you almost wanted to strangle them. At least to say, "Excuse me, you can't go scampering up the mountain so gleefully with wild abandon. There is such a thing as real life, with limits and consequences and responsibilities and cares."

Does that make any sense? I doubt it. The point is, the young couple unwittingly trigger the jealousy that's in us all, and sub-consciously one cannot help but long to see them taken down.

So the sight of the woman in tears was actually wish-fulfillment.

For one split second.

Followed immediately by shame and guilt.

Add in the fact my wife was needling me about finding the young woman attractive, and the whole thing was not a pretty picture.

We reached the car in nothing flat, and within five minutes we were safely out of Champney Falls and on the road again.

Still, all things considered, it was just not my day.

FOUR

"IT'S A BED-and-breakfast."

"No, it's not. It's an inn."

"The guidebook says it's a bed-and-breakfast."

"The guidebook is wrong."

"How can the guidebook be wrong?"

"Don't be silly," Alice said. "Guidebooks are wrong all the time."

"It's listed under *Bed-and-Breakfasts*."

"It's listed wrong."

"No, no," I said. "You don't understand what I mean. It's not like they listed it and then said it's a bed-and-breakfast. There's a whole section in the guidebook for bed-and-breakfasts. And that's the section it's in."

"That's the wrong section."

"How do you know?"

"I *know*," Alice said. "Do you really think I don't know?"

"I didn't say that. All I said was—"

"I bet you don't even know what a bed-and-breakfast is."

"Huh?"

"You know what it is? You're telling me this place is a bed-and-breakfast. You know what that is?"

"I'm just telling you how it's listed."

"You don't know what it is, do you?"

"Sure, I do. A bed-and-breakfast is a place that serves breakfast."

"So is an inn."

"Huh?"

"An inn serves breakfast. What's the difference between an inn and a bed-and-breakfast?"

"Ah . . ."

"I don't believe it. Here you are, insisting the place isn't an inn, it's a bed-and-breakfast, and you don't even know the difference."

"What's the difference?"

"A bed-and-breakfast just gives you breakfast. It doesn't serve dinner."

"An inn serves dinner?"

"Of course."

"And a bed-and-breakfast doesn't?"

"That's right."

"So why don't they call it a bed and no dinner?"

"Don't be dumb."

"Is that the only difference?"

"Not at all. A bed-and-breakfast is run by homey folks who introduce themselves to you, and sit on the porch with you, and tell you stories of how they came to buy the place and the tribulations they've had in running it."

"You're kidding."

"It's all right. We're not staying in a bed-and-breakfast. The Blue Frog Ponds is an inn."

"Then why isn't it called the Blue Frog Ponds Inn?"

"It was probably too long to fit on the sign."

"Fit on the sign? Inn has three letters, Alice. I mean, it's not like this was the Blue Frog Ponds University of Psychoanalytic Studies or something."

"Stanley, it's an inn. I booked it. I know. This is a new addition to the guidebook, and whoever added it, added it wrong. Trust me, it's an inn."

Oh, dear.

Those dread words.

I must explain. I'm a private detective, but I don't really see myself as one, it's just what I do to pay bills. I'm also an actor and a writer, and once I even got a screenplay produced.

For anyone who's ever worked in the motion-picture industry, the words *trust me* have a very unpleasant connotation.

So, it was with some trepidation that I watched Alice turn into the Blue Frog Ponds. Was this really an inn, or might it be after all the dreaded bed-and-breakfast?

From the outside it was hard to tell. A circular drive led up to a large white house with blue trim. It was surrounded by grass, and flower beds, and a wooden front porch with table and chairs, suitable for telling guests long stories of how one had acquired the building.

Hmmm.

A sign hanging off the porch said BLUE FROG PONDS. But I knew that didn't mean anything, because after my talk with Alice I had been poring over the guidebook, and not only did not all the inns call themselves inns, but some of the bed-and-breakfasts called *themselves* inns.

I followed Alice up on the front porch, went inside. We found ourselves in a living-room/foyer/hallway sort of deal. In the back right corner was a short wooden bar with three stools, behind which a rather frumpy-looking woman in a print dress was waiting on a middle-aged couple. The man was drinking Bud Light, and the woman was drinking wine.

And they were paying.

That seemed like a very good sign.

Now if we could only check in. But there didn't seem to be a front desk.

The frumpy woman said, "Just a minute, I'll be right with you." She finished making change and came out from behind the bar, which redefined frumpy as plump frumpy. She said, "Can I help you?"

"Yes," Alice said. "We have a reservation. Hastings."

"Of course," she said.

She marched to a breakfront on the wall, flipped down a panel of what proved to be a pull-out desk, consulted a ledger, and said, "Yes. You're in room twelve. You reserved this on MasterCard. You want to pay for it on that?"

Alice produced the card.

I expected the woman to put it in one of those machines you pull the bar across and make an imprint on a form. Instead, she flipped open another breakfront, revealing a computer-and-modem setup, and scanned the card electronically, just as if we'd been staying in some hotel chain.

"There you go," she said, handing the card back to Alice. She bent down, peered at a pegboard in the first breakfront. There were a series of hooks numbered one through twelve. She selected two keys from hook number twelve.

I must say, I found the whole transaction encouraging. First off, we were in room twelve. Surely a house with twelve rooms for rent couldn't be a bed-and-breakfast, could it? No, anything that extensive had to be an inn.

Then there were the two guests at the bar. They were not being offered drinks by a gracious host, they were *paying* for them.

But the payoff was the MasterCard. It was not just a MasterCard, but an *electronically scanned* MasterCard. Surely that had to mean inn.

I was feeling so good I smiled at the woman as she handed me the keys.

She smiled back. "My name's Louise."

Uh-oh.

Bed-and-breakfast.

FIVE

ROOM TWELVE OF the Blue Frog Ponds Inn, Bed-and-Breakfast, or whatever it happened to be, wasn't even in the building. It was out the side door, up the driveway, in a two-story frame house off to the right. It was also white with blue trim, and there was a blue frog on the front door. It occurred to me, at least it wasn't a cartoon, just a simple overhead shot of a frog, accurate in every aspect with the exception of being blue.

To the left of the door, a blue-and-white sign read EAST POND. A sign below that read 9–12.

"Here we are," Alice said. "Rooms nine through twelve."

"Or those are the hours the building is open."

Alice gave me a look, tried the door.

The building indeed had rooms nine through twelve. Nine and ten were apparently on the ground floor, because Alice and I were immediately greeted by a narrow staircase with the sign 11–12 and an arrow pointing up. We went up the stairs to an equally narrow hallway, which also featured a low, slanted ceiling, running as it did the length of the building under the eaves. Alice was able to walk upright, but I had to duck slightly. A small annoyance, but for someone lugging a suitcase, enough to grate.

The first door we came to was room eleven.

I stopped and blinked.

"Oh, dear."

There was a frog on the door. But it was not like the frog downstairs. This frog would have been happy at Disney World. It was a cartoon frog, with big eyes and a big smile, standing on its hind legs and acting human, just like Mickey Mouse or Goofy.

The frog, of course, was blue. He was wearing red shorts and a white T-shirt. Stitched onto the pocket of the shirt was the name Freddie.

Freddie had one thumb and three fingers, just like a Disney character, and with his left hand he was making a big okay sign, with his thumb and index finger curled into a circle and his two remaining fingers pointing up into the air.

He was also winking.

"Uh-oh," I said. "Do you suppose we have our own frog?"

We did. He wore yellow shorts and a white T-shirt with the name Frankie on the pocket. Frankie was standing with his hands in his pockets and his head cocked to one side. He wasn't winking, but his eyes were bright, and he had a sort of enigmatic smile.

"Hey," I said. "I think our frog's better than their frog."

"Don't start with me," Alice said.

"Did you know this when you booked the room?"

Alice didn't answer, just opened the door and went in.

I followed, lugging the suitcase.

It was a simple room. A double bed. A dresser. A chair. A closet and a small bath. The floor was wood, and there was wallpaper on the walls. A simple floral design. The only hanging picture was a landscape. The was a relief. I'd half expected to see poker-playing frogs. But no, the room was simple and spare and—

"Hey," I said. "Where's the TV?"

"Stanley, this is not a motel. It's an inn. They don't have TV in the rooms."

"Sure they do."

"No, they don't. Don't be silly. Nobody goes to an inn to watch television."

"But—"

"Does the guidebook say this place has TV?"

"It doesn't say one way or another."

"There you are."

"But most of the inns have TV. I can show you."

"What's the big deal?"

"Bed-and-breakfasts don't."

"Are you going to start that again?"

"This is listed as a bed-and-breakfast."

"Stanley, what's the big deal about television?"

The big deal about television was I'm a Red Sox fan, and living in New York City all I get are Yankee and Mets games. For me, getting to see the Sox was one of the main attractions of vacationing in New England. They were playing the Blue Jays this afternoon, and I must confess I'd been looking forward to getting up to the room and switching it on.

"Well," I said, "there's a Red Sox game."

"Now?" Alice said.

"Yeah. It's on now."

"So go watch."

"Huh?"

"They'll have a TV in the inn. Go watch the game and stop being such a cranky puss."

"But—"

"Go on, go on. I'll be fine. You go watch the game, and I'll unpack for us."

With Alice being so nice it was hard to point out that a TV in the inn wasn't nearly the same thing as a TV in the room. I was still horribly disappointed with the whole affair, and couldn't shake the nagging suspicion that I had been somehow manipulated into a bed-and-breakfast against my will.

On the ground floor I couldn't resist checking out the other rooms. Unless they happened to have televisions, their main advantage seemed to be that one could stand upright in the hallway outside 'em.

Of course, each room had a frog. For my money, Felix, green pants, room nine, looked rather smug, while Fredericka, pink dress, room ten, looked rather coy.

I let myself out of the front door of East Pond and briefly considered checking out the frogs in the West Pond building opposite.

Very briefly.

I headed for the main pond, or building, or whatever, in quest of the TV.

I figured the most likely place would be the bar. Naturally, I figured wrong. No one actually sat at the bar, it merely dispensed alcohol for people to carry out onto the porch. Not that there were a lot of people out there—in fact, the only ones were the couple that I had observed earlier buying drinks.

While I stood there looking stupid, halfway between the bar and the porch, Louise suddenly appeared behind me, which was a bit disconcerting—I had not seen her make an entrance, and there did not appear to be any door.

"Can I help you?" she asked.

"Is there a television?"

"Oh, yes, of course." She pointed. "Through the living room, and it's the door on the right."

"You have cable?"

"Sure do. Seventy-two channels."

That was a relief. I had been envisioning a worthless pair of rabbit ears, or some ancient antenna on the roof I'd have to climb up and try to turn.

"Do you get NESN?"

"New England Sports Network? We sure do."

"Great," I said. "Thanks a lot."

I went through the living room, which was empty but which featured a number of chairs and couches of which Alice could tell you the period but which I could only classify as old, and into the TV room.

Which was almost empty.

There was one occupant. A young girl, maybe five or six. She had blond curls, a pink dress, and a Barbie doll.

But she wasn't playing with the Barbie doll.

She was watching TV.

Nickelodeon.

The children's channel.

She heard me, turned, looked up. From her expression, I must have impressed her as that man her mother had taken great pains to warn her about.

I smiled ruefully, beat a hasty retreat back to the room, where Alice was arranging clothes in one of the dresser drawers.

"What's the matter?" she said. "No TV?"

"There's a TV. It's being watched by a six-year-old child. I didn't ask her if she might prefer baseball."

"Were her parents there?"

"Not so you could notice."

"Then they can't have left her long. I'd try back in a little while."

"The game'll be over in a little while."

"Don't be a grouch. Go do something else."

"Like what?"

"There's a swimming pool and a putting green."

"How do you know?"

"It's in the guidebook."

"What guidebook?"

"Not the guidebook. The directory. The brochure. The list of services." Alice pointed. "There. On the table."

I picked up what proved to be a two-page booklet, or four-page, if you were counting sides. On page three, or the front of page two, depending on how you figured, was a listing of recreational services. These included a TV room, swimming pool, and putting green.

"There's also shuffleboard," I said.

"Yes, I know."

"Would you care for a game?"

"I'm not sure we're old enough."

"We could use phony IDs."

"I'm still unpacking," Alice said. "Why don't you go swim or putt?"

That seemed better than watching her unpack. I put on my swimsuit, went out to look for the pool. It wasn't near East Pond, and it wasn't near West Pond either. But from there I could see a pool where South Pond would have been, just around the far side of the inn. On my way I detoured past the TV room, but, as expected, Nickelodeon was still on. I gave up on the Red Sox as a lost cause, and headed out to the pool.

It was sunny and warm, and I would have expected the pool to be crowded, but apparently the Blue Frog Ponds didn't have that many guests. Uncharitably, it occurred to me that was probably due to bad word of mouth.

The pool was surrounded by a wooden fence. I opened the gate, went inside.

The pool was not entirely unoccupied. There was one person there. The woman was sunbathing. She was lying on her stomach on one of the lounge chairs.

She was nude.

At least, she looked nude. There was no bikini strap across her back. And that certainly was her bare behind. Good lord, she must have thought she had the place to herself. Maybe I should leave.

Then I saw the string around her waist. She was wearing a thong bikini. At least the bottom of it. And she'd probably just untied the top. So, for all intents and purposes, she was a fully dressed sunbather, and I could just ignore her and enjoy my swim.

I dropped my towel on a chair, kicked off my flip-flops, and pulled off my shirt. Stepped to the edge of the pool and dove in.

When I came up, it was only natural to see if the sunbather had reacted to my presence.

She had.

The young woman had raised her head to see who had joined her in the pool enclosure.

It was her. You know. The young, attractive, Swedish brochure, blond, crying hiker from Champney Falls.

And she smiled and said, "Hi."

I didn't want to talk to her. When we'd found her crying behind the big rock, Alice couldn't help whispering, "Looks like you broke her heart." And here she was, half naked, alone with me in the swimming pool enclosure, not half an hour after we'd checked in, and I could imagine what Alice would make of that.

But I couldn't be out and out rude, could I?

So I smiled and said, "Hi."

"You're new here, aren't you?"

"Just checked in."

"I thought so. I hadn't seen you here before."

The young woman had craned her neck to talk to me, revealing that she was indeed lying on an untied bikini top.

I pulled myself out of the pool and sat on the edge. Not to get a better view, merely to allow her a more comfortable position.

Honest.

"So, you've been here for a while?" I said.

"Since yesterday. It's nice, but there's not much to do."

"Except swim."

"Yes." She smiled, then put on a mock pout. "But, you know what? I don't really like the water. I just want to get a tan."

Oh, dear.

That was my cue, if ever I'd heard one, to compliment her on her body. Which would suddenly, instantly, and irrevocably have transformed the conversation from casual to flirting. Already, I was acutely aware of the fact the young lady had avoided the use of the pronoun *we*. From her conversation, the young man did not exist, and she was staying there alone.

I was even more acutely aware of the fact that I had not mentioned Alice. Which I certainly wanted to do. It just seemed so clunky to say, "Yes, I'm here with my wife."

On the other hand, it would have been easy for me to say, "Yes, we just checked in." Only I hadn't done it. In light of which, it was impossible to deny this girl's allure.

She actually seemed quite innocent. Aside from being half naked. There was a warm, puppy-friendly quality about her.

While avoiding the compliment, I didn't swim off. Instead, I deflected her remark with a joke. "You've been sunbathing since yesterday?"

She giggled at that, feeble joke though it was. "No, I went hiking. At some waterfall or other. I forget the name."

I could have told her. But if she hadn't recognized me from Champney Falls, I wasn't about to remind her. Embarrass her with the realization I'd seen her crying behind the rock.

"Yes," I said, "I'll probably be doing some hiking too. Well, enjoy your tan."

I slipped into the pool and swam off, aware of the fact I'd, once again, neglected to mention Alice. It occurred to me life was incredibly complicated. At least mine was.

I swam to the other side of the pool, pulled myself out, and toweled off. I noticed the young woman was no longer watching me, had gone back to working on her tan. She certainly made lying in a deck chair look desirable. I lay back in my deck chair, closed my eyes.

It was a gorgeous day. The sun was warm, but there was a cooling breeze. Lying there felt great. I was tired after hiking all day. It occurred to me I might fall asleep. I don't think I actually did, but rather drifted in a sort of blissful, semiconscious state, where there weren't any responsibilities, or decisions, or cares, or woes, and everything was kind of lazy, carefree, sunny, and bright.

"Look who's here."

The words snapped me back to reality. I opened my eyes to find Alice standing next to my deck chair.

Great. Look who's here, indeed. I know who's here, Alice. I didn't invite her, I didn't know she was coming, I didn't expect to see her, and I'm not going to take kindly to being blamed for it.

I was mulling over in my mind just how much of that I wanted to put into words, when Alice was suddenly bumped aside by something floppy and brown, and the next thing I knew I was being licked unmercifully again by the large, sandwich-eating dog.

SIX

"SHE'S FROM BOSTON," Alice said.

"Oh?"

"Well, just outside it, actually. She has a house with a yard, which is perfect for Prince. She said she wouldn't want to keep a dog in the city."

"Certainly not that dog," I said.

"She's divorced, runs an antique shop on Boylston Avenue. Her husband left her for a younger woman. He's a doctor, she's a manicurist."

"She runs an antique shop *and* gives manicures?"

"Don't be dumb. The younger woman's a manicurist. The one her husband left her for."

"Uh-huh," I said. "And how long ago did this happen?"

"I'm not sure," Alice said, and looked disappointed at herself at having failed to glean this bit of information in the full fifteen minutes she'd had talking to the woman while I was changing for dinner.

Alice and I were seated at a booth in the dining room of the Blue Frog Ponds. I had been more than a little reluctant to dine there, figuring the menu would be completely inedible on the one hand, or feature blue frog legs on the other, but Alice had told me not to fear. Whatever else the Blue Frog Ponds might be, its dining room was famous, listed in the guidebook as a four-star restaurant. Or, as Alice explained, it wasn't just for the guests, it was a place people actually came to eat.

I couldn't argue with that. There were two booths and about a dozen tables in the dining room, and almost all were full. We owed our booth to Alice's foresight in checking out the dining room on her way to the pool and making a reservation. I could see why she had. The booths were semiprivate, partitioned alcoves for two, with plush, cushioned benches, and a table of some dark wood or other of which I'm sure Alice would know the name. All in all, a very pleasant place to dine.

I looked at my menu. "Any tips on what to eat?"

"Huh?"

"Did the guidebook make any recommendations?"

"It said pay attention to the specials."

"I don't see any specials."

"Of course not. The waitress tells you the specials."

"So where's our waitress?"

"They're busy. I'm sure she'll be right over."

Our booth, though semiprivate, had a clear view of the dining room. Both the waitresses I could see were indeed busy. One of them was young and somewhat pretty, though not in the blond, Swedish, sunbather, hiker category. The other was middle-aged, and looked rather severe.

Naturally, that's the one we got. She strode up, whipped out a pad and pencil, and said, "Would you like to hear the specials?" Her tone implied if we didn't, we would be taken outside and shot.

"Yes, please," Alice said.

Our waitress had black hair streaked with gray, pulled back into a bun. The expression on her face gave the impression the bun was way too tight. "Very well," she said. "Our fish today is maki shark, with the chef's special sauce, mint potatoes, and fresh corn off the cob. We also have prime rib with horseradish. It comes with baked potato and mixed vegetables."

"What do you recommend?" Alice asked.

"The shark is excellent. But if you're really hungry, the prime rib is thick."

"I'll have that," I said.

"And I'll try the shark," Alice said.

"Would you like anything to start?"

"Are there any specials for appetizers?"

She shook her head. "There's a wide variety on the menu. Our barbecued ribs are famous." She cocked an eye at me. "But it's a large portion. You won't want to order it with the prime rib."

Damn. I'd been about to, and now I couldn't. I had half a mind to order it, just to show her. But I wasn't going to win Alice's heart by picking a fight my first night there.

"Maybe just a house salad," I said.

She nodded. "Good choice. Now, you, with the shark, might want something more substantial."

"I'll try the scampi."

"Fine. And a house salad?"

"Sold."

"Can I get you anything to drink?"

Alice ordered a white wine, and I ordered a Diet Coke. From the look on the waitress' face I might as well have ordered poison, but she wrote it down and went away.

"Cheerful," I said.

"I'm sure she's perfectly pleasant," Alice said. "They're just very busy."

"Even so."

"I bet she smiles when she brings us the drinks."

She didn't, but I scored no points in the matter, because our drinks were actually brought to the table by a boy who looked too young to be doing it. Whether he was a waiter, or a busboy, or even the bartender, I had no idea, but if he'd shown up in my bar I'd have carded him. Anyway, he brought the drinks to the table, asked which was which, and at least had the decency not to sneer when I claimed the Diet Coke.

Alice took a sip of wine, said, "So anyway, she seems very nice."

"The waitress?"

"No, not the waitress. The woman with the dog. You know, that dog likes you."

"He liked my sandwich."

"You never should have given it to him."

"I didn't expect to see him again. What is she doing here?"

"Hiking in the mountains."

"No, I mean *here*. At this bed-and-breakfast."

"It's an inn."

"Fine. What's she doing at this inn?"

"What do you mean, what's she doing here? She's staying here."

"Yeah, but why here? Did she follow us?"

"Well, of course not. Why would she follow us?"

"I don't know. We just wound up in the same place."

"Maybe so, but she certainly didn't follow us. She's been here since yesterday."

"Really?"

"Yes, of course, really."

"Then what was she doing at Champney Falls?"

"Hiking."

"Yeah, but—"

"But what?"

"You mean she went there to hike?"

Alice looked at me. "Yes, of course," she said. "So did we. What's so hard to understand?"

"I'm sorry," I said. "It's just we went there because we were driving by. So, in my mind, I didn't think of it as something important enough to actually drive to. See what I mean?"

"Yes, I see what you mean," Alice said. "You have the most convoluted thought process. Tell me something, what could it possibly matter?"

Our waitress suddenly materialized, slid salads in front of us, and stalked off without a word. That was the only problem with the booth—the side partitions acted like blinders, allowing people to sneak up on you.

I picked up my fork, said, "Damn."

"What's the matter?"

"She forgot to ask us what dressing?"

"Stanley, it's house salad. Comes with house dressing."

"Yeah, but I bet they have others."

"It looks good. Try it."

I tried it. As expected, it was some sort of vinaigrette. It wasn't half bad. Still, given a choice, I would have opted for something more along the lines of blue cheese.

Alice's scampi hit the deck a moment later, accompanied by the admonition, "Don't touch it!" from the Miss Congeniality of the serving set. I'm sure she just meant it was hot, still I couldn't suppress the image of me reaching out for a shrimp and her smacking my knuckles with a ruler.

"What are you smiling at?" Alice said.

"Just a thought. What do you suppose her name is?"

"What do you mean, what do I think her name is?" Alice said. "You want me to guess her name?"

"I mean, how does she strike you? From her attitude."

"As a rather hassled waitress. What's your point?"

"No point. I was just playing a game. Like it occurred to me maybe her name was Olga and she used to moonlight as the head of a concentration camp."

"Nice guy," Alice said. "Is this just because she wouldn't let you have the barbecue ribs or put cheese glop on your salad?"

"Not at all," I said. "It's just if you were writing a murder mystery, she'd be the chief suspect."

"And therefore innocent," Alice said.

"Huh?"

"If she were as suspicious as you say, she'd have to be innocent. Otherwise there'd be no mystery. It would be too easy."

"Aha," I said. "But that's the double twist. You think it's too easy because she looks so guilty. So you figure she couldn't possibly be. But in point of fact she is."

"No good," Alice said.

"Why not?"

"Too convoluted. The double twist is the same as no twist at all. You wind up with the person who looks guilty being guilty. Wow, what a surprise."

"It is if you're led to think otherwise."

I was grateful the conversation had moved into a nonserious discussion of murder mysteries. I munched on my salad, and cast covetous glances at Alice's scampi. It was cool enough for Alice to eat, but I wasn't about to risk the ruler.

Our entrées arrived just then, and I found myself hard-pressed any longer to wish our waitress ill. Alice's shark was indeed a small portion, but my prime rib was an inch and a half thick and filled the plate. I kid you not. The potato and mixed vegetables came in side dishes. The beef stood alone.

I had just begun sawing into my mountain of meat when I heard, "Oh, to die for."

Alice had just tasted the shark. Evidently it was to her liking.

"Oh, Stanley, you have to try this. The sauce is magnificent."

To be honest, tasting shark is not a high priority in my life. I also had a mouthful of meat. Still, I was trying to be a good sport. I chewed, swallowed, took a sip of water.

Alice dipped a bit of shark in the sauce, held the fork out to me. I accepted it rather tentatively on long teeth, but had to admit it was quite good.

"See?" Alice said. "It's the sauce. The sauce is to die for."

I wouldn't have gone that far, but it was rather tasty. Still, I was happy enough to return to my prime rib. I attacked it vigorously, and polished it off about the same time Alice finished her shark.

"And how was everything?" demanded our waitress.

It struck me as a perfunctory and practically rhetorical question. I couldn't help wondering how the woman would react to anything but abject praise. On the other hand, I couldn't think of a single thing to complain about.

And Alice was still sky-high. "The shark was to die for." she said. "That sauce. What is in that sauce?"

"It's our chef's own recipe. Isn't it good?"

"It's to die for. I don't suppose . . . ?"

"What?"

"Would it be possible to get the recipe?"

She shook her head. "The chef does not make a policy of giving out his recipes."

There was something in the way she said it, and she and Alice exchanged a look. At least, that's how it seemed to me, but maybe I just imagined it, because a second later she said, "Would you care for dessert?"

"What do you recommend?" Alice said.

"The cheesecake is quite good. But if you prefer chocolate . . ."

"Yes?"

"Our chocolate cake is very popular. It's all chocolate, and very moist. It's so rich it has no frosting."

"I'll try it," Alice said.

"And I'll have the cheesecake," I said.

Alice and the waitress exchanged looks, as if to say, "How predictable." I must say, I felt somewhat picked on. What was wrong with having cheesecake?

I was about to voice that very thought when the blond hiking couple hoved into view. They were escorted across the dining room by the other waitress, and seated at a table right in our line of fire.

The young man was dressed in sneakers, shorts, and a white polo shirt, and looked as if he might have just stepped off center court at Wimbledon. The young woman was dressed in a two-piece pink sunsuit. While not nearly as revealing as her swimsuit, it still looked pretty good.

At any rate, it was impossible not to note their entrance.

"Ah," Alice said, "the floor show has arrived."

Having already taken a ribbing about talking to the girl by the pool, I was not looking forward to going through it again.

"Yes," I said. "And don't you find it a little strange?"

That caught Alice up short, and at least postponed whatever remarks she'd been about to make about the young lady's attire and my possible appreciation of it. She frowned, said, "What?"

"I mean, that they're here. Don't you find it strange that they're here? I mean, they're here, we're here, the woman with the dog is here. We were all at Champney Falls, and we're all here. It's like a bad mystery novel that's full of coincidences, where all the people in it keep bumping into one another for no apparent reason."

"I'm sure they have a reason."

"That's not the point. The point is, how did we all wind up here together? The girl says they checked in yesterday. But that doesn't have to be true."

Alice stared at me. "What are you getting at?"

"Well, did *they* follow us here?"

"Oh, for goodness' sakes."

"No, they couldn't have. When we left, she was still crying behind a rock. But what about the woman with the dog. They could have followed her here."

"Stanley . . ."

"See what I mean? They're not involved with us, but they could be involved with her."

"Stanley, what do you think you're doing?"

What I was doing was kidding around and trying to forestall any more husband-bashing.

"Shhh," I said. "Here comes the waitress. Don't let on. Just act natural."

Fortunately, that had the desired effect. Alice wasn't about to let a total stranger in on how goofy a moron she'd happened to marry. She just smiled and said, "Thank you," when the chocolate cake was slid in front of her.

Alice took a bite, and suddenly all was forgiven. Or at least forgotten. The look on her face approached ecstasy.

"Oh, my god," Alice said. "I don't believe this."

Alice's dessert was so moist and soggy it looked almost more like pudding than cake.

"Good?" I asked.

"Good? Stanley, I don't believe this cake. It's heaven."

It was, indeed. It had rescued me from the conversation. I took a bite of cheesecake—which wasn't heaven, but wasn't bad, either—and enjoyed a brief respite while the two of us drank our coffee and ate our dessert.

Unfortunately, having placed her order, the young woman got up and headed in the direction of the ladies' room, which of course led her right past our booth.

Alice watched her go, turned back, and said, "You were saying?"

"I don't remember what I was saying."

"Oh, yes, you do. You were advancing some insane theory

about how that young woman happened to be here. Probably to cover up the fact that she's actually here to see you."

"Oh, I'm sure she is. I just thought you might find that hard to accept."

"Not at all," Alice said. "I'm sure she *isn't*. Although you probably *think* she is."

"Thanks a lot."

"Anyway, do tell me your fascinating theory—what was it?—that they're here because they followed the woman with the dog. And just why would they do that?"

"Why, I have no idea. I was just saying they had the opportunity. When we left, the woman was still crying behind the rock. The woman with the dog was still up at the falls. By the time she came down, the boyfriend could have showed up, and the two of them could have followed her."

Alice looked at me. "What is this, a busman's holiday? You're a detective and you're on vacation, so you're going to make up a mystery wherever you go?"

"I'm just kidding around, Alice. All I'm saying is it's quite a coincidence, all of us winding up at the same place."

"Exactly," Alice said. "And that's all it is, coincidence. We came here because the other inn I called was full. I don't know why our friend with the dog came here, but I can certainly find out.

"And as for them," Alice said, jerking her thumb in the direction of the young woman, who had just walked by on her way back to her table, "they are probably staying here because they stayed here before, because it's a cheap place to stay, or because the other inns were full. All right, we all happened to be at Champney Falls. It's a coincidence, and that's all it is. And there's no reason to make anything more of it than that."

"Yeah, I know," I said.

And in walked the grumpy, overweight hiker with the bald head.

SEVEN

WHEN WE GOT back to the room after dinner, I suggested that since there was no television we find some other means by which to amuse ourselves.

To Alice, who knows me well, this was none too subtle a suggestion. She gave me her there-he-goes-again look, designed to make me feel like a moronic, sexist pig, incapable of controlling his base, primitive urges. But, as I pointed out, this was the first time in years we'd been vacationing alone, and it was somewhat like a second honeymoon. And I was gentle and romantic and suave and tender and caring and loving, and in every way, shape, and form, the epitome of a perfect gentleman, and the long and the short of it was Alice was moved by the sentiment, and before you know it she was in my arms, and I was nuzzling her hair, and things were looking awfully good.

And someone in the next room coughed.

You couldn't mistake it. It was as loud as a pistol shot.

Alice stiffened and pulled away, and I knew I was dead.

"Did you hear that?" she whispered. "The walls are paper-thin. You can hear everything. *Everything.*"

I whispered something about how I could be quiet, but it was a lost cause, Alice was having none of it. And just like that, our romantic evening went down the drain. And, I realized, so did all of them. Good lord, how many nights were we staying here? And I thought not having a TV was bad. Say it ain't so, Alice. Say it ain't so.

Unfortunately, it was so, and after a few more whispered arguments, entreaties, and pleas, I gave up the fight and accepted Alice's invitation to go for a walk. A walk wasn't exactly what I had in mind, but anything beat hanging out in a room so devoid of creature comforts.

First off, we stopped by the inn to see if anything was going on. Surprisingly enough, there was. From the tinkle of glasses and silverware coming from the door of the dining room dinner was still being served. And the bar was absolutely jumping with two, count 'em, two patrons sitting on bar stools sipping drinks, two young men who sat there chatting happily as if no one had told them sitting at the bar simply wasn't done. On the other hand, the middle-aged couple I'd previously seen on the porch was back on the porch, demonstrating the approved method of sipping drinks at the Blue Frog Ponds.

As if that weren't enough, a sign by the front desk announced that at nine o'clock there was a movie in the game room.

"Where's the game room?" I said.

"Right out back between East and West Ponds," Louise said.

Once again, I hadn't noticed she was there, and had no idea where she came from. I made a mental note to ask Alice about that later.

"How do you show movies?" I asked.

"There's a big-screen TV and a VCR."

"You mean you have *another* TV?" I said.

"Yes."

"On the cable?"

"Of course."

"Nice to know," I said.

Alice and I went to check out the game room. It was in a small building that I hadn't noticed before, probably because someone had neglected to put a frog on the door. Inside was a single room with a pool table, a ping-pong table, and a big-screen TV.

As an attraction, the game room was only slightly less popular than the swimming pool. Alice and I were the only ones there.

Of course, it was only eight-thirty, and the movie wasn't scheduled to start until nine. Still, aside from the dining room, I was beginning to feel like I was in a ghost town.

"Well, Fast Alice," I said, doing my best Jackie Gleason as Minnesota Fats, "whaddaya say you and me shoot a game of eight ball for ten cents a game?"

Alice has seen *The Hustler* too. She cocked her head at me, à la Paul Newman, and said, "I hear you're a big hustler, Fats. Whaddaya say we make it twenty cents a game?"

"Now I know why they call you Fast Alice," I said, and racked up the balls.

By the time people started showing up for the movie, Alice was up forty cents. I had won one game and lost three. Not that Alice is that much better than I am—actually, we're pretty evenly matched—but two of the games I'd been ahead and lost by scratching on the eight ball.

Anyway, the people who showed up to watch the movie were three women, including the one with the dog. Of course, the dog wasn't with her, that's the only way I know to describe her.

"Hi," she said. "Who's winning?"

I jerked my thumb. "The hustler."

She smiled. "Why am I not surprised?"

"He's setting me up," Alice said. "He lets me win a few games and then raises the stakes."

"Won't you have to stop playing when the movie starts?"

"Well, I'm not the brightest of hustlers," I said. "I'm Stanley, this is my wife, Alice."

"I'm Florence," the woman said.

"Really," I said. "You should have your own room."

She blinked. "I *have* my own room."

"No, I mean your name starts with *F*. You could have your own frog, like Frankie or Freddie."

"Stanley has a strange sense of humor," Alice said.

The woman smiled. "I hadn't thought of that. But now that you mention it, I'm in Fenwick."

"Fenwick?" I said.

She smiled again. "I guess they were running out of *F* names. But, yes, I have Fenwick frog on my door."

"We're in Frankie," I said.

She frowned. "I don't think I've seen Frankie."

I jerked my thumb. "East Pond, second floor."

"Oh, that's why. I'm in the inn."

"Where's Prince?" Alice asked.

"Up in the room. He didn't want to watch the movie."

Neither did I. The movie that night was *Bridges of Madison County,* which was probably why the customers were all women. In my present mood, it was a movie I seemed unlikely to enjoy, so when Louise showed up and slid a videocassette into the VCR, I excused myself and slipped out the door.

I had no idea what I was going to do. There was no Red Sox game, since they'd already played that afternoon, but it occurred to me there might be something on TV, so I wandered back to the inn to check it out.

The young hiker was standing on the front porch. Ordinarily, I'm shy at initiating conversations with people I don't know, but having talked to the girl, I didn't want to avoid talking to him.

So I walked up on the porch and said, "Hi."

If I'd made his day, you wouldn't have known it. He looked at me as if I couldn't possibly be speaking to him. In spite of the fact there was no one else there.

He said, "I beg your pardon?"

That was a conversation killer. As I say, I'm not particularly outgoing. And I'm certainly not one to force a social situation. I had ventured "Hi." As to his response, "*I beg your pardon*" was about as cold as one could get. *Hi* is not ambiguous. *Hi* is relatively simple and straightforward. *Hi* does not require an explanation. Under the circumstances, *I beg your pardon* could be translated as "I don't know you. Why are you talking to me? Leave me alone."

His body language said so also. He seemed fidgety, impatient. He never really focused on me, and kept looking around.

He was obviously waiting for the girl. Impatiently waiting. Which bothered me. I kept remembering the sound of the slap.

Which prompted me to ease my way out of the situation as quickly as possible.

"Anyone in the TV room?" I said.

His slight pause told me what a stupid question that was. He smiled coldly, said, "I have no idea."

I mumbled something about checking it out, gave him up as a lost cause, and went inside.

The dining room was just closing. I saw the young man who had served us our drinks go by with a tray of dishes. So he wasn't the bartender, just the busboy, which certainly made more sense. Unless he *was* the bartender, and in an establishment this small everyone helped with everything.

"He's my son," Louise said, startling me both by her presence and by reading my mind. "It's a family affair, and we all pitch in."

"Oh, really?" I said.

"Yes," she said. "We've only been open for two years, but we're doing very well. The dining room's the key. You run a good dining room, the rest takes care of itself."

And there I was, suddenly stuck in the dreaded bed-and-breakfast personal account of "how I came to buy the place." The crowning blow. The last straw.

Still, I couldn't be out-and-out rude. Something was called for. "That's very interesting," I said. "Who's your chef?"

Louise's eyes narrowed. "Why do you ask?"

I blinked. Because I'm inept in social situations, and I'm trying to make polite conversation was the actual point in fact, but probably wasn't about to charm her. "Because the food was so good," I said.

"Oh? What did you have?"

"I had the prime rib, and my wife had the shark."

"You must try the barbecued ribs," she said. "They're famous. Excuse me, I have to help out."

And she disappeared through the door of the dining room.

I stood there, somewhat bemused. On the one hand, I was pleased to have missed the how-we-came-to-buy-the-place lecture. On the other, it occurred to me the woman had avoided discussing the chef.

I shook my head. Good god, Alice was right. I was getting a little stir crazy, making mysteries out of everything. It occurred to me I'd better find myself something to do.

I checked out the TV room. The six-year-old girl wasn't there, but the middle-aged couple I'd observed earlier having drinks on the porch was. They were watching a TV movie of a fairly predictable variety—just a few minutes were enough to assure me it either had something to do with date rape, incest, or sexual harassment, or else someone's wife, mother, or daughter would turn out to be a call girl.

"Care to join us?" the woman on the couch asked, when the exciting drama paused for a commercial.

"Just checking out the room," I said. "My wife's watching *Bridges of Madison County.*"

"Seen it twice," the woman said. "I could see it again, but Johnny thought twice was enough."

Johnny, who was somewhat pudgy faced, smiled what I took to be a rather long-suffering smile. I must say, my heart went out to him—not being able to stand the movie a third time, he'd been paid back with this.

"Yeah, well I'm just looking around," I said. "Tell me, are there any other things here that aren't in the guidebook?"

"Guidebook?"

"I don't mean guidebook. You know, that little brochure about the inn. It listed the swimming pool and this TV room, but it didn't say anything about the game room. You know, where they're showing the movie. So I'm wondering if there's anything else at Blue Frog Ponds the brochure neglected to mention."

"Can't think of anything," the woman said.

"There's the pond," Johnny offered.

Johnny's wife was rather small and thin compared to him. Still, there was little doubt as to the pecking order. She turned on Johnny now. "The *pond,* for goodness' sake?" she said. "That's not what the man means. The man doesn't mean the pond."

"Well, now, how do you know what he means?" Johnny said.

"Well, didn't he just say so? The brochure didn't mention the game room, what else did it leave out? The man is talking about features of the inn."

"The pond's not a feature?"

"The pond's not even on the property. And what do you think about that?" the woman said. "They call the place the Blue Frog Ponds, and the pond's not even theirs."

"Where is the pond?"

Johnny jerked his thumb. "On the other side of the road. The stream widens out, forms a little pond. There's a path down to it from the parking lot. You can't miss it."

"Hush, now," Johnny's wife said. "It's starting again."

If that wasn't an exit cue, I never heard one. The movie was indeed starting again, and I didn't want to see it. I beat a hasty retreat outside.

The cranky young man was gone, and the front porch was deserted. I stood in front of the Blue Frog Ponds and looked around. The sun had just gone down, and there was an orange glow over the top of the mountains in the west. Farther east, you could see the crescent of the moon in the sky, and the stars starting to come out.

I enjoyed looking at the sky, which I guess labeled me as a tourist—if you live in New York City, it's a big deal to look at the sky.

I looked at the parking lot across the road where we'd left our Toyota. Johnny'd said there was a path leading from it. I crossed the road and took a closer look.

There it was, down by the far end. A dirt path leading off through the trees. It didn't appear to be overgrown, and it wasn't really that dark. And the stream couldn't be that far away. In fact, I could hear the sound of running water. So I figured, *what the heck, it's an adventure,* and set off down the path.

After a couple of minutes I came to the stream. It was a narrow stream, not more than ten to twenty feet wide, which came twisting and turning down the hill through a series of rocks. In spring it might have been a raging torrent, but it was quite tame now. It looked shallow enough to wade across, if one had a mind. I wasn't about to get my feet wet. I set off downstream, looking for the pond.

It didn't take long. It was right around the first bend. I came through the trees, and there it was. An actual pond, no doubt about it, a good forty to fifty feet wide, just off the far side of the stream.

When the stream was high it probably fed the pond. At the moment it was separated by a little bank of mud and rocks. It was just dark enough that the moonlight reflected off the pond made the little grove in which it stood seem like an entirely romantic setting.

Or maybe it was the young couple embracing in the shadow of the pine trees beside the stream. I didn't see them at first, and they clearly didn't see me, because they went on about their business as if I wasn't there. But some movement or other caught my eye, and suddenly there they were, necking to beat the band.

I couldn't see them clearly, and I had no idea who they were. Nor did I care. All I wanted to do was get out of there as quickly as possible, before I embarrassed them by my presence.

Then they turned slightly, and moonlight fell on the young woman's hair.

It was blond.

A blond page-boy cut.

Just my luck. And what did I do to deserve it? Here I am, minding my own business, and I happen to stumble over the Swedish hiking couple and wind up spying on their love life. What was Alice going to make of that?

I'd just had that thought when the young couple swung around sideways and light fell on their faces.

It was indeed the Swedish hiking beauty, she of the infinitesimal swimsuit.

But the young man kissing her didn't have blond hair.

His hair was dark.

Uh-oh.

He was the young man who had brought us our drinks.

The busboy.

Louise's son.

EIGHT

I DREAMED SOMETHING was treading on my chest. It was one of those dreams where you're afraid you're going to wake up and find out it's true.

I opened my eyes.

Blinked.

A large, orange, striped cat was kneading up and down on my chest with its paws, clearly tromping down a spot on which to lie. While I gawked at it in amazement, the cat completed its task, made a 360-degree turn as if screwing itself in, and plopped down on my chest and proceeded to purr.

The door opened, and Alice came in.

"You have a cat on your chest," she said.

"I see that."

"Why do you have a cat on your chest?"

"I'm not entirely sure. I guess I left the door unlatched. Was it open just now?"

"Yes, it was."

"Then I must not have closed it all the way. Either that, or this cat has mastered doorknobs."

"How long has he been there?"

"I woke up, and he was tromping on my chest. He lay down, and you came in."

"You look adorable."

"I'm glad to hear it. How was the movie?"

"You wouldn't have liked it."

"Yeah, I know. Thank you."

"For what?"

"Not making me see it. Johnny's wife made him sit through it twice."

"Who's Johnny?"

"The couple having drinks on the porch. They didn't go to the movie because they'd already seen it twice."

"Really?" Alice said. "You actually introduced yourself to them?"

"Not really. I just went in the TV room, and they were there. Watching some god-awful movie of the week."

"You watched with them?"

"Not if you paid me. I'd have rather watched your movie. Boy, is this strange."

"What?"

"You ever try talking with a cat on your chest?"

"Not that I recollect."

"Well, he's vibrating with my voice box, and the effect is a little weird. Anyway, that's not what I did tonight."

"What did you do?"

I told Alice about my adventure finding the pond. It was not easy with the cat on my chest, but I did my best.

"You found her necking?" Alice said. "Stanley, what is it with you and this girl? Are you following her around?"

"Don't be silly. I had no idea she was there."

"And yet she turns up everywhere you go."

"I wasn't the one necking with her, Alice."

"So who was?"

"The busboy," I said. It was my trump card, and I played it casually. "Louise's son."

Alice's eyes widened. "Randy?" she said. "She was making out with Randy?"

So much for my victory. I gave Alice a pained look. "His name's Randy?" I said. "How do you know that?"

"Don't be silly," Alice said. "Louise's son is named Randy. He went to Dartmouth two years, dropped out for a year, and bummed around, but he's going back in the fall. In the meantime he's living at home, helping out at the inn."

I snorted in disgust. The cat raised its head, gave me a dirty look, then got to its feet and stretched and yawned, digging its claws into my chest. It was not painful, just annoying. I cocked my head at the cat, said, "Is that really necessary?"

In answer, the cat swung a one eighty and managed to smack me in the face with its tail, in the process of going through the whole stretching routine again. Then, thoroughly satisfied with itself, it climbed down off me, curled up in a ball next to me, and began purring loudly.

"You have such a way with animals," Alice said.

"I didn't do anything," I said. "I'm just lying here. Would you mind telling me how you know all about Louise's son?"

"Everyone knows about Louise's son," Alice said. "Jean and Joan told me, but Florence knew it too."

"Jean and Joan?"

"Yes. The two women who came in together. To the movie."

"What two women who came in together?"

"Stanley, we were shooting pool, and Florence came in with those other women. That was Jean and Joan."

"Oh?"

"You didn't notice the women who came in?"

"Not particularly. Was there any reason that I should?"

"Absolutely not," Alice said. "None of them were young and attractive and practically naked. So there was no reason for you to notice them at all."

"Give me a break."

"So Randy was making out with Christine. How interesting."

"Her name's Christine?"

"You didn't know that? Yes, her name's Christine, and her boyfriend is Lars."

"Boyfriend?"

"More than likely. Of course some married women retain their last names. But they're registered as Lars Heinrick and Christine Cobb."

I blinked. "How in the world do you know all this?"

"Are you kidding?" Alice said. "An attractive young couple like that, you think people aren't going to notice them?"

I opened my mouth, closed it again. After all the grief I'd been getting for noticing them, what could I possibly say to that?

"Anyway," Alice said, "Jean snuck a peek at the registration book—Jean's the nosier of the two, even before I knew she did that, you could just tell—and that's how they're registered." Alice cocked her head. "Would you like their room number?"

"I'd prefer their frog."

Alice frowned. "I don't know their frog. It's not listed that way in the register. I think to find out, you'd have to go and see. Anyway, their room's in the main building. Room four."

"I'd go look, but I don't want to disturb the cat."

"Of course not."

"You wouldn't know its name, would you?"

"I didn't even know there was a cat."

"I'm surprised. What about the chef?"

"What about him?"

"You happen to know who he is?"

"That's rather sexist."

"What?"

"Assuming the chef is a man."

I blinked. "Alice. You said, 'What about him?' "

"So?"

"*You* assumed he's a man."

"No, I didn't."

"What?"

"I didn't assume he's a man. I *know* he's a man. It's not sexist to call the chef a man if you know he's a man."

"You know who the chef is?"

"Of course I do."

"Why am I surprised?"

"I don't know. I don't even know why you were asking."

"Because I asked Louise about the chef, and she changed the subject."

"You asked Louise about the chef?"

"I wasn't prying. She asked me about dinner. I had to say something. I asked who the chef was, she didn't answer and excused herself."

"He's her husband."

"Oh?"

"They're not getting along. That's why she didn't want to talk about him."

"Alice."

"Well, it's common knowledge. You can tell just to look at her, that is not a woman in a happy relationship. Anyway, Charlie's the cook."

"Her husband's named Charlie?"

"Didn't I just say that? And there's no way she'd divorce him, because his recipes are to die for."

I sat up a little too quickly for the cat, which sprang to its feet and arched its back, its tail lashing furiously.

"Alice," I said. "How could you say something like that?"

"Well, it's true. The only reason they're making a go of it is the dining room. Without that, the whole place goes under."

"You're suggesting Louise stay with a husband she doesn't love just to keep a business venture afloat?"

"You think she should divorce her husband?"

"I don't think anything of the sort."

"Then what are you talking about?"

"About what you said."

"I didn't say anything."

"Yes, you did. You said she couldn't divorce her husband."

"So?"

"What do you mean, so? That's the whole point. You're the one who brought up divorce."

"I didn't bring it up. I said it was out of the question."

"For financial reasons?"

"Of course."

"Alice, you can't admit that. That's the whole argument."

"What argument?"

I had no idea. My mind was mush, and I couldn't keep anything straight in my head. Which usually happens when I try to argue with Alice. After years of marriage, you'd think I'd know better.

I sighed, scratched the cat under the chin. It regarded me suspiciously a moment, then, mollified, lay down, and curled up again.

I looked at Alice. "So," I said, "here we are, once again, in our TV-less room with nothing to do."

"I'm going to bed," Alice said.

"My thought, exactly."

"I'm going to sleep. We have to be up early in the morning."

"Why?"

"We have a seven-thirty breakfast reservation."

"Seven-thirty?"

"Sure. We don't want to sleep all day. It's not like in the city. We're in the country. When the light comes in the window, you're going to want to get up."

"I'll get up," I said. "I promise you, I'll have no problem getting up. Whether I go to sleep right now, or just a little bit later."

Alice smiled and slipped out of her hiking shorts, which I thought was a promising sign.

It wasn't.

She went in the bathroom, emerging minutes later in her flannel pajamas.

"Good night," she said, getting into bed.

I made one last feeble attempt, which earned me nothing but a reminder that the walls were paper-thin, after which Alice rolled over and went right to sleep.

It's amazing how she can do that. I have trouble falling asleep. Usually, what helps me go to sleep is watching television.

I sighed, got up, trying not to disturb the cat, and rummaged through the suitcase for my book. It was a murder mystery I'd brought along at Alice's urging—when we were packing she said, "Bring a book," so I'd brought a book. But I hadn't expected to read it, so I'd just plucked it off the shelf almost at random. It was an Agatha Christie that I'd probably read before, but didn't really remember the title.

As soon as I began reading I realized why. The paperback had been published with its British title. I knew it under its American one. So *4:50 from Paddington,* which I thought was a Hercule Poirot novel I had never read, was really *What Mrs. McGillicudy Saw!,* a Miss Marple novel I had not only read before, but also remembered who did it.

Oh, well. At least it ought to put me to sleep.

Only it didn't. I have trouble adjusting to new surroundings, and my first night in a new bed I usually have a devil of a time.

Tonight was no exception. I tossed and turned, fussed with the blankets, readjusted the pillows, apologized to the cat, and worried about whether I should leave the door open so it could go out.

And reread Agatha Christie. Every now and then looking over at Alice and cursing the paper-thin walls.

Unfortunately, the state of the walls was a fact I could not dispute. When our next-door neighbors returned twenty pages later, I could hear them quite clearly. I could hear them moving around the room, washing up, and getting into bed.

I could hear them in bed.

And they either had no inhibitions whatsoever, or else they were totally unaware they could be heard.

It was so distracting, I couldn't read. All I could do was listen. And hope they wouldn't wake the cat.

As I lay there, next to my attractive-yet-sleeping wife, listening to their nocturnal activities, which seemed to be going on for quite some time, it occurred to me that Frankie, the frog on my door, had his hands in his pockets and a rueful smile, while Freddie, on their door, was winking and signaling, A-okay!

NINE

"I **HAVE A** cat in my room."

"An orange, stripey cat?" Louise said.

"That's the one."

"That's Max. He's a sweetheart. Is he bothering you?"

"No. I was just afraid someone might be missing him."

"Don't worry. He's not that type of cat. Very independent. Likes to hang out with the guests. If you get sick of him, throw him out. He'll show up at the kitchen door when he's hungry."

"He's your cat?"

"In a manner of speaking. He belongs to the inn. Oh, here's your wife."

Alice came in from the porch where she had stopped to talk to two women on her way to breakfast. As usual, I had misread the situation. Like a fool, I had assumed that people on their way to breakfast intended to eat breakfast. At the door to the inn I had gone inside, only to watch Alice veer off in the other direction. This had left me inside the inn but outside the dining room. Hence the conversation with Louise about the cat.

"Good morning, Mrs. Hastings," Louise said. "Seven-thirty breakfast reservation, right this way."

She led us into the dining room and sat us at a table. "Your waitress will be right with you."

When she left, I jerked my thumb in the direction of the porch. "Jean and Joan?"

"Uh-huh."

"Which is which?"

"Jean's thinner."

That did it for me. Jean was the one with leathery skin and short, frosted hair. Joan was the plump one with the glasses and curly, blond permanent.

"Uh-huh," I said. "Am I to assume you stopped to gossip about what I observed last night by the pond?"

"Gossip?" Alice said. "My, what a rude word."

"I'm sorry," I said. "You mean you didn't tell them?"

"I may have mentioned it," Alice said. "In passing. But I don't see the big deal. It's the sort of thing you'd comment on. After all, you told me."

"You're my wife."

"Exactly," Alice said. "If it's something you'd tell your wife, it's certainly worth repeating."

"Certainly," I said. "So that's Jean and Joan. Do you know there's a song about them?"

"There is?"

"Well, not about them. But there's a Jean and Joan in a song. As I recall, the chorus goes, *You've got to change your evil ways, baby.*"

"You're just making that up."

"No, I'm not. Don't you remember the song. It goes—"

"No. Don't sing. Not at the breakfast table."

"Just a chorus."

"Stanley."

Our waitress appeared. She couldn't sneak up on us the way she could when we were in a booth, still there was something in the way she approached our table that made her seem like something out of an old movie. Something furtive. A spy, perhaps, or secret agent.

I chided myself for having such a vivid imagination.

She set a pot of coffee down on the table.

Then, to my utter amazement, she glanced left and right, palmed a piece of paper from the pocket of her apron, and surreptitiously slid it under the corner of Alice's plate.

"I'll be back to take your order," she said, and hurried off to another table.

"What in the world?" I said.

"Shh," Alice said. "Act natural."

I got it. Of course. Alice was getting back at me for the way I'd acted at dinner last night. How she'd gotten the waitress in on it I had no idea, but somehow she had, and now she was playing it for all it was worth, opening and reading the paper under the table.

"Okay, I'll bite," I said. "What's the secret message?"

"You can see it. Just don't make a big deal out of it. Here, take a look. Just don't let anyone else see."

I took the paper Alice handed me and unfolded it.

It was a Xerox copy. There was writing on it in longhand. I squinted to make it out.

MIRIAM'S CHOCOLATE CAKE

1 can of Hershey syrup

4 eggs

1 cup self-rising flour

¼ pound butter

⅔ cup sugar

Cream butter and sugar. Add eggs, syrup, and flour, and stir. Pour into greased 9" square. Bake at 375° for 35 to 40 minutes.

Serve unfrosted.

I looked up at Alice. "A recipe?"

"Shh. You don't have to shout it all over the place. Of course it's a recipe. For the cake I had last night."

"I thought you couldn't get the recipe."

"You can't. I slipped Lucy ten bucks to get it for me."

"Lucy?"

"Our waitress."

"You paid ten bucks for the recipe?"

"Stanley. Did you taste that cake?"

I had, and it was rather good. Still, ten bucks is ten bucks.

Lucy returned to take our order. She made no reference to the recipe. Indeed, there was nothing in her manner to indicate anything out of the ordinary had occurred.

Nor was there in ours. We merely placed our orders. Alice had waffles, and I had the French toast.

Lucy went out, and Johnny and his wife came in. They must have missed Louise somehow, because they came in alone. With no one to show them to a table, they stood and looked around. After a few moments they spotted us and came over.

"Good morning," Johnny said. "You find that pond all right?"

"As a matter of fact, I did. Ah, this is my wife, Alice."

"Pleased to meet you. I'm Johnny. This is my wife, Clara."

"So," Clara said to Alice, "you went to the movie last night?"

"Yes."

"I wanted to go, but stick-in-the-mud here wouldn't see it."

"Seen it twice," Johnny said.

"We've already ordered, but would you care to join us?" Alice said.

"Oh, we wouldn't want to intrude," Johnny said.

Clara sat right down, said, "Thank you so much," and proceeded to pour herself a cup of coffee.

I couldn't quite believe that Alice had offered or that Clara had accepted. I'm not sure Johnny could either, but he sat down, and his wife poured him a cup of coffee too.

Lucy returned with our orders. Alice's waffle was covered with berries—strawberries, raspberries, blueberries, and even had a slice of melon. My French toast was thick and cinnamon-sugar glazed.

"That French toast sure looks good," Johnny said. "I'll have that."

"You will not," Clara said. "Look at that sugar glaze. You want to drop dead on me, you go ahead and eat like that. Now, I'll have the waffles and berries. There's a sensible meal."

After a moment's hesitation, Johnny sheepishly ordered the waffles too.

I didn't know whether to gloat. After all, I had the French toast. On the other hand, when I'd ordered it, Alice hadn't seen what it was like.

Florence came in with the two women I now recognized as Jean and Joan. Louise seated them at a table across the room. Florence, who was facing us, smiled and waved.

"You know Florence?" Clara said.

"We met her yesterday," I said. "On a hike. At Champney Falls. Nice woman."

"Yes," Clara said. "But she has that awful dog."

"Prince?" Alice said. "Oh, he's a sweetheart."

"Yes, but he's not trained. And he sheds. And drools. And he's a terrible beggar. God forbid you should give him any food."

"Did you hear that, Stanley?" Alice said. "Stanley gave him a sandwich." She managed to make it sound like a crime.

"Excuse me," I said, "but I'm going to eat this while it's hot."

I cut off a piece of French toast, dipped it in maple syrup.

"Gee, look who's here," Alice said.

I looked over my shoulder to see Louise ushering in the Swedish hiking couple. It took me a second to realize I knew their names. Another second to realize I wasn't quite sure what they were. Oh, yes, he's Lars. Not that surprising. She's Christine. Though I'd imagined her more an Inga.

Louise seated them in one of the booths. They must have reserved it. It occurred to me if we'd only had the foresight to do so, we would have escaped dining with Johnny and Clara.

Once Lars and Christine were seated in their booth, they were out of sight. Which should have put them out of mind.

Except.

A pot of coffee was delivered to their booth.

And it wasn't the waitress who brought it.

It was the busboy.

Louise's son, Randy.

Whom I had seen kissing Christine last night by the pond.

That certainly made for an interesting dynamic. A glance at Alice showed that she thought so, too, but wasn't about to mention anything in front of Clara and Johnny.

The table across the way was far less restrained. Jean, Joan, and Florence had their heads together whispering furiously, and every now and then one of them would glance in the direction of the booth.

Lucy returned with Johnny and Clara's waffles, then headed to the booth to take the young couple's order. There was a lull in the conversation while Johnny and Clara dug in. I accepted it gratefully, settled back, sipped my coffee, and surveyed the room.

The dining room was not as crowded as it had been for dinner. I assumed breakfast was primarily for the guests. At any rate, aside from those I've already mentioned, the only other people in the room were the men I'd seen last night in the bar. This morning they looked more like tourists, in shorts and hiking boots. They sat in the corner, finishing up breakfast and reading the paper. I wondered where they'd gotten the paper, which appeared to be *The New York Times*.

I also wondered if they were gay. And chided myself for the thought. Surely two men could travel together without being gay. On the other hand, maybe they were.

I wondered what their frog looked like.

Prompted by the thought, I turned to Johnny. "Who's your frog?"

He stopped with a forkful of waffle halfway to his mouth. "Huh?"

"The frog on the door of your room. What's his name?"

"Name?"

"Yeah. All the frogs have names. Ours is Frankie. What's yours?"

Johnny looked at Clara. "What's our frog's name?"

She stopped sawing her waffle and impaled him with a look. "Well now, Johnny McInnerny, how would you expect me to know that?"

Well, I guess that told me. Granted, Clara'd felt far more free to smash her husband down than if I'd been the one asking her, still the original question was mine.

Which sort of drew the line in the sand. So, don't care to know the name of your frog, eh? Well, Clara, baby, you and Johnny just lost a chance to go on my list of the all-time great fun couples.

Nonetheless, part of her answer I liked—calling her husband by his last name. Now, instead of constantly saying Johnny and Clara, I could refer to them as the McInnernys. It occurred to me what minutely small satisfactions I was managing to glean from this vacation.

Out of the corner of my eye I saw Lucy usher another couple in. They came right by our table, and I got a closer look. I was impressed. They were a most attractive couple. Not as young and perfect as the one in the booth, but still. The man was maybe thirty-five, but his face was smooth and unwrinkled, and his hair was jet-black, and all in all he looked like he'd just stepped out of high school.

The woman looked equally young, but gave the opposite impression—that the bright eyes and curly brown hair belonged to the vice president of something. Something big, like an airline or movie studio.

Anyway, the pair looked mismatched. It occurred to me, maybe they *were* mismatched. That this man and this woman were having an affair.

I looked at Alice, to see if this had registered.

Alice had indeed noticed the couple. To the McInnernys she said, "Who is that?"

"I have no idea," Clara said. "I haven't seen them before."

"Me, either," Johnny said. "You suppose they just got here?"

"Either that or they don't get out much," I said.

It had just occurred to me, maybe they were the couple I had heard next door. I hadn't mentioned them to Alice. I figured it would just give her more ammunition for invoking the passion-free zone.

I'd just had that thought when a little girl came bounding into the dining room, and went bubbling up to their table, squealing, "Mommy! Daddy!" and establishing the fact that what we were observing was your basic stable family unit.

"They didn't just get here," I said. "That's the kid who was in the TV room yesterday when I wanted to watch the Red Sox game."

"You should have thrown her out," Johnny said.

"Absolutely," Clara said. "People have no business bringing children to a place like this."

That did it. That was the last straw. I had had it with the McInnernys. They didn't like children, and they didn't like dogs. Well, I didn't like them.

I was not about to be rude, you understand. Or even start an argument. I just made a mental note to be sure to tell Alice never to invite them again.

Not that there was any danger of that. Alice was clearly as eager to get away from the McInnernys as I was. She attacked her breakfast at what had to be a record pace, and said, "Well, we better be going if we're going to get any hiking done."

"Start at Pinkham Notch," Johnny said. "They'll fit you out with everything you need."

"Where's that?"

"Pinkham Notch Visitors Center. It's on the way to Mount Washington. You can't miss it. A great big lodge by the side of the road. Information center, dining room, lodge, what-have-you. Everybody starts out there."

"Uh-huh," Alice said. "And that's right on the way to Mount Washington?"

"Uh-huh. Can't miss it. As a matter fact, we're going there ourselves, we could show you the way."

"Oh, that won't be necessary," I said.

"Don't be silly," Clara said. "We're hiking there ourselves. Johnny, we should show them Pinkham Notch."

"Absolutely," Johnny said. "We know the best trails to hike. Stick with us, and you can't go wrong."

"But you've already hiked those trails," Alice said. "You wouldn't want to do it again."

"Oh, that's no problem," Clara said. "Some of those trails are beautiful."

"See," Johnny said. "She's willing to see that stupid movie three times, you think she can't hike a trail again?"

"So, it's settled," Clara said. "Johnny and I will show you Pinkham Notch."

I looked at Alice for help, saw she was at a loss.

I looked at Johnny, smiled weakly.

Kill me now, vengeful gods. Kill me now.

TEN

SAVED BY THE dog.

In the nick of time, Prince saved the day. A true hero, just like Lassie or Rin-Tin-Tin.

You see, Florence and Jean and Joan came along to Pinkham Notch. And Florence brought Prince. And the McInnernys didn't like dogs.

What a relief.

As they made their excuses and scuttled down some trail or another, I could hardly keep from cheering. Florence and Prince were lifesavers. I even felt a fondness for Jean and Joan. I didn't know them at all, but compared to the McInnernys they had to be saints.

So, having dispensed with our would-be guides, we were now left to happily work things out on our own.

Alice, Jean and Joan, and I went into the visitors center and came back armed with instructions on what were described as easy but fun hikes.

The first one was across the highway just beyond the far end of the parking lot. We crossed the road with Prince on a leash, and found a narrow trail leading off into the woods. For a while it was easygoing. Then about a hundred yards in, the trail began to slope up, first gradually, then steeper and steeper, and before you know it we were scrambling over rocks, bracing ourselves against tree trunks, and climbing from one ledge to another.

Prince seemed to have no trouble with the terrain, but I found it hard going. I wasn't about to complain, though, what with Jean and Joan scampering up the hill as happy as clams. I gritted my teeth, and scampered along with 'em, wondering just how high this damn mountain was.

Not very. At least, not where we were going. In about twenty minutes we emerged from the woods on the top of a cliff.

"Wow, look at that," Alice said.

Alice, of course, was well ahead of me and had reached the edge of the cliff. I stepped out gingerly—heights are not one of my favorite things.

Prince rocketed by me, and I nearly jumped a mile. I was pretty far back from the edge, still I had a moment of panic as I envisioned the dog taking a flying leap and sailing off into nowhere. Fortunately, Prince skidded to a stop and proceeded to look out with all due caution. I made my way to the edge of the cliff, where Jean and Joan had already joined Florence and Alice.

Wow. Even for a skeptic, I had to admit it was pretty impressive. Below the cliff, the mountain we had just climbed fell away as a slope of rocks dissolved into a slope of treetops that leveled off into a sea of green that stretched out and eventually reached the road. Across the road, and a little to the right, was the sprawling Pinkham Notch recreation center. And behind it, rising majestically up to the sky, was the Mount Washington mountain range.

I'd seen it, of course, from below, but not like this. At Pinkham Notch you were surrounded by mountains towering around you, too close to see. Here, from the perspective of height and distance, was an entire panorama.

"Hey," I said, "this is spectacular."

"Worth the climb?" Alice said.

"Absolutely," I said. I was rather cocky, knowing how much easier the trip down would be.

We enjoyed the view a little longer, then moved back from the edge and sat down on the rocks for a drink.

Joan had a water bottle on her waist, and she and Jean drank out of that. They drank right from the bottle.

Alice and I had a bottle in the backpack, and paper cups.

Florence had a paper cup for herself, and a plastic bowl for Prince. He lapped his water gratefully and sloppily, spilling as much as he drank.

After that, we packed up our gear and headed out, which seemed sensible to me. It was a spectacular view, but we'd seen it, so on to something else.

"So, what's next?" I said, after we'd clambered down the rocks and were back on level ground.

"Glen Ellis Falls," Alice said.

"Uh-huh," I said. "And that's listed as . . ."

"Short, easy, ideal for the grumpiest husband," Alice said.

Florence, Jean, and Joan laughed. I realized in this group I had lost my identity, been subjugated to the role of Alice's husband, a notorious stick-in-the-mud, to be humored and gotten around.

It was a bit of a surprise to realize I didn't really mind.

Glen Ellis Falls was just a mile down the road. We pulled into the parking lot, piled out of our cars, and took the tunnel under the highway to the trail.

It was the easiest hike yet. A gravel path twisted down into the ravine. We followed it about a quarter of a mile, and suddenly we were there, at the top of Glen Ellis Falls.

Which was a mighty impressive sight. It was a high falls, formed by a stream of water flowing between two boulders and cascading down the mountain into a pool below. I whipped out the guidebook and was able to announce that the falls was sixty-four feet high, and had been originally called Pitcher Falls because the rock formation at the top made it look like water flowing out of a pitcher.

As I made these announcements, I realized I was losing my audience. Prince had not stopped at the top of the falls, and the women were now following him down the stone steps toward the bottom. I stuck the guidebook in the backpack and tagged along.

At the base of the falls, we climbed out on the rocks. This is one of the attractions of Glen Ellis Falls. In good weather, you can leave the stone steps and scramble around on the flat rocks surrounding the pool. Everyone else seemed to be doing it, so we did too. Alice climbed out, followed by Jean and Joan. Florence even brought Prince. She kept him on the leash, but let him climb. He seemed more surefooted than I would have given him credit for.

Not wanting to be an old stick-in-the-mud, I stashed the backpack behind a rock, and climbed out too.

It was fun scrambling from rock to rock. I could see why this falls was such a tourist attraction. Aside from the great view, you really felt you were part of it. Leaving the path. Climbing around. It had just the right sense of adventure, of doing something you weren't really supposed to do. Although, of course, you were. Scrambling on the rocks was even advertised in the guidebook.

Be that as it may, Glen Ellis Falls was a pretty good time, and I sort of hated to leave.

I hated to leave for another reason. The path was up. When we started back to the car, that was the main thing in my mind.

The fact we were going up. The other falls we'd climbed up to, and then come down. Not this time. This time we'd climbed down to the falls, and had to go up. Which was really a shame, and put a damper on what was otherwise a perfectly enjoyable outing.

The thing is, that was in my mind, but I wasn't saying it. And I was making a very conscious effort not to say it. Because it certainly seemed a normal thing to say, but seemed too grouchy even for the old grouch role I'd been reduced to playing.

Anyway, the point is, I had all that in my head when we left the falls.

Preoccupying me.

Distracting me.

Making me careless.

Which is why I felt like such a fool when we finally reached the top of the hill and headed for the parking lot and Alice said, "Where's the backpack?"

Uh-oh.

I knew where the backpack was. Right there at the base of the falls where I'd taken it off to go scrambling around on the rocks. I hadn't given it a second thought.

I explained the situation to Alice with as much dignity as I could muster, and hurried off down the path, trying to ignore the laughter and comments emanating from Florence and Alice and Jean and Joan.

At least going down to the falls was easy. Though it didn't seem easy, with the foreknowledge of what the climb back up was going to be. Still, going down was a breeze. I reached the bottom in no time at all, came around the corner into the alcove where I'd left my backpack.

And bumped right into her.

Like a fool, I hadn't been looking where I was going, I'd been looking at my backpack.

I stepped back, put up my hands, said, "Excuse me."

She said, "You."

I blinked.

It was her. My nemesis. The Swedish hiker. What's-her-name. Not Inga. Christine.

Good lord.

Christine.

"Yes," I said. "I'm sorry. I left my backpack. I wasn't looking where I was going."

She kept looking at me. "It was you, wasn't it?"

"Huh?"

"Last night. By the pond."

"Oh."

"It *was* you," she said. "I thought so. You saw me, didn't you? Didn't you?"

What could I say? "Yeah, that was me."

"I knew it. Promise me something. Promise me you won't tell anybody. You won't, will you? Promise me you won't."

"Okay," I said. "I won't."

All right, so it wasn't an exact truth. But what was I going to tell her? That half the people in the place knew anyway? That her romance with Louise's son was probably the number-one gossip topic at Blue Frog Ponds? That certainly seemed a little harsh. All she'd asked me was not to tell anybody. Well, I certainly wouldn't tell anybody.

Else.

ELEVEN

GRILLED MAKO SHARK WITH MANGO SALSA

2 mako shark steaks, approximately ½ pound each

1 tablespoon extra-virgin olive oil

MANGO SALSA

2 ripe mangoes, peeled and diced into ¼ inch pieces

3 tablespoons chopped red onion

2 cloves garlic, finely chopped

1 tablespoon jalapeño pepper, roasted and chopped

¼ teaspoon kosher salt

3 tablespoons lime juice

3 tablespoons chopped fresh cilantro

Makes 2 cups

To prepare the Mango Salsa: Seed and derib the jalapeño. Roast at 500° for 10 minutes. Peel off skin and chop. Combine with remaining ingredients.

To prepare the fish for grilling: Coat with 1 tablespoon of extra-virgin olive oil on each side. Salt and pepper. Grill to taste approximately 4 to 5 minutes on each side.

Garnish fish with a slice of lime and a sprig of cilantro. Serve with Mango Salsa.

Serves 2.

I looked up at Alice. "You paid ten bucks for this?"

She frowned, glanced around the dining room. "Please. Be a little discreet."

"I don't understand. Why do you want this recipe?"

"Stanley. Did you taste that sauce?"

"It was good."

"It was to die for."

"Whatever. The point is, when are you ever going to cook shark?"

"You don't understand." Alice turned to Florence. Smiled. "He doesn't understand."

"What's to understand?" I said. "You either cook shark or you don't. If you don't, why pay ten dollars for a sauce."

"Five dollars."

"Huh?"

"Florence and I are splitting it."

"Oh, is that right?"

"That's right," Florence said.

"You mean you cook shark?"

Florence smiled. "You don't understand."

I certainly didn't. But then I was approaching the problem from the warped male viewpoint of one used to buying things one intended to use. Even so, I probably wouldn't have made such a big deal of it if I hadn't been subjected to rather unmerciful husband-bashing all day long.

"So," I said. "Let me be sure I understand this. The two of you have joined forces to purchase a recipe for a dish you have no intention of ever preparing. Just because you happen to like the recipe."

"See, he does understand," Florence said.

I blinked. "No, no. I wasn't being serious. I was ridiculing the concept."

"And very amusingly too," Alice said. "Now, if you could just do so in a slightly lower voice."

I don't know if I might have pursued the topic, but at that moment my girlfriend came in with her boyfriend. I use the terms loosely. My girlfriend was of course Inga/Christine, my bathing companion and confidante. The boyfriend I was referring to was Lars, cranky Swedish hiking companion. Not unhappily married Louise bed-and-breakfast owner's busboy son, Randy.

They were shown to their booth by the younger, less severe-looking waitress, who to the best of my knowledge was not augmenting her income by peddling Xerox copies of pilfered recipes of Louise's husband, the chef's specialties to the guests.

Anyway, she showed the happy couple to a booth directly behind me, for which I was eternally grateful. I didn't want to be constantly glancing at the young woman, wondering if she was glancing at me.

You see, I hadn't had a chance to tell Alice yet. About our meeting by the waterfall. Because when I got back to the parking lot, Florence and Jean and Joan were there. And I'd promised. Given my word. And I couldn't see telling everybody after I'd promised. Even though they already knew, still, it didn't seem right. It was like compounding a felony, adding insult to injury, rubbing salt in the wound. I don't know exactly, but the point is, I didn't feel comfortable telling people.

Except Alice. I had to tell Alice. I meant to tell Alice. I intended to tell Alice. And I was going to tell Alice.

I just hadn't had a chance to tell Alice.

So, since I hadn't been able to tell Alice about the waterfall rendezvous, I certainly didn't want her to catch the young lady in question trying to flash me secret, unspoken messages with her eyes.

If you can't understand that, you are undoubtedly single.

"Are you ready to order?" Lucy said.

I hadn't even realized she was there. She'd disappeared earlier, after slipping the recipe under Alice's plate.

"Yes," I said. I wasn't about to blow it this time. I went right for the appetizer. "I'd like to start off with the barbecued ribs."

"Uh-huh," Lucy said. "You mean the special, or off the menu?"

Good lord. She'd told us the specials, and I hadn't heard a word. I'd been too preoccupied with other things. But it probably wouldn't be prudent to admit that now.

"From the menu," I said. "The ribs on the menu. The ones you said were famous."

"Uh-huh," she said. "And for the main course?"

"I'll have the petite filet mignon," I said, with complete confidence. It was a small portion, described as lighter fare, and would not open me to ridicule, like ordering the prime rib.

Lucy blinked. "But that *is* the special," she said. "The barbecued ribs and petite filet combination. Of course, you can order it à la carte if you want, but it's exactly the same thing, and it'll cost you about six dollars more."

"I'm sorry," I said. "I misunderstood you. Yes, of course, that's exactly what I want. I'll have the special."

"Space cadet," Alice said, shaking her head.

Fortunately, she and Florence still had to order, which kept them from giving me too much grief. Florence had the salmon filet. Alice had some sort of veal dish I had a feeling we'd wind up with the recipe for tomorrow.

When Lucy left, the husband-bashing got a little heavy, so I excused myself to go to the bathroom.

The minute I got up, I realized I'd forgotten where the bathroom was. That's not exactly right. I knew where it was. I'd forgotten who I had to walk by to get there. Fortunately, when I went by their booth, they were being served drinks, so no one noticed me.

But I certainly noticed them. Particularly since the one again serving them was none other than the busboy, Louise's son, Randy. It still made for an interesting dynamic. Of course I couldn't see much, what with the booth being semiprivate and all, but in my split-second window of opportunity as I passed by, I could swear I saw boyfriend Lars looking suspicious and Inga/Christine looking concerned.

Then I was by them and out the door of the dining room, and I couldn't for the life of me swear if I was making the whole thing up.

I stood there a second, laughed, and shook my head. The two guys traveling together whom I thought might be gay were back in the bar, and looked up. I smiled a completely impersonal, noncommittal, meaningless smile, turned and beat a retreat to the men's room.

I went in, splashed water on my face, had a little talk with myself. I'm not sure exactly what I told me, but I seem to recall a somewhat sarcastic observation that it was a good thing I hadn't opted for a job in the secret service.

On my way back into the dining room I had to pass by their booth again.

Oh, boy.

They were having a fight. Or at least an argument. Or at least a disagreement of some kind.

Not that I heard anything. They weren't loud. In fact, they weren't even talking. All I saw was the tableau.

The girl sat up straight, staring ahead with a blank look, as if seeing nothing. A tear ran down her cheek. Or had run down her cheek—it had stopped now, suspended in the hollow of her cheekbone. She looked like she had just lost her last friend in the world.

The young man sat glaring at her. His chin set, his eyes hard. He looked positively murderous.

Neither moved.

Well, so much for my little attempt to compose myself.

I went back to my table, sat down, said, perhaps a little too heartily, "How's tricks?"

No one noticed.

"Did you see?" Alice said.

"See what?"

"When you were going out." She lowered her voice. "Randy serving them drinks."

I didn't have to ask who *they* were. "Is that right?" I said.

"Uh-huh," Alice said. "I wish the angle were better. You can't see into that booth at all."

"Aren't they entitled to a little privacy?" I said.

"If they kept to themselves, they'd have it," Florence said. "If they're going to run around with the staff . . ." She waggled her hand.

There was no way I was coming out of the conversation a winner. Fortunately, our appetizers arrived just then, driving all other thoughts from our minds.

Oh, my goodness.

When I saw the barbecued ribs, I understood why Lucy had advised me against ordering them with the prime rib. I must admit, most of my experience with spare ribs comes from Chinese takeout. Still, I have had barbecued ribs on occasion, and knew generally what to expect.

But not this. This was a huge basket of ribs, piled high in three to four rows—that's right, rows—of thick, meaty ribs in a sauce that smelled absolutely sensational.

Florence and Alice, accepting comparatively modest portions of shrimp cocktail and soup, regarded the ribs with raised eyebrows.

"Good lord, Stanley," Alice said. "How can you possibly eat all that?"

"Are you telling me you'd like a rib?"

"I'm worried about your health. I mean, look at all that food."

"Uh-huh," I said. "How about you, Florence? Care for a rib? There seems to be plenty to go around."

"And then some," Florence said.

We all proceeded to eat our appetizers. Florence and Alice, despite numerous disclaimers, consented to sample the ribs. Alice had two, and Florence had at least three.

While all this was going on, the dining room was filling up. The two guys from the bar came in and were shown to a table. And the man and woman from breakfast, once again minus the little girl, were seated at a table next to Jean and Joan, who had sat down before us, and were already on their main course.

It was somewhere in there, and long about the time Alice and I were negotiating over some sparerib or other, though whether it was one I felt she should eat or one she felt I should not, I couldn't say, the bald, overweight hiker from Champney Falls came in. From my seating position, I couldn't see where he went. He walked behind me out of my line of sight, and never reappeared. So, unless I wanted to turn around and look, I was out of luck.

Not that I cared, you understand. Still, as far as I knew, he wasn't staying at the inn, so I had to wonder why he was always here. Of course, it could have just been the food.

"You know who that is?" I said.

"Who?" Florence said.

"The man who just came in."

"What man?"

"Bald. Overweight. He was here last night."

"Uh-huh. And where is he now?"

"I assume he's right behind me. I hate to turn and stare."

"There's no one behind you," Florence said.

"I don't mean *right* behind me. He came in, walked behind me, and I assume he sat down."

"Well, he's not there now."

"Alice, help me out here. The hiker from Champney Falls—where is he?"

"I have no idea."

"Didn't you see him come in?"

"No, I was talking to Florence. I wasn't watching who was going in and out."

"And he's not here now?"

"No, he's not."

That did it. Rude or not, I turned my head to look.

And he wasn't there.

To my right was the table with the two men from the bar. To my left was the table with the man and woman minus the little girl. Along the far wall, slightly at an angle, so, as Alice said, you couldn't see in, was the booth with the Swedish hiking couple, Lars and Inga/Christine.

At that moment, Lars came out of the booth. He did not look happy. He glanced back inside, as if to say something, but didn't. Then he turned and walked purposefully out the door.

I wondered if she would follow him. Somehow I hoped she wouldn't. I think in the back of my mind I was recalling the sound of that slap at Champney Falls, and then seeing her crying behind the rock. At any rate, I hoped she'd stay put.

She did. At least in the few seconds before I felt compelled to turn back to my table before I made a complete moron out of myself.

Even so, Alice said, "Stanley, what are you staring at?"

"I was looking to see where that man went."

"Well, he must have gone out, because he's clearly not here."

"Uh-oh," Florence said. "Look who's coming."

I looked, and quite agreed. The McInnernys were bearing down on us. And while there wasn't room for them at our table, they looked inclined to talk.

"So," Johnny said, "how did it go? You manage to get along without us?"

"Of course they did," Clara said. "My goodness, Johnny McInnerny, you think you're the only one knows how to read a map?"

"Nothing of the kind," Johnny said. "It's just we've done it before. So, what did you guys see?"

Florence, whose tolerance of the McInnernys was even less than ours, said, "Excuse me, I have to check on Prince," and got up.

I had a moment of panic, realizing that left two chairs free, but the McInnernys made no move to sit down.

"We did a few easy hikes," Alice said. "Square Ledge Trail. Glen Ellis Falls."

"You should try Mount Willard," Johnny said.

"Not Mount Washington?"

"Not for hiking. You do that in the van. Mount Willard you can climb."

"That's a good tip," I said, and let the conversation lie there, hoping they'd move on.

Fortunately, Louise arrived just then, functioning as the maître d', and ushered them to a table.

"That was lucky," I said.

"Luck had nothing to do with it," Alice said. "Louise is very sharp. I'll bet she read the situation, and that was a rescue."

"Oh, come on."

"You don't think so? A very smart woman. It takes an awful lot to run a place like this."

"You give her all the credit?"

"Huh?"

"Isn't her husband responsible for some of it?"

"He's the cook. It's a full-time job."

Of course. Louise's husband was the cook, which was a full-time job, and therefore he couldn't have anything to do with running the inn. On the other hand, it occurred to me if Louise was the cook, Alice would be telling me how remarkable it was the woman was able to run the inn and do the cooking too.

Florence came back to the table.

"How's Prince?" I said.

"Just fine. How are the McInnernys?"

"Same as ever," I said. "Well, that's too bad."

"What's too bad?" Alice said.

"We didn't get our entrées. Florence is back, and we didn't get served yet. Usually, if you leave the table, your food arrives."

Alice said to Florence, "He's not always like this."

"But I know what he means," Florence said. "It's like hopping in the shower when you're expecting a phone call."

"Yeah, but that works," Alice said, and the two of them laughed.

I picked up the last rib.

"You're not going to eat that," Alice said.

"I certainly am."

"You won't have room for your steak."

"I'll have room," I said, taking a bite. "Aren't these good, though?"

"They're all right," Florence said.

"Say," I said, "why don't we get the recipe for these?"

"Don't be silly," Alice said.

"Why is that silly?"

"You want a recipe for ribs? Everyone knows how to cook ribs."

"Not like this."

"You think I can't cook this?" Alice said.

"I didn't say that. I just said you didn't have the recipe."

"Stanley, I don't need a recipe for ribs."

"You're telling me you'll cook me these ribs when we get home?"

"Absolutely."

"You've never cooked barbecued ribs."

"No, but I can. It's perfectly easy."

"Uh-huh," I said. "You're saying that barbecued ribs is something that you *would* make?"

"Yes."

"On the other hand, shark is something you wouldn't."

"Are you going to start that again?"

"So, it makes sense to get a recipe for something you wouldn't cook, but no sense to get a recipe for something you would?"

"Don't be silly," Alice said. "You just don't understand."

Previously that had been Florence's cue, but fortunately she didn't seem to be picking up on the banter this time around. I was glad. I didn't want to have to excuse myself to go to the bathroom a second time.

Yeah, I know. This time I'd started it, asked for it, and brought it on myself. But those ribs sure were good.

Lucy came into view with a tray of serving dishes, and expectations were high, however, like everyone else, she veered off and passed behind me and out of view. That was depressing—our food couldn't possibly arrive until Lucy had served whoever it was she was serving.

A couple of minutes later she passed by, heading for the kitchen again. I kept an eye out hopefully, the last rib now but a fond memory. Unfortunately, the next person to emerge from the direction of the kitchen was the other waitress, so the tray of food she was holding couldn't possibly be ours. Nevertheless, I watched her as she took the route behind me out of sight. I even turned slightly in my chair to watch the tray go.

I saw her stop in front of the booth where Inga/Christine was waiting for boyfriend Lars. So, they were getting served, and he hadn't come back yet. His food would be getting cold. Somehow, that pleased me.

"What are you smiling at?" Alice said.

I hadn't realized I was smiling. "Oh, nothing," I said. "It's just sometimes things work out."

There came an ear-splitting scream. You read about them in books all the time, but it's something else to encounter one in real life.

For a second I had no idea what was going on.

Then I realized.

I jumped up, wheeled around.

The waitress who had just brought the food to the booth was shaking and crying hysterically.

It was easy to see why.

Inga/Christine was slumped half in, half out of the booth, her head loose, her blond hair dangling, her eyes glassy.

She was clearly dead.

TWELVE

THE POLICEMAN DIDN'T seem in any hurry. He stood in the middle of the dining room, cocked his head, and said, "Tell me again."

"There's nothing to tell," Louise said. "The young lady and her boyfriend are guests at the inn."

"Boyfriend?"

"Yes. They've been staying with us for three days."

"No problems up till now?"

"None whatever."

"No suspicion anything was wrong?"

"I don't think anything *is* wrong. The poor woman just had a heart attack."

"That's not what the doctor says."

So I gathered. The doctor, a rather prissy-looking little man with gray hair and a tiny mustache, had arrived within minutes, which I guess is one of the advantages of living in a small town. He'd come bustling in and taken charge in a manner which I initially thought of as efficient, an assessment I had later changed to officious. Because the man, for no apparent reason, had deemed this a suspicious death and called in the police. Which would have been all right in itself, had he not gone further and closed the dining room. Or, rather, the kitchen. The dining room was still open, in fact we were still in the dining room. We just weren't eating.

I know that's a cold and callous thing to say under the circumstances. But if we were going to be held captive by an overzealous cop, it would have been nice to have our food.

The cop in question was a human traffic jam. The type of person who could walk up to a man on fire and say, "What seems to be the trouble?" It could be he only gave that impression because he was keeping me from my meal, but I don't think so. I think it was just him.

He had a way of moving that suggested that part of his body was probably asleep. Or perhaps underwater—maybe that was it—he moved as if underwater.

The cop, whose name I didn't know, and didn't seem likely to find out, was probably my age, if not younger, a horrifying thought. He was a large man with a gleaming bald head, and ears that stuck out on each side of his head like the handles of a pitcher.

A pitcher of molasses.

"Just one more time," he said.

Louise frowned.

The doctor came in, took the cop aside and whispered to him. The cop listened patiently, then asked the doctor something. Probably to repeat what he'd told him just one more time. The doctor frowned, whispered some more. When he was finished, he straightened up and stepped away. That left the cop with the choice of talking out loud, or conceding the conversation was over.

He did neither. He raised his hand, and, slowly with one finger, gestured to the doctor to come closer again. The doctor did, though, it appeared to me, rather reluctantly. This time when he was finished, he straightened up and went out the door.

The cop lumbered over to Louise. "So," he said, "let's go over this one more time."

Louise never got a chance because Lars came in. He wasn't weeping, but he was certainly distraught. He came in the door, fighting off the young police officer who was attempting to restrain him, and barreled up to the cop.

"Please, please," he said. "Tell me what's going on. They won't let me see her. They won't tell me anything. They keep holding me in that room and telling me to wait. I'm tired of waiting, and I want to know what's going on."

"Well, now," the cop said, "I can understand you're upset. Anyone would be. Terrible thing."

"A terrible thing? That's what you call it, a terrible thing? She's dead. Christine is dead. Oh, my god, I can't believe it."

"Try to get a hold of yourself."

"Stop telling me to get a hold of myself. That's all anyone's told me since it happened. First the doctor and now you. Tells me she's dead, and won't let me near her. Do you understand? Stood in front of me and wouldn't let me near her. Then they take her away and hold me here, and no one tells me what's going on. Doesn't anyone care about my feelings at all?"

"We most certainly do. And I'd like to make this as painless as possible. Unfortunately, I have to do my job. You do understand what's going on here?"

"Understand? What's to understand? Christine is dead."

"Yes, she is. And we have to find out why. I don't mean to upset you further, but you have to understand there's every indication her death was not from natural causes."

"What are you saying?"

"Simply that. I'm sorry, but the medical findings seem to indicate that she was killed."

"Killed!"

"It's preliminary and only a suspicion until proved by the autopsy. But for the moment, we have to go on the assumption that she was killed."

"Killed? How?"

"That's something I prefer to go into in private."

The cop turned and looked over to where two officers who apparently comprised the local crime scene unit had been processing the booth. "You guys about done?"

"All yours if you want it. We're just packing up."

"Fine," the cop said. "If you don't mind, we'll talk in there." He turned and addressed the room. "Ladies and gentlemen, I'm sorry to hold you here, but you understand what's happened. You are all witnesses to an apparent crime. A young woman has been killed. Apparently. But it is unlikely that this was a natural death. It might be accidental, it might be self-inflicted, it might be murder. It's up to us to sort it out, which is why you're here. Do you understand?"

We certainly did, since the cop had made the identical speech shortly after he'd arrived and ordered us all to resume our original seats. All except Lars, of course, whose seat was part of the crime scene, and who'd been held incommunicado in the TV room, once the cops had managed to pry him away from the body.

The cop gestured to the booth. "Mr. Heinrick," he said.

Lars blinked at him. "You want me to sit in there?"

"Yes, I do. I understand why that might make you uncomfortable. But the fact is, I would like you to sit exactly where you were sitting during dinner, and describe for me what happened."

"I don't understand."

"You don't have to. That's my job. Come along now. Let's get it over with."

The cop put his arm gently but firmly around Lars' shoulders and led him over to the booth. After a moment's hesitation, while Lars looked at the cop, they sat down.

Of course, as soon as they did, they disappeared from our line of sight.

And, like unruly students when the teacher leaves the room, everyone began talking at once.

"Damn," Alice said.

"What's the matter?"

"What's the matter? We're not going to be able to hear what he says."

We most certainly weren't. And I couldn't help wondering whether that was the whole idea, if that was why the cop had assembled us here, instead of holding us like Lars in some other room. That we were there merely to provide background noise, to make sure his interrogations were not overheard.

"It's all right," I told Alice. "I happen to know what he's saying."

"What's that?"

"He's asking Lars to tell him what happened just one more time."

THIRTEEN

ALICE WENT FIRST.

I don't mean first after Lars. I mean first from our table. She was maybe the tenth, overall.

The interrogation of Lars took no time at all, maybe ten minutes, though it seemed like an hour and a half. When he was done, he was consigned to the TV room again, in the company of a young cop. While that certainly didn't look good, it was a notch above being hauled off to jail in handcuffs.

After Lars, a parade of witnesses was summoned to the booth. The cop who fetched them had a droopy mustache and a droopy face, giving him a sad-sack look. He also had an irritatingly polite manner, ending almost every sentence with, "If you wouldn't mind." Since we were in effect being held in police custody, minding was hardly an option.

Anyway, the first witness summoned had been the busboy, Randy. This caused considerable comment in certain circles, notably our table and that of Jean and Joan. In short, all those who knew of his liaison with the deceased. The fact that he'd been summoned first led to speculation—had the police learned of the affair?

Apparently not, since he was out in five minutes.

Next up was Louise's husband. I'd never seen Louise's husband, but I recognized him instantly. I took no credit, however, as he was hard to miss in his chef's apron and hat. Other clues were the fact that he came from the kitchen, and was protesting to the sad-sack cop that his food was going to burn. I was right with him there—if the man was still cooking, he should return to the kitchen and look out for my steak.

He was in twice as long as the busboy. Which seemed to confirm the theory—Randy's liaison was not yet known, they were merely concerned with who prepared the food.

This concept was not lost on the guests. The word *poison* began to reverberate throughout the room.

Next up was the waitress who found the body. Followed by our waitress, Lucy. Their interrogations were equally long, which made no sense. While the waitress who found the body might have something to say, Lucy knew nothing at all.

Which confirmed my worst fears.

The cop just loved to talk.

Next up was Louise, who hadn't even been in the dining room, and should have had nothing to say at all.

She said it for six-and-a-half minutes. By then I had taken to timing them.

After Louise, they started in on the guests. First up were the McInnernys, who objected to being taken one at a time. At least Mrs. McInnerny objected—I'm sure Johnny didn't mind. In fact, going alone was probably a relief. At any rate, we had four minutes of him and eight minutes of her. More than ten minutes of the McInnernys, who in all likelihood knew absolutely nothing at all.

After that were a couple I didn't know, a man and woman who presumably had stopped in for dinner and weren't even staying at the inn. They were followed by the two men who could be gay, another couple presumably just there for dinner, and the man and woman with the little girl.

The little girl herself was not interrogated. That struck me as a wise, humane move. It also occurred to me, when the dust had cleared and the case was finally solved, it would probably turn out that she had had the key clue all along.

After that came Alice.

She set a record, sixteen and a half minutes.

I sat there feeling most uncomfortable. Not that I was worried about what she was saying. It's just as the interview stretched on, the grumbling in the dining room became less and less restrained. The sentiment was abundantly clear—who the hell was *she*, and why was *she* so all-fired important?

Finally Alice emerged, which meant Florence would be next— at all the tables Sad Sack had been observing ladies first, part of his annoyingly mannered Emily Post routine.

I hoped Florence would be quick. Though, from what I'd observed, she seemed even more likely to gossip than Alice.

However, I was not to find out.

"Mr. Hastings?" Sad Sack said. He smiled and gestured toward the booth. "If you wouldn't mind."

FOURTEEN

EVEN THOUGH I had not yet said a word, somehow I expected the cop to begin with "Just one more time."

He didn't.

He said, "You're a private detective?"

Oh, dear. I'd been afraid of that. Alice had bragged about me. "Is that what my wife told you?"

"Among other things."

"I see," I said. "Did she tell you what *type* of private detective?"

"I beg your pardon?"

"Did she mention I work for a negligence lawyer?"

"No, I don't believe she did."

I groaned. "Then I'm afraid you've got the wrong impression."

"Oh?"

"I work for a personal-injury lawyer who handles negligence cases. Mainly trip-and-falls. I drive around New York City interviewing accident victims and photographing cracks in the sidewalk." I smiled. "Now, if Alice has told you I have an expertise in murder cases, you have to take it with a grain of salt. It's really a matter of circumstance, and not me. I must say, I have always found the police to be much more clever and resourceful than I am. If Alice has been telling you not to worry because I'm here to solve your murder case for you, I assure you it's just a case of a wife being somewhat overzealous in praising her husband's professional skills. I'm really no expert, and my accomplishments are minimal. So I hope my wife hasn't been boring you with tales of my exploits."

The cop cocked his head, looked at me sideways. "Actually, she hasn't, Mr. Hastings. She *did* mention you did negligence work—in fact, she told me all about it. She just didn't say you worked for an attorney. I believe she described you as being self-employed." He frowned, squinted at me. "But the idea that you have a knack for solving murder cases—and, do I understand you correctly, that you might help me with this one?—that certainly is a fascinating premise. Though your wife didn't mention it at all."

I rubbed my head. Oh, dear. That ought to teach me to lead with my chin.

"I'm sorry," I said. "I should have let you do the talking. Please, go ahead."

"No, no. I find this immensely interesting. Would you care to illuminate on how you've managed to be of use to the police?"

"I'd rather be shot dead."

"I beg your pardon."

"I was trying to *downplay* my worth as an investigator. I'd assumed my wife had been in here singing my praises."

"Well, she wasn't. At least, not in that manner. I don't mean to imply your wife is not proud of you. She just never made that particular suggestion."

"I get the point."

"Good. Then, please, fill me in. How did you come to acquire such a working knowledge of police procedure that you were afraid your wife might be inclined to brag about it?"

I took a breath. "My detective work has sometimes led me into criminal cases. Not often, but enough that I've become acquainted with a few homicide cops."

"Really? And you've helped them solve crimes?"

"I'd say I've *watched* them solve crimes."

"Excellent," the cop said. "And now you'd like to watch me solve this one?"

"Is it a crime?"

"It is indeed. I'm Chief Pinehurst, by the way. You'll want to know that, of course, the next time you're listing your accomplishments."

I took a breath. Refrained from comment.

"Anyway, getting back to what your wife said. She wasn't promoting you so much as an investigator as a witness."

"Oh."

"Yes. *Oh.* Do you suppose you could elaborate on that?"

"I assume my wife has done a fairly good job."

"That she has. Still, we do prefer eyewitness accounts to hearsay."

"I understand."

"Good. Could you tell me what you saw?"

"I saw the decedent kissing a young man."

"Decedent?"

"Yes."

"You're not in court, and no one's taking this down. You don't have to be so formal. You can call her by name."

"I'm blanking on her name."

"You're blanking on her name?"

"I have trouble with names."

"And you're a private detective?"

Good lord. No wonder the interrogations had taken so long.

"I'm not a private detective by choice. It's a job. I admit I'm not as qualified as I might be."

"And yet you manage to assist the police. How extraordinary." Chief Pinehurst consulted his notebook. "The young woman's name is Christine Cobb. Was that the young woman you observed kissing someone?"

"Yes, it was."

"And who would that person be? The person she was kissing?"

"That would be the busboy, Randy. Who, I understand, is the son of the people who run the inn."

"Louise and Charles Winthrop. Well, that certainly is interesting. You observed Christine Cobb and Randy Winthrop having a romantic encounter?"

"I saw them kissing."

"And that's all?"

"That's all I saw. And only for a moment. I withdrew immediately."

"What do you mean by immediately?"

"A matter of seconds. As soon as I saw who it was, I left."

"Why?"

"So as not to embarrass them."

"I see. How come you say only a few seconds?"

"That's all it was. I saw them there. I recognized her first. I thought she was with her boyfriend. Then the light fell on his face, and I saw who it was."

"Which is when you left?"

"That's right."

"To save them embarrassment?"

"Yes."

"Because she was kissing another man?"

"Yes, of course."

"So, if it was her boyfriend, Lars, she'd been kissing, you would have stayed?"

"No, of course not."

"But you just said the reason you left was because she was kissing another man."

I said nothing.

"Was that statement false?"

"It was not."

"That statement was true?"

"Yes, of course."

"So, if you left because she was kissing another man . . ."

"It does not imply I would have stayed if she wasn't. It's faulty logic. The one thing does not imply the other. I left because she was kissing another man. I would have also left if she had been kissing Lars."

"But you didn't leave until you saw who she was kissing. Is that correct?"

"I saw who she was kissing."

"And not at first. Isn't that what you said? You recognized her first. Then the light fell on his face, and you saw him."

"That's right."

"That's right?"

"Yes, of course."

"That doesn't jibe with your current statement."

I blinked. "I beg your pardon?"

"You maintain it makes no difference to you who she was kissing, you would have left in any case. If that were true, you would not know who she was kissing, because you would have left before you found out."

"Oh, for goodness' sakes."

"You have a quarrel with that logic?"

"I find it hard to follow."

"Oh? Well, let's go over it one more time."

I put up my hand. "Let's not. I see the point you're making. It's a good one. Possibly even a great one. It may well crack the case. I admit I am incapable of explaining my inexplicable tardiness in leaving the scene of the decedent's assignation."

"Well said." Chief Pinehurst nodded approvingly. "Very impressive. You rattled that off quite expertly. The only slight fumble was forgetting the victim's name and having to refer to her as *the decedent*." He rubbed his head, pursed his lips, frowned. "Though I can't say I join you in characterizing your behavior as inexplicable. There is indeed a perfectly logical explanation that springs to mind."

"What's that?"

"Natural curiosity. You saw the woman kissing someone, you wanted to know who. While it did not matter who she was kissing, with regard to your intention to leave, still you wanted to know who it was before you did."

"If that's so perfectly obvious, I don't see why you're making such a big deal of it."

"Because you did. I asked for your reason, and you couldn't give me one. If you'd just said, I wanted to see who it was, I would have found that perfectly natural. And we wouldn't be discussing it now. But you, perhaps embarrassed by your own natural curiosity, decline to do so."

I took a breath. "Tell me, Chief, are you punishing me for being a private detective?"

"Not at all. I'm just trying to get your story. It's always difficult when a witness is evasive."

I took another breath. "Believe me, I'm not trying to be evasive. In fact, if I could get a word in, I'd like to volunteer something."

"Oh? What's that?"

I told him about talking to Christine/Inga at Glen Ellis Falls. Of course, I didn't call her Christine/Inga—explaining why would have sent the investigation off on another unproductive tangent. But I told him everything else.

"Interesting," Pinehurst said. "So the young lady was actually aware that you had seen her."

"Yes, she was."

"Somewhat extraordinary, considering what a brief time you were there. At least, according to your account."

"It was a brief time."

"Yet long enough to be seen. And Miss Cobb asked you not to tell anyone?"

"That's right."

"Which you promised to do. Although, at the time, you had already told everyone."

"That's not true. I'd told my wife."

"Which had the same effect." He cocked his head, raised an eyebrow. "Your wife didn't mention this incident."

"That's because she didn't know about it."

"You withheld this from your wife?"

"I didn't withhold it. I hadn't had an opportunity to tell her."

"Oh? When did the incident occur?"

"Early this afternoon."

"Uh-huh. And you say you left your backpack and had to go back and get it?"

"That's right."

"So, you went back down the hill, found your backpack, and encountered Miss Cobb. She recognized you as the person who had seen her kissing Randy Winthrop. She asked you not to tell anyone. Which you promised to do. Although, in point of fact, you had already told. You then returned to the parking lot, encountered your wife, and refrained from telling her of the incident."

"I didn't want to tell her in front of Jean and Joan."

"Why not?"

"Because I'd promised I wouldn't tell."

"But Jean and Joan already knew."

"Not from me. If my wife told them, what difference does that make? I promised I wouldn't tell. I wasn't going to rush up the hill and immediately tell."

"Yes, but they already knew."

"That's not the point. Well, it *is* the point. I felt bad about that, and I didn't want to discuss it."

"That's why you withheld it from your wife?"

"No. That's why I withheld it from Jean and Joan. I was going to tell my wife at the first opportunity. I just never got one."

"Uh-huh. And is that the only thing you kept from your wife?"

I found myself taking a breath again. "It was the only thing I had not had an opportunity to tell her. I am confident that every-thing else I observed, she knew."

"And what else *had* you observed? With relation to the young woman?"

"I assume my wife told you about the incident at Champney Falls?"

"You can assume anything you like. I'd rather hear it from you."

"Okay. I'll tell you this as if you knew nothing. On the day we arrived here, which was yesterday, on our way we stopped off at Champney Falls. Christine Cobb and Lars Heinrick were there. They passed us on our way up. While we were stopping to rest. When we got to the falls we did not see them. However, there was an incident where we thought we heard the sound of a slap."

"Coming from where?"

"Somewhere in the woods. It was impossible to tell."

"But you and your wife both heard the slap?"

"Yes, we did. Didn't she tell you?"

"I'm concerned with what you're telling me. Did anyone else hear the slap?"

"Yes. Florence. The woman at our table."

"She was also at Champney Falls?"

"Yes."

"You went there together?"

"No. We met her there. Quite by accident. We didn't know her, didn't know she was staying at the inn. We began talking to her because of her dog, which was attracted to my sandwich."

"Uh-huh. And is that the only incident? The sound of the slap?"

"No, it wasn't." I told him about seeing Christine Cobb crying behind the big rock with the tree on it.

"So," Pinehurst said, "at some time after you heard the sound of a slap, you saw the decedent, Christine Cobb, crying behind a big rock. When was the next time you saw her?"

I put up my hand. "Before you get to that, there's one other significant thing about Champney Falls."

"What's that?"

"There was a hiker there who later turned up at the inn. Although he doesn't appear to be staying here."

"Yes, your wife mentioned him too. He was here tonight?"

"Yes, and I don't think he ate. Because he's not here now. He came in, and must have gone right back out."

"But you didn't see him go?"

"No, I didn't. He came in, walked behind my chair out of my line of sight. That's the last I saw of him."

"Uh-huh. And can you describe this man?"

"He was bald and overweight." As I said it, I realized the description fit Pinehurst.

If that offended him, he didn't show it, just said, "Would you care to elaborate on that?"

"On the trail he looked out of place. Like hiking wasn't a natural thing for him to do."

"Uh-huh. You think overweight people shouldn't hike?"

"Not at all. I thought *he* shouldn't hike. At least, he gave the impression he wasn't enjoying it."

"And what was he wearing?"

"On the trail, a T-shirt and shorts. Either a blue or dark gray suit at the inn."

"I see."

"Does that jibe with what my wife told you?"

"Actually, I think it does. Let me see." He flipped through the notebook again. "Let's see. Bald on top. Fringe of light brown hair. Sideburns to middle ear, short, barber cut, recently trimmed. Hazel eyes, thin eyebrows—lighter than hair. Thick lips, bulbous nose. Pale blue, Lands' End pocket tee. Tan shorts, cuffed, brown leather belt."

Pinehurst flipped a page. "And in the dining room, dark blue suit, light blue shirt, red patterned tie with gold diamond studded tie clip." He looked up from his notes. "I would assume we were discussing the same man."

"My wife is far more observant than I am. I would credit anything she tells you."

"Thanks for your opinion. But getting back to my question."

"What question?"

"The one I asked you before you chose this particular tangent. Not that it's not important, and not that I didn't want you to tell me about this man. However, right now I'm concerned with Christine Cobb. Could we go back to the time you saw her crying behind the rock? My question was, when was the *next* time you saw her?"

"Later that day at the swimming pool."

"Swimming pool?"

"Yes. The one here at the inn. My wife and I came here and checked in. We went up to our room and got settled. I went out to the swimming pool to swim, and she was there."

"Oh?"

"What do you mean, *oh?*"

"I don't mean anything. I just said *oh*. Why did you think I meant something?"

"You said *oh* as if you didn't believe me."

"Not at all. I was merely surprised. That is, if I understand you correctly. Are you saying the woman was there when you got there?"

"That's right."

"Well, that's certainly interesting. You leave the woman crying behind a rock, drive here and check in, go out to the swimming pool, and there she is. The woman seems to magically pop up wherever you go."

"Not at all. I admit I was surprised to find out she was staying here."

"Were you?"

"I certainly was. But coincidences happen."

"Yes, but at the speed of light? The way you tell it, you left the falls, drove straight here, checked in, went out to the pool, and there she was. Now, does that make any sense to you?"

"Of course not. That's not what happened. When we got here, we had to check in. Then we had to go upstairs and unpack. Discuss what we were going to do. As a matter of fact, I didn't go swimming right away. I went to watch TV. There was a ball game on. There's no TV in the rooms here. So I had to go to the TV room in the main building—" I broke off, looked at him. "But why are we talking about this? What does it matter?"

"It's important that things make sense. When something doesn't make sense, it needs to be explained. And if it can't be explained, there must be a reason why it can't be explained, and that in itself may be important. At the moment, I'm trying to establish your relationship with Christine Cobb."

"I didn't *have* a relationship with Christine Cobb."

"And yet she shows up everywhere you go. Who else was also at the swimming pool at the time?"

"No one."

"No one?"

"That's right. When I got there, she was sunbathing in one of the deck chairs."

"Sunbathing?"

"Yes."

"She was nude?"

"No. She was wearing a bikini."

"You recognized her as the woman from the falls?"

"Not at first. She was lying on her stomach, and I couldn't see her face. I went for a swim, later I saw it was her."

"Did you speak to her?"

Oh, dear.

I didn't want to talk about it. I'm not sure why. Maybe I still felt guilty about the fact I'd had a conversation with her without mentioning Alice. Or maybe I didn't want to talk about it because it was totally unimportant. Or maybe I didn't want to talk about it because it was only a one-minute conversation, but I knew we'd be talking about it forever.

Already my interrogation was running even longer than Alice's had.

And we hadn't even gotten around to discussing the murder yet.

FIFTEEN

"YOU WENT OUT?"

"I went to the bathroom."

"You went to the bathroom?"

"That's right."

"Why?"

"Chief, I wouldn't want to accuse you of overintellectualizing, but this doesn't require that much thought. I had to go to the bathroom, so I went."

Well, we'd finally gotten around to discussing the murder. Not that it made any difference. Since I didn't really know anything, I had little to contribute.

Not that Pinehurst was willing to leave it at that. Naturally, he wanted to know every little thing.

"When was it that you went to the bathroom?"

"I don't know."

"You don't know."

"I'm not in the habit of consulting my watch on such occasions. Doubtless there are people who are."

"I'm not concerned with your watch. I was hoping you could tell me relative to your meal."

"That I can do. I went to the bathroom after we placed our orders."

"See. That wasn't so hard. And on your way to the bathroom, did you happen to pass by this booth?"

"Yes, of course."

"Why *of course?*"

"Don't be silly. Look where my table is. The bathroom's out there. To get to it you walk right by."

"And as you went by did you look in the booth?"

"Actually, I couldn't see in the booth."

"Why was that?"

"The busboy was in the way. He was serving the drinks."

"The busboy, Randy?"

"That's right."

"Whom you'd observed kissing Christine Cobb?"

"That's the only busboy Randy I know."

"Uh-huh. And did that register with you at the time—I mean who all those people were?"

"Yes, it did."

"So you are absolutely certain it was the busboy, Randy, you saw at their booth?"

"That's right."

"He was serving them drinks?"

"Yes, he was."

"You saw that too?"

"Yes, I did. He had a tray with drinks. He was placing them on the table."

"And did you notice what those drinks were?"

"No, I did not."

"You don't know what Christine Cobb was drinking?"

"No, I don't."

"Or Lars Heinrick?"

"Or Lars Heinrick."

"Were they both in the booth when the drinks were being served?"

"Yes, they were."

"How can you be so sure?"

"As you say, I was aware of who these people were. I saw who it was who was serving them drinks. The significance was not lost on me. I took note of it. If Lars had *not* been there, that would have been very interesting, and I would have taken note of *that*. But I didn't. I did not see the busboy, Randy, *alone* with Christine Cobb at the booth. I saw him serving drinks to the two of them."

Pinehurst nodded. "Very convincing. I'm sure that you're right. Now, when you returned from the bathroom, what did you see then? Assuming you went by the booth?"

"Yes, I did."

"So what did you see?"

I told him about Lars Heinrick glaring at Christine Cobb, and about seeing the tear running down her cheek.

"Interesting," Pinehurst said. "Particularly in terms of the sequence. The busboy serves them drinks. They immediately have a fight. Lars is angry, and she's tearful. Can we conclude he was aware of what was going on?"

"Of course not," I said. "It could have been any number of things."

"Yes, yes," Pinehurst said. "That question was rhetorical, still I thank you for answering it. Anyway, after that you went back to your table?"

"Yes, I did."

"And immediately told your wife and her friend what you saw?"

"No, I didn't."

"I didn't think so. Or your wife might have mentioned it. Why didn't you tell your wife what you'd just seen?"

"I told you that."

"Don't be silly. How could you have told me that? The subject just came up."

"No, no. I mean the other thing. Seeing her at whatjamacallit— Glen Ellis Falls. I hadn't had a chance to tell my wife about that, and I didn't want to bring up the subject."

"What subject? This is an entirely different matter. Talking to her at Glen Ellis Falls and seeing her at dinner in the booth."

"Even so. I didn't want to talk about her at all. I simply didn't mention it."

"But your wife did. At least she says she did. She said the three of you noticed and commented on the fact it was the busboy, Randy, who was serving them drinks."

"Yes, I guess we did."

"So there you are. Wouldn't that have been the perfect time to have mentioned that right after that you'd seen the young woman with a tear in her eye and the young man looking somewhat less than pleased?"

"If I'd wanted to get into it. As I say, I was avoiding the topic until I had a chance to talk with my wife."

"You felt you needed to explain?"

"No. I *wanted* to explain. I wanted to tell my wife exactly what the young woman said, so she'd realize the position I'd been put in."

"You thought you were in a bad position?"

"Haven't I said that? The woman asked me to keep a secret. One that had already been told. It was a very uncomfortable position."

"And that's all there was to it—this uncomfortable feeling of yours?"

"What do you mean?"

"Your only real concern with this woman was keeping or not keeping her secret? She wasn't a threat to your relationship with your wife?"

"Don't be silly."

"Why is that silly? An attractive young woman like that. If she were to make a play for you . . ."

"Yes, but she didn't. She barely noticed me at all. She was involved with the busboy."

"So you say."

"What do you mean by that?"

Pinehurst shrugged. "Well, we only have your word for it. Everyone else, it's all hearsay. They're all repeating stories told by you. You're the only one who actually saw anything. So, in the event you were mistaken . . ."

"I'm not."

"Or in case you didn't happen to be telling the truth . . ."

"I beg your pardon?"

"No offense meant, but I'm a policeman. And I can't take anyone's story at face value. All these things have to be checked. Now, your story is not corroborated. Other people may know of it, but you're the only source of the information. So what if this rendezvous never took place? What if the busboy wasn't there? What if you were the man Christine Cobb was kissing?"

"Are you serious?"

"Works for me. You see her at Champney Falls. You're immediately smitten—and who could blame you. An attractive young woman, and crying, too. A damsel in distress. You arrive at the inn, spot her at the swimming pool. Sunbathing alone. You can't resist. You go out, strike up a conversation. Your wife arrives to interrupt, but not before you've established a relationship, leading to your rendezvous later that night."

"Oh, for goodness' sakes."

"You have a problem with that? It certainly works for me. Here you are, your first night at the inn, and yet you leave your wife and go stumbling around in the dark. One would think a man would have to have a motive."

"One would be wrong. I did not leave my wife. My wife left me. She went to watch *The Bridges of Madison County* in the recreation room. I did not wish to see *The Bridges of Madison County*. If that's a crime, I plead guilty as charged. I did not wish to go back to my room alone because it is somewhat cheerless and does not have a television. I went in there, to the TV room— where you're holding Lars Heinrick now—I went in there to see what was on, but there were some people watching some dreadful TV movie. It was the McInnernys, that couple at the table over there. If you want to check, they were the ones who told me about the stream and the pond. That's why I went out there to take a look, and that's how I happened to see the busboy, Randy, kissing Christine Cobb."

"Uh-huh," Pinehurst said. If he was convinced, you wouldn't have known it.

"The McInnernys will confirm everything I've just said."

"By that, I assume you mean they will confirm telling you about this pond. So," Pinehurst said, "you leave your wife at the movie. You come back to the inn, looking for Christine Cobb. You look in the TV room, but she's not there. Of course you can't tell the couple watching TV you're looking for Christine Cobb, so you become involved in a brief conversation with them about the grounds, during which they tell you about the pond.

"You leave the TV room and encounter Christine Cobb. Naturally, you want to take her someplace you won't be seen. You've just been told about this pond across the road. It sounds romantic to you. You tell the young woman about it, suggest you check it out. Which you do."

"Chief?"

"Yes?"

"Not to tell you your business, but have you considered *asking* the busboy if he was involved with Christine Cobb? If he admits it, you're done. Even if he denies it, I can't imagine a callow youth like that fooling you for long."

"Thanks for your vote of confidence. I certainly intend to question the busboy again. It's on my list."

"Your list?"

"Yes, of course. At the moment, I'm concerned with you. Now, you admit you passed by the booth twice. The time you got up and went to the bathroom."

"Admit?"

"You did pass by the booth twice, didn't you?"

"Yes, I did."

"There you are. Now, was that the *only* time you got up from the table during the meal?"

"Yes, it was."

"Well, that's something I can check with your wife. And with the other woman at the table. But say it's true. Say you only got up that one time. On your way out of the dining room the busboy was serving the drinks. That's fairly well established both by you and by your wife. So let's assume that that's true.

"So, on your way *back* from the bathroom the drinks have already been served. They're there on the table. Now, according to your story, as you pass by the booth, you see the young man glaring at the young woman and a tear running down her cheek. Is that right?"

"Yes, it is."

"Yet, here again, we have only your word for that. There's no corroboration of any kind. In this case, it's *worse* than your story of her kissing the busboy by the pool. Because you didn't even tell your wife. You didn't tell anyone. So here's a story you chose not to tell until after the crime. After the murder, questioned as to what you did, you suddenly spring this tale. That on your way back from the bathroom, this is what you saw.

"Well, it could have happened like that. What you describe is certainly in keeping with the situation. Not too inventive, of course, but seeing the woman crying is what you've described before. If you're making something up, it's hard to be artistic. It's better to be sound. The soundest thing is something that fits in with what's gone before. One would describe something similar to, or identical to, a past event, in order to give the story validity, make it seem real.

"So, you say you saw a tear running down her cheek. And the boyfriend glaring at her. Like the incident from Champney Falls. The fact she was crying and the sound of the slap. You put that together in your head, and you create the scene you describe in the booth."

"Oh, is that right? And why do I do that?"

"To cover what you actually did. Which was to stop at the booth and put poison in her glass."

"Poison?"

"Surely you've guessed that poison was involved. Assuming you're guessing. And don't know for sure because you did the deed. But, yes, that is the apparent cause of death."

"There was poison in her glass?"

"That's what I suspect. Of course, I have to await the report from the lab. But, let us assume for the sake of the discussion the young woman was poisoned. And let us assume that you stopped by her booth to put poison in her glass."

"And why would I do that?"

"Because she's a woman."

"I beg your pardon?"

"I'm sorry. That was a sexist remark. I was generalizing, and one should not generalize. But say you were having an affair with her. And say she was not willing to leave it at that. Say she wanted you to leave your wife, which you weren't willing to do, so she threatened to tell her. You can see the whole sorry pattern begin to emerge."

"I certainly can." I rubbed my head. "Chief, is there any way we could move this along? We could always come back to the matter, should any of these unfounded suspicions pan out."

Pinehurst pursed his lips. "So, you're somewhat touchy on the subject of poison."

I took a breath, exhaled. "I'm somewhat exasperated by the suggestion I might have administered it."

"Uh-huh. Well, help me out then. Show me a reason why you couldn't."

"How about this? When I returned from the bathroom, both Lars Heinrick and Christine Cobb were in the booth. If I had stopped by to drug her drink, don't you think Lars might have wondered why?"

"Sure, if your story's true. If Lars was indeed in the booth at the time."

"But he was."

"According to who?"

"There's no according to who about it. He *was*."

"How do you know?"

"Because I saw him get up and go out."

"When was that?"

"Later. After I'd returned to my table."

"And who saw him go out?"

"I did."

"There again, we have your unsubstantiated word."

"Didn't anyone else see him go out?"

"Actually, people did. But no one's that accurate on the time. And, as to whether he went out before or after you came back, well, I don't think anyone can help us there."

"Try my wife."

"Oh?"

"I'll bet she'd remember."

"Perhaps. But then a wife will alibi her husband."

"Alibi?"

"Yes, of course."

"But, but, but—"

"But what?"

"But you say my motive for killing her was to keep my wife from finding out. So why would my wife give me an alibi for the killing?"

Pinehurst shrugged. "I could be wrong. You could have another motive entirely. And you and your wife could be coconspirators."

"Give me a break."

"But let's not get off on a tangent," Pinehurst said.

I blinked. I couldn't quite believe he'd said that.

"The point is, so far no one can confirm the time Lars Heinrick went out. So it's entirely possible you could have had a moment alone in the booth with Christine Cobb. Long enough to lean over, whisper something in her ear, and administer the poison."

"Are you telling me I have to find someone who remembers when I came back, *and* who saw Lars Heinrick go out?"

"That would be nice. Though it wouldn't solve your problem."

"Why not?"

"Because you could have done it anyway. Say Lars Heinrick hasn't left yet when you come back. You stop by the booth under some guise of talking to the *two* of them. You distract their attention in some way, and slip the poison in the glass."

"Yes, but Lars Heinrick is alive."

"Yes, of course. You only poison one glass."

"No, no. You miss the point. He's alive, so you can ask him. If I stopped by the booth while he was there, he will remember it. Ask him if I came by the booth. Ask him if I had any opportunity to put the poison in that glass."

"Are you sure you want me to do that?"

"Yes, I'm sure. Why do you ask?"

"I thought you were a private detective. Well, I guess it takes all kinds. Perhaps you haven't had time to think this over. But try the concept on. As good a murder suspect as you happen to look right now, Lars Heinrick looks better. He's the one with the best motive, and he's the one with the best opportunity.

"Now, assuming that he's guilty—or assuming that he's intelligent enough to realize that he *looks* guilty—his natural reaction would be to pin the crime on someone else.

"So, if I put the idea in his mind—if I suggest to him that the police might suspect you of this crime by asking him whether you stopped by the booth and had an opportunity to tamper with the glass—well, wouldn't that make it awfully tempting for the young man to say yes? Particularly, if he suspected you of being the one who had alienated the young lady's affections?"

I tried to keep my exasperation from showing. It was difficult, talking through clenched teeth. "Couldn't you manage to ask him a question somehow without tipping your hand?"

"Actually, not very well. If he's guilty, he knows what's up. Even if he's innocent, he suspects what's going on. He'd be apt to grasp at straws."

"Then don't *give* him one. Ask him if *anyone* stopped by the booth. If he names me, I'll buy you dinner."

"Sporting of you," Pinehurst said. "I assure you I will try to eliminate that as a possibility. Not the dinner, the chance he saw you in the booth. But even if I can, that leaves the much more likely possibility that when you stopped by he wasn't there."

"I don't suppose you could manage to eliminate *that* possibility?"

Pinehurst smiled. "In all good time, Mr. Hastings. In all good time."

That's what I was afraid of.

SIXTEEN

"THAT COP IS not too bright."

"Why do you say that?"

"He thinks I did it."

Alice smiled. "That would certainly account for your opinion."

"That's not what I mean."

"What do you mean?"

"He sent me back here. To sit with you. If he really thinks I did it, he's giving us a chance to compare notes and patch up our stories."

"Stories?"

"In case we were in it together—one of his scenarios. The other is I did it alone. In that case, I would now have a chance to cloud your recollection."

"As if you could."

"Yeah, but he doesn't know that. Leaving me alone with you is a bad move, if he seriously thinks I did it."

"Well, obviously he doesn't."

"Don't bet on it. And even so, it makes no sense leaving us alone."

Alice and I were alone at our table because Pinehurst was questioning Florence. If leaving us alone made no sense, questioning Florence made even less. I mean, fine, maybe the guy had to take everybody's statements and eventually he'd get to Florence, but surely there are priorities. And from what I just told him, he had to want to talk to Lars or the busboy.

But, no, that would be too easy, that might lead somewhere. That could get us out of the dining room before midnight, which wasn't apt to happen. Dawn seemed much more likely.

"So what is it we shouldn't be comparing notes on?" Alice said.

I sighed, shook my head. "You wouldn't believe me."

I told Alice about meeting the girl at Glen Ellis Falls, seeing the tear running down her cheek in the booth, and Chief Pinehurst's assessment of all that.

Alice was understandably shocked. "Oh, dear," she said when I was through.

"Yeah," I said. "What a horrible situation."

"I'll say. And the worst part is, it sounds so logical."

"Oh?"

"Well, you were alone with her at the swimming pool. And you were the only one who saw her kissing the busboy. And then you meet her at the waterfall and don't even tell me about it."

"I explained why."

"Yes, but it's an explanation that wouldn't convince a cop. You promised not to tell, so you didn't want to tell, although you'd already told. That's too convoluted reasoning for most people. As for me, I know you, I know that's exactly how you think. But a policeman?" Alice shook her head. "You're lucky you're not on your way to jail."

126

"I certainly am. I'm clearly his chief suspect. With the possible exception of Randy or Lars."

"Randy couldn't have done it," Alice said.

"Why not?"

"Are you kidding? Just look at him."

"He's in the kitchen."

"You know what I mean. You've seen him. Can you imagine him killing that girl?"

"Why not?"

"Why not? Are you kidding me? He was absolutely infatuated with her. Killing her was the last thing on his mind."

"Yeah, but you don't know his story."

"Story, schmory. He didn't kill her."

"What about Lars?"

"What about him?"

"Could he have killed her?"

"Sure."

"Why? Because his mother doesn't run a bed-and-breakfast?"

"It's an inn."

"Don't start that, Alice. Do you see the point I'm making? Here's Randy and Lars. Two nice, clean cut–looking young men. Nothing much to choose between 'em. But you flat out tell me Randy couldn't have done it and Lars could."

"That's just my opinion."

"Yes, but you have it. And you also have a tendency to state your opinions as facts.

"Well, that's a nice thing to say."

"You know what I mean."

"I suppose I'm responsible for making you the number-one suspect?"

"No, I seem to have done that on my own. Anyway, since the cops made the mistake of letting us confer, you think you could help me with my alibi?"

"I beg your pardon?"

"The theory is I put poison in her glass on my way back from the bathroom. My argument is how could I have done that while Lars was still there? Unfortunately, no one knows when Lars went out. Relative to when I returned from the bathroom."

"It was after."

"How do you know?"

"I saw him go. And it was a long time after you came back to the table."

"That's not good."

"Why not?"

"If it was a long time, he could have gone out and come back in the meantime. You see what I mean. He could have been out when I went by his table. Come back shortly after that, and then left again when you saw him."

"What are you doing, trying to break your own alibi?"

"Actually, yes. Because if I can do it, he can do it. I'm trying to find answers to all his objections."

Something hit me on the cheek. It bounced off, fell to the table.

It was a green pea.

I looked at it, then at Alice. Then in the direction from which it came.

At the far table, either Jean or Joan was waving at us—at the moment I was blanking on which was which—but the thinner of the two was trying surreptitiously to attract our attention.

I say surreptitiously because she was obviously trying to do so without also attracting the attention of the sad-sack cop with the droopy mustache, who seemed to have appointed himself in charge of maintaining discipline in the dining room. Talking was permitted, and all the people at the tables certainly were. But intercourse *between* tables was something Sad Sack simply wouldn't allow. Whether those were Pinehurst's orders, or whether this was something Sad Sack had decided for himself was not entirely clear, but at any rate talking between tables was strictly forbidden.

Once again, I had the feeling of being in school—the teacher's back was turned, and one of the students had just hit me with a spitball.

Once she had our attention, Jean/Joan looked a question and pantomimed a kiss. When I looked puzzled, she repeated the sequence.

Alice got it. Nodded yes.

Then Sad Sack turned around, and suddenly we were all on our best behavior again.

"What was that?" I said.

"She wanted to know if we told them about Randy kissing Christine."

"You mean if we hadn't she wasn't going to bring it up?"

"How should I know?"

"Otherwise, what's the point in asking?"

"Don't be silly."

"Why is that silly."

"You think a person wouldn't just want to know?"

"Sure. But communicating behind a policeman's back is probably not the smartest move to make in a murder investigation."

"How could it hurt?"

"What if he saw you and wanted to know why?"

"I'd tell him. I mean, it's not like there's anything we're withholding from the police. Is there?"

"No, I guess not. Who is it who waved at us, by the way?"

"Stanley. You don't know who that is?"

"I know who it is. But is that Jean or Joan?"

"It's Jean."

"Oh."

Alice shook her head. "You're hopeless."

"I know. You think you could discourage Jean from further attempts at communication. She's only going to get us in trouble."

"How much trouble can we be in? You're already the prime suspect."

129

"That's just my point. The police already suspect me of murder. Let's not make them angry."

Alice shook her head, pityingly. Obviously I had once again proved myself to be an old fuddy-duddy.

Fortunately, Jean gave up trying to communicate, so there was no harm done.

Florence emerged from the booth. Instead of returning to our table, she looked around, caught Sad Sack's eye, and went over to him.

With the noise in the dining room I couldn't hear what she was saying, but she was talking animatedly and gesturing and pointing, and once I thought I heard the word *dog*.

I did.

Florence returned to our table with a chip on her shoulder.

"He won't let me walk Prince," she said in disgust. "If they're going to keep us here all night, the dog has to go out."

"Did you ask Pinehurst?" I said.

"Who?"

"The cop who questioned you. His name's Pinehurst. Didn't he tell you that?"

"I don't believe he did."

"He only tells the chief suspects," Alice said.

"Huh?"

"Stanley's a suspect. Couldn't you tell from the questions he was asking?"

"He mentioned the two of you. But I didn't get that impression."

"Oh? So who did it sound like he suspected?"

"It wasn't like that?"

"What do you mean?" I said.

"It wasn't like he suspected anyone. It was like he just wanted to ask questions."

"Exactly my impression," I said. "Except in my case, he acted as if he suspected me."

"Maybe that's just his way," Florence said.

"Oh, yeah? Didn't he ask you what I told you?"

"Yes, of course."

"About seeing her and Randy by the pond—did he ask you about that?"

"No, he just asked me what I knew."

"Did you tell him that?"

"Of course."

"Did he ask you any questions, try to break the story down?"

"Break it down?"

"Yes."

"No. Why would he do that?"

"Under the theory I made it up."

Florence blinked. "What?"

"That's the theory," Alice said. "Stanley made up the story about the busboy kissing her to cover up his own affair."

"Are you kidding me?"

"That's the theory," I said.

Florence exhaled, shook her head. "Poor Prince."

"Prince?" I said.

Florence nodded. "Uh-huh." She shrugged. "Looks like we'll be here all night."

SEVENTEEN

IT WAS NEARLY one o'clock before Chief Pinehurst was done. By then he had questioned everybody in the room, and had a second helping of Randy and Lars. What he had learned from all that was not entirely clear, but the bottom line was when he was finished no one was in custody, but all residents of the Blue Frog Ponds had been instructed not to check out.

My heart sank when I heard it. I felt like a man in a shaggy dog story, trapped forever in a cheerless, sexless, TV-less room in an inhospitable bed-and-breakfast, while a painstakingly pedantic policeman slowly and methodically sifted an endless spiral of clues, never drawing one whit closer to any solution.

That seemed to be Alice's assessment of the situation also. "You have to solve this," she said, when we finally got back to the room.

"I beg your pardon?"

"Come on, Stanley. You can see how it is. That cop hasn't got a clue."

"I admit his style is not reassuring."

"Reassuring? It's positively frightening. He doesn't know what he's doing. If he were to arrest Randy, it would break Louise's heart."

"I don't think he's about to do that."

"Oh, yeah? The guy questions everyone in the room. Then he asks for Randy and Lars. Well, Lars is the grieving boyfriend, but who is Randy? Who is he possibly except suspect number one."

"I thought I was suspect number one."

"Don't be dumb. Anyway, the whole thing's ridiculous. The only real suspect is Lars."

"Why?"

"Because he's the only one with a motive. He's the only one involved with her who could possibly want her dead."

"What about Randy?"

"Why would he want her dead?"

"I don't know. To shut her up?"

"Shut her up about what? The affair? Why would he care about that? What's the worst that could happen? Mommy gets miffed and gives him a lecture about keeping his hands off the guests? Would he kill to protect against that?"

"Of course not," I said. "But what about Lars?"

"What about him?"

"I would think his motive's pretty thin. He found out the girl was seeing someone else, so he killed her? I don't think so. Packed up, drove off, and left her stranded here I could buy. But took her out to dinner and slipped poison in her drink? It simply doesn't make it. If this is a crime of passion, poison just isn't that passionate. Shoot her, stab her, strangle her, that fills the bill. But poison doesn't. You don't poison someone in the heat of passion. It is a cold-blooded, premeditated crime."

"Exactly."

"What do you mean, *exactly?* That destroys your argument."

"No, it doesn't. It casts some doubt on the fact he killed her because she was having an affair with Randy, but that doesn't have to be his motive."

"So what does?"

"I have no idea. All I said was they're the ones with the relationship, so he's the one most likely to *have* a motive. But that's not important right now. What's important is keeping the cops from arresting Randy."

"You want to keep your voice down a little? The walls are thin, and this is not the type of thing I want to spread around."

Alice waved it off. "Oh, they're not back yet."

My eyes widened slightly. "Hey, you're right. They aren't."

Alice looked at me reprovingly. "Stanley. How could you even think that at a time like this?"

"A time like what? You just pointed out our neighbors aren't home."

"I don't believe you. A woman has been killed."

"Yes, but—"

"And it's one in the morning, and we have to get to bed."

"Exactly."

"Stanley. Don't joke. A woman has been killed, and someone close to us did it. That's pretty scary."

"Yeah, I know."

A floorboard creaked.

Just outside the door.

I immediately turned to look, then looked back at Alice.

Her eyes were wide.

I put my finger to my lips.

She nodded. Gestured toward the door.

I was closer. I took two steps on tiptoe, trying not to make a sound. I stretched my arm out, reached the doorknob.

Looked to Alice.

She nodded.

I twisted the doorknob, stepped back, swung the door wide.

And—

Nothing.

There was no one there.

Then Max the cat came walking in, his tail swishing proudly back and forth like a windshield wiper. He padded right by me, dropped his hindquarters, and sprang lazily onto the bed. He stretched, inspected the bedspread, then gave Alice and me a critical stare, as if reprimanding us for not warming the bed for him.

I closed the door, went over, and scratched Max under the chin. After a few moments he lay down and began purring, though, it seemed to me, rather reluctantly, as if not willing to seem readily appeased. I sat on the bed next to Max, scratched him behind the ears.

"Now then," I said. "Before we were so rudely interrupted."

Alice put up her hand. "Don't start. I'm not in the mood."

"I can see that."

"I mean for joking. This is serious. A woman has been killed. A young man is under suspicion. And the cop in charge doesn't seem to know what to do."

"I wouldn't worry about it."

Alice looked at me. "Why not? What are you saying? Is there something you're not telling me?"

"I just don't think you have to worry about the cop."

"Why not?"

I smiled. "Think about it. Here we are in a New England bed-and-breakfast—fine, call it an inn if you want to, that's not the point. Anyway, here we are in this bed-and-breakfast inn sort of place. Someone's been poisoned, the local cop's been brought in, and he's a bumbling sort of fellow. And he's ordered us not to leave, so we're all stuck here together, all the suspects under one roof—yes, I know, they're separate buildings here, I was speaking metaphorically. But you see what I'm getting at?"

"No, I don't," Alice said. "What are you talking about?"

I pointed to the Agatha Christie on the night table. "Well," I said, "we would appear to have all the elements of your basic, cozy crime novel."

"So?"

I shrugged. "Isn't it obvious?"

I scratched Max behind the ears, smiled at Alice.

"The cat will solve the crime."

EIGHTEEN

"WHAT'S THAT?"

"What?"

"That."

"Nothing."

"Alice. What's that paper in your hand?"

"Oh, that," Alice said. She brought it up from under the table rather reluctantly. "It's really not important."

"Uh-huh," I said.

I held out my hand. Alice passed the paper over. I unfolded it, read:

SUMMER GARDEN SOUP

1 spring onion
2 cloves finely chopped garlic
2 tablespoons unsalted butter
2 Yukon Gold potatoes
10 spears asparagus
2 cups chopped spinach
2 cups chicken broth
1 cup water
Reggiano Parmesan
Salt and pepper to taste
rinds of Parmesan (optional)

Snap off the tough ends of the asparagus and discard. Cut spears diagonally into 2 or 3 pieces. Sauté onion and garlic in 2 tablespoons of butter until translucent. Add 2 cups of chicken broth, 1 cup of water, and Parmesan rinds, if you wish.

Peel and slice the potatoes, add to the soup mixture, and simmer for 20 minutes. Then add the chopped fresh asparagus, simmer for 5 minutes. Be careful not to overcook. Add 2 cups of chopped spinach. Simmer 2 minutes. Remove Parmesan rinds. Salt and pepper to taste. Puree.

If served hot, drizzle with *extra-virgin olive oil* and grated Reggiano Parmesan.
If served cold, garnish with *plain yogurt* and *fresh chopped chives*.

Serves 2–4.

I looked up from the paper. "I don't believe this."
"Stanley."

"There's a murder investigation going on, and you're still buying bootleg recipes?"

"So what? One thing has nothing to do with the other."

"It's the principle of the thing."

"Now we're talking principles?"

"How about priorities?"

"What priorities? Life doesn't stop because there's a murder investigation."

"I just don't see how you could even think of a recipe."

"Did you taste that soup?"

"No."

"Case closed."

Alice and I were talking in low tones. As was everyone else in the dining room. In addition, eye avoidance was at a max. Granted, neither Florence, Jean, Joan, nor the McInnernys were there—in short, all the people we knew and might have acknowledged—still, of the people in the dining room, no one was looking at anyone else. That is, anyone at any other table. Those at the tables were, as I say, conversing in low tones.

Which was to be expected. It was eerie sitting in the dining room. Knowing a young woman had died there just the night before.

Ordering food was downright spooky.

When Lucy arrived to announce the special was blueberry pancakes, I had to stifle the urge to say, "With or without poison?" Alice and I ordered them, however, on Lucy's high recommendation.

She had just left with our orders when Louise swooped down. For a moment I thought she was going to bust us for the recipe. Naturally, that was the last thing on her mind.

Louise actually sat down at our table, leaned over, grabbed me by the arm, and said, "You have to help me."

It was so abrupt I could only blink. "I beg your pardon?"

"I hear you're a detective. My son is in trouble. Serious trouble. He needs your help."

"I'm not a lawyer."

"He doesn't need a lawyer. He needs a detective. Someone to get the facts."

"Why?"

"Why? That policeman thinks he had something to do with it."

"Why would he think that?"

Louise blinked. "I don't know. But he obviously does."

"What does your son say?"

"I don't know. He won't tell me."

"Uh-huh," I said. "So, you have no idea why he might be a suspect?"

"Well . . ."

"Well what?"

"What if he knew the girl?"

"What makes you think he did?"

Louise grimaced. "Please. One hears things. One wonders if they're true."

"And what does one hear?"

"You're not making this easy for me."

"I'm sorry. But I need to know what you want. If your son isn't talking to you, and you're asking me to help you based on what other people are saying, then I need to know who those other people are."

Louise hesitated a moment, then said, "Actually, Florence hinted there might be a connection."

"Uh-huh. And did she hint what that might be?"

"You should know."

"Oh?"

"She said you saw something."

"Did she say what?"

"Yes."

"Then you don't need to ask, do you?"

"Are you saying it's true?"

"Is that what you want—when you say you need my help—just to confirm whether the story is true?"

"Is it?"

"Ask him yourself. You expect me to rat a guy out to his mother?"

"It's for his own good."

"It always is. If it's a family affair, I'm keeping out."

Louise took a breath. Sighed. "Fine. Keep out," she said. "Don't tell me anything. Leave me in the dark. All of that's fine, if you'll just do one thing."

"What's that?"

"Talk to him. Talk to my boy. He won't talk to me, maybe he'll talk to you. He has to talk to someone."

"What about the cop?"

"What about him?"

"What did he tell the cop?"

"I don't know. Don't you understand? That's the whole point. He won't tell me."

"Then he's not going to tell me, either."

"He might."

"Why?"

"You're not his mother."

"True."

"Then there's the other thing."

"What's that?"

"What you saw. If what I hear is true, you're the one who saw it. So he'd have a hard time denying it to you."

The McInnernys arrived just then, boisterous, brash, and over-bearing, just as if there hadn't been a crime. They descended on our table with their usual lack of tact.

"There you are," Johnny said. "Are you doing Mount Washington today? We are. It's crystal clear. You won't get a day like this two or three times a season. You'll see a hundred miles. You'll see five different states. You'll see Canada."

"Canada?"

"It's the day to go. You want to reserve a space?"

"Reserve?"

"In the van. We're going at ten o'clock. Want us to sign you up?"

"I don't think so," I said. "I can't guarantee we'll make it. Can we, Alice?"

"I'm not sure what we're doing," Alice said. "Maybe we'll see you up there."

"That would be nice," Mrs. McInnerny said. It occurred to me her name was Carla or Clara, though I couldn't recall which.

At any rate, that completed the conversation and left the McInnernys with nothing more to say to us. They stood there, smiling awkwardly to fill the silence, until Louise finally realized they were waiting on her, and got up to show them to their seats.

Florence came in while Louise was still seating the McInnernys. She hesitated a moment, seemed ready to select another table, but Alice waved her over. She came, I thought, rather reluctantly. I wondered if she felt guilty for having finked on me to Louise.

"Good morning," I said. "If you can say that under these circumstances."

"Yeah," Florence said. "What a night."

"How's Prince doing?" Alice asked.

"I just walked him. He seems none the worse for wear. Of course, he has no idea what's going on."

"I bet he knows something's going on," Alice said. "Animals pick up a lot."

"Sure," I said. "From your manner. He can tell from your manner you're acting different."

"I'm not acting different."

"I'm not saying you're acting different. But this had to affect you. It's affected all of us. And the dog can sense that. See what I mean?"

Florence rubbed her head. "What a nightmare."

"Yes," I said. "But it doesn't concern us. We're just observers, watching it all go by."

As if on cue, Lars came in. He stopped in the doorway and stood there, a blank look on his face.

It was hard not to feel sorry for him in that moment. He was practically a parody of a man in despair. He was unshaven, and his hair was uncombed. His shirt was buttoned wrong. His shoelace was untied.

He looked oblivious to his surroundings. There was no chance of him finding a seat. Indeed, it was obviously a miracle he'd managed to find the dining room at all.

Louise, who had finished with the McInnernys, went over and took him by the arm. As she guided him into the dining room, I saw her hesitate as she approached the booth, then guide him to a table on the opposite side of the room.

It was not until he was seated that I was aware of what had happened.

It was quiet. There was a dead silence in the room. All talk had stopped. Even the McInnernys held their tongues. Everyone had stopped talking, and all eyes were on Lars. If he was aware of it, it must have been living hell.

Louise was aware of it. She turned away from his table, looked around. Seemed embarrassed by the shared spotlight. She hurried back to us.

Louise must have been really upset, because she didn't ever acknowledge Florence, just bent down, grabbed my arm, and said, "Please. He's in his room out back. He won't come out. He won't talk to me. You have to help me, and—Oh!"

I looked around to see Chief Pinehurst bearing down on us. That did not bode well. Since he had chosen our table over Lars' he was undoubtedly about to order Louise to produce Randy.

He didn't.

He stopped at our table, drew himself up formally, and announced, "Alice Hastings?"

NINETEEN

RANDY WAS LYING curled up in bed, the covers pulled up under his chin. His blanket was old and worn, a security blanket, perhaps, from when he was a boy.

"Hi," I said. "May I come in?"

Randy's room was in back of the kitchen with its own outside entrance. It was a small room, and gave the impression of having once been a shed. Indeed, the door had a latch rather than a knob. I had knocked, got no answer, and stuck my head in.

I got no answer again. Not even an acknowledgement of my presence.

I was in no mood for such behavior. I stepped in, closed the door behind me. "All right, look," I said. "You can talk to me or not. That's entirely up to you. But you would do well to listen.

"The police suspect you of a crime. I don't know what you've told them, and I don't really care. I doubt if they care, either. They've got their information anyway, so they don't need much from you.

"You were having an affair with the victim. You served her the drink that killed her. The cops know that. Doubtless they've asked you about it.

"If you've admitted the affair, it's bad. It makes you suspect number one.

"If you've denied it, it's worse. Why? Because the cops know about it anyway, and they know that you're lying.

"They know because they have a witness. I'm the witness. I saw you kissing her down by the pond. Now you can deny that if you like, but in the cops' eyes that establishes only one thing—it means you're a liar. And when a chief suspect lies in a murder investigation, it is not good. Not when it's a transparent lie that wouldn't fool anyone. That is not the way to go. That is not the prescribed method for beating a murder rap."

Randy rolled over, faced the wall. "Get out," he said.

Aha. The clever detective had elicited a response. It occurred to me I'd nearly broken him. Could a confession be far behind?

"Your mother's worried about you, Randy, because you won't talk to her. I can understand that. It must be hard discussing your affairs with your mother. But that's no reason to clam up on everyone. Particularly the police."

Randy lay still, said nothing.

"Okay, if you don't want to talk, you don't want to talk. But I have to report back to your mother. So what am I gonna tell her? I guess I'm gonna tell her that there's nothing I can do. Because you're not talking, period.

"Well, that's fine. If that's the way you wanna play it, that's the way to go. But if you're gonna do it, do it right. Get a lawyer. Act on his advice. Let *him* be the one telling you not to talk. That takes the onus off of you. The cops can't regard your silence as an admission of guilt. So talk to a lawyer now. You're gonna need one anyway, to make statements for you at the time of your arrest. So get a good attorney, and let him take charge."

Again Randy said nothing.

"You ever have her here? In this room—in this bed, I mean? The cops are gonna go over it, and when they do, they're gonna use a fine-tooth comb. A single hair, that's all it will take. You wouldn't believe the things they can do nowadays with DNA.

"On the other hand, I'm sure they'll be watching to see if you try to wash the sheets. So dashing out to the laundry would probably not be the swiftest move."

Randy offered no reaction whatsoever, continued to ignore me.

"On second thought, you probably didn't bring her here. Not a particularly romantic setting. No, I would imagine you had more of a taste for the great outdoors. So examining the sheets would be a waste of time. The police would do better looking for grass stains on your clothes."

"Shut up."

"See," I said, shaking my head, "you're no good at this. The things that aren't true don't bother you, but the things that are touch a nerve. You might as well have a sign on your forehead that flashes CORRECT every time I get something right."

Randy rolled over, glared at me. "Why don't you get out of here. Go on. Get out."

"I'll tell you why, Randy. That cop came back to talk to my wife. He's talking to her right now. And you know what they're talking about? Me. They're talking about me. And do you know why? Because I'm the one who told them about you. So he's checking on my story. He wants to find out if it's true. And guess what's gonna happen if it is? Go on. Take a guess."

Whether Randy would have risen to the bait I was not to know, for at that moment the door swung open, and his father, Louise's husband, the cook, whose name for the life of me I couldn't remember, stuck his head in and said, "Randy. Come on. Get up. I need help. The dishes are stacking up. There's coffee to be served. Your mother can't do everything. You've gotta help. I don't have time to argue. The pancakes are on. Just get up."

And with that he was gone again.

"You see how it is?" I said. "If you just lie here feeling sorry for yourself, your problems aren't going to go away. In fact, they're just gonna increase, because everybody's gonna wanna know why you're doing it. You may not be guilty, but you sure look guilty. And it's not gonna take much more to convince that cop. Yes, he's slow, but he's putting it together piece by piece. And what you're doing only helps him. Why don't you give yourself a break?"

The door swung open again.

I turned to look, but there was no one there. And the door had not opened very wide.

Before I had time to think, there was a flash of orange, and Max sprang up on the bed. He climbed on Randy's chest, treaded down a spot, curled up, and began purring.

Randy let him, which said something for the boy. Most men as hassled as he was would have brushed the cat aside. Randy let him lay, actually reached up, stroked his fur.

It was a bizarre scene, the prime murder suspect lying there, refusing to talk, petting a cat.

I admit to being somewhat disconcerted, losing my train of thought. What had I just been talking about?

I realized whatever it was, it was the same old song. Randy was doing himself no favor by refusing to talk. So now I had to snap him out of it.

"Come on, Randy," I said. "You are this close to going to jail. When my wife gets done talking, you are going to be under arrest. And I hate that. I don't want your arrest on her head, or on mine. But there's no help for it if you refuse to explain. So why don't you tell me what you know? You're gonna have to tell your story to the cops. A little rehearsal might help. Whaddya say?"

Once again, I was not to know, for at that moment the door swung open, and Chief Pinehurst walked in.

I felt bad. I'd done everything I could to warn Randy, but it hadn't worked. I'd failed him, failed his mother. With him not talking, this was the inevitable result.

"All right, let's go," Pinehurst said.

Randy said nothing, just lay there petting the cat. He looked as if he were about to cry.

"Come on, Randy," I said. "It's better not to resist."

"I'm glad to hear you say that," Pinehurst said. "But I don't want him." He put his hand on my shoulder. "All right, Mr. Hastings. Let's go."

TWENTY

"I DON'T UNDERSTAND."

"Of course you don't. It's not your case. You don't have to understand."

"No. I don't understand why you want to question me."

"You don't?"

"No, I don't. I already told you everything I know."

"Well, that's a trifle broad. I think you'll find that isn't quite the case. Particularly after what your wife said."

"My wife?"

"Yes, of course."

Pinehurst and I were in the TV room: I guess he'd gotten sick of the booth. Either that or Louise had refused to let him have it during breakfast. At any rate, Pinehurst was sitting in an over-stuffed chair, and I was sitting on the couch, right where I'd found the little girl watching TV my first day there. I wondered vaguely if there was a Red Sox game today. If so, I wondered if I'd be free to watch it.

"I beg your pardon," I said, "but what could my wife have possibly said that made you suspect me?"

"Now, now," Pinehurst said. "Did I say I suspected you? I don't recall ever saying that."

"Actions speak louder than words," I said. And grimaced. Good god, the man had me talking in clichés.

"I'm sorry if I gave you that impression. Well now, what do you say we kick this around some, and I'll let you go. Your wife indicated a desire to see Mount Washington. I'd hate to hold you up."

"What was it you wanted to kick around?"

"Getting back to the scene of the crime. I find myself interested in your movements during dinner."

"We went over that."

"Yes, we did. But it certainly is interesting. Sifting through the varying accounts. It's yours now I'd like to pin down. How many times did you get up from your table during the meal?"

"Once."

"Are you sure?"

"Absolutely."

"And that's the time you went to the bathroom?"

"That's right."

"And when was that?"

"If I recall correctly, it was after I'd placed my order and before my food arrived."

"If you recall correctly?"

"When we discussed it last night it was fresh in my mind. If I should forget some trivial detail this morning, I hope you will not pounce on it as if you'd cracked the case."

"That was not my intention," Pinehurst said. "These questions are preliminary. Perhaps if we could speed things along."

Pinehurst speeding things along? The word *oxymoron* hung unspoken in the air.

"Fine," I said. "What do you want to know?"

"To the best of your recollection, you left the dining room after
you placed your order and returned before your food arrived?"

"That's right."

"And that is the only time you got up from your table until
after the body was discovered?"

"That's right."

"When you first arrived at your table, were Christine Cobb and
her boyfriend already there?"

"No, they were not."

"How are you so sure?"

"Because I saw them come in."

"You are certain of that?"

"Yes, I am."

"Why did you note their arrival?"

"I told you that. Because I had the conversation with her by
the waterfall that I hadn't had a chance to discuss with my wife.
So I had reason to note her entrance."

"Uh-huh. That would seem to be convincing. Now, as to the
rest of dinner. I believe you said that Florence got up to walk her
dog?"

"That's right."

"And how long was she gone from the table?"

"I don't know. Five minutes, maybe. She just went to walk the
dog."

"Uh-huh. Now, your wife—when did she leave the table?"

"She didn't leave the table."

"She didn't?"

"No."

"You mean she didn't leave the table while you were there?"

"She didn't leave the table at all. She came in with me, sat there
the whole time."

"But you went to the bathroom."

"So?"

"So, how do you know what your wife did while you were out of the room?"

I blinked. "I beg your pardon?"

"You certainly can't vouch for your wife's whereabouts while you weren't there."

"Vouch for her whereabouts? What are you talking about?"

Pinehurst frowned, shook his head. "See, that's the problem with people's recollections. Everybody remembers something slightly different. Your wife remembers that you got up. And you remember that Florence got up. And Florence remembers your wife got up."

"What?"

"Which you don't remember. So, can I assume that this was something that happened while you had left the room?"

"What do you mean, my wife got up?"

"Your wife got up from the table. Moved around the dining room. According to the woman who was sitting with you. And, according to your wife, by the way. She remembers getting up, going over and talking to two women at another table. The women you'd been hiking with that afternoon. Which is certainly interesting when you consider where the tables are."

"What do you mean?"

"Do you recall where you were sitting? In relation to the room? To get to the other table you have to pass right by the booth. If your wife actually conferred with these women, she would have walked right by. Which she obviously did, since both of them confirm the conversation."

I put up my hands. "Wait a minute, wait a minute. What has this got to do with anything?"

"We're talking opportunity here. Opportunity and motive. You had the opportunity because you left your table. The woman with the dog had the opportunity because she left the table. And your wife had the opportunity because she left the table."

"Why are you talking about my wife?"

"I'm talking about everybody. She's just one of the people I'm talking about. No reason to get upset." Pinehurst shrugged. "On the other hand, when we start comparing motives, you must admit your wife had more than most."

I stared at him. "What?"

"If we are to assume that you and the girl were involved. That you were making the story about her and the busboy up. Now, if you were the one who was involved, which seems likely when you start adding up all your personal connections—swimming with her, meeting her by the pond and the waterfall—well, if you're the one with the connection, it doesn't necessarily give you that good a motive.

"But your wife. Well, your wife might want to kill that woman very much."

"Are you accusing my wife—"

Pinehurst put up his hands. "Please. No one is accusing anyone. We're examining possibilities. Jealousy is certainly a motive. A woman scorned."

I took a breath. "I am going to try to be calm and discuss this rationally. Which is a little difficult under the circumstances. Because I hate to dignify this with a response. But I would like to point something out. If my wife did indeed leave the table to go over to talk to Jean and Joan while I was in the bathroom, well that was long before Lars left the room. So, if my wife passed by their table, they were both there. And Lars would certainly remember if she had stopped to talk."

"I'm sure he would. On the other hand, we have the same problem that I pointed out when it came to you. Lars is no dope. He may have a convenient memory when it comes to such things."

"What do you mean, *may have?*"

Pinehurst grimaced. "Ah, well, you got me there. That's one of the problems with murder investigations. People who are the most likely suspects tend to take offense." When I opened my mouth, he said, "Not that I am suggesting that you are taking offense. No, no. I was referring to Lars."

"What about him?"

"As I say, he's taken offense. At least to the point where he's withdrawn his cooperation."

"You mean he's not talking?"

"That's right."

I blinked. "Your chief suspect isn't talking, and yet you're still questioning all of us?"

Pinehurst shrugged. "This is America. A man is innocent until proven guilty. He also has the right to remain silent. Lars Heinrick is exercising that right."

"Does he have a lawyer?"

"Not yet. Though I assure you he has been made aware he has that option. But for the moment he's merely declining to talk."

"I see."

"I'm sure you do. And I'm sure you understand the implications. With Mr. Heinrick not talking, I've been unable to corroborate the claims of the various witnesses. For instance, your claim that you did not stop by his booth. Or anyone else's claim for that matter. Which includes both your wife and the woman with the dog."

I rubbed my head, exhaled. "Fine. For the moment, you have no conclusive proof. I'll grant you that. Will you grant me the concept of reasonable doubt? Not in a legal, courtroom sense, but just in terms of *common* sense. Won't you concede that it is *unlikely* that someone stopped by the booth and put poison in the glass while Lars was still there?"

"Of course," Pinehurst said. "I'm a perfectly reasonable man.

For instance, I would be the first to admit that between your wife and the other woman at your table—Florence, the woman with the dog—your wife had less opportunity. Because when Florence went to walk the dog, Lars, by most accounts, had already left the dining room. Whereas, when your wife went by the booth, Lars was presumably still there."

I exhaled. "Thank you for that assessment."

"That is correct, is it not?" Pinehurst said. "That when the woman went to walk the dog, Lars Heinrick had already left the booth?"

"To the best of my recollection, that's true."

"And it's also true that Lars Heinrick and Christine Cobb arrived in the dining room together, prior to the time you went to the bathroom, so that at the time your wife went by their booth, Lars was presumably there?"

"Absolutely," I said. "Of course, I have no knowledge of what happened when I was out of the room, but if Alice got up then, it was at a time when Lars Heinrick was there. Because I know for a fact he was there when I left the room."

"I'm glad to hear it," Pinehurst said. "And while I'm not ready to concede the point, I have to admit it seems entirely likely. In which case your wife's opportunity is certainly lessened. Which should undoubtedly knock her down a few notches on my list of suspects. Unfortunately, her motive is rather strong."

I opened my mouth, closed it again. Talking to Pinehurst was immensely frustrating. I began to sympathize with Lars Heinrick for declining to do so.

"And if your wife got up at that time, to visit the women at the other table, she would have walked right by the booth. Isn't that right?"

"I suppose."

"And she did do that. By her own statement. So, I put it to you. If your wife saw the busboy serving them drinks, and was curious, and wanted to take a closer look, is it possible she might have chosen that moment to talk to the two women at the other table, just so she'd have a chance to go by the booth?"

I frowned. While that seemed entirely possible, it also had nothing to do with the investigation. "Maybe so," I said. "In which case when she passed by the booth, not only was Lars there, but the busboy would have been there also."

"On the way *to* the women's table, perhaps. But not on the way back. The busboy would have been gone. And it's entirely possible Lars was gone also."

"No, it isn't. I saw him in the booth. On my way back in."

"So you say. But, as I've pointed out, I only have your word for that. And if you were lying to protect your wife . . ."

"Oh, is that what we've come to? Now I'm lying to protect my wife?"

"I said *if*. The hypothetical. I'm trying to prove things here. A fact is not a fact, if it can be contradicted by a hypothetical. Anyway, your wife did not mention the fact that she'd been to the other table to talk to the two women?"

"No. Why should she?"

"No reason. But the fact is, she didn't. She didn't mention it to you, and she didn't mention it to me."

"I beg your pardon?"

"When I first questioned her. Last night. We talked about many things, but that wasn't one of them. She completely neglected to mention the fact that she got up."

"Did you ask her?"

"I asked her if she left the room. She told me she had not."

"And she hadn't. Her answer was absolutely correct."

"Yes, as far as it went. But that would have been an excellent opportunity for her to tell me she got up. Which she neglected to do. It was not until I jogged her memory this morning that she mentioned it at all."

I put up my hand. "Whoa. Hold on, here, Chief. Just hold on.

There's a huge, *huge,* difference between forgetting to mention something, and lying to the police. Which is the inference you seem to be drawing here. My wife did not lie to you. She did not mislead you. She did not attempt to trick you. If she didn't mention the fact that she talked to Jean and Joan, it is only because you didn't ask her. And because it was an irrelevant, trivial detail that totally slipped her mind."

"I never said it wasn't," Pinehurst said. "As I say, I am merely assembling facts. The fact is your wife didn't mention it. And might not have, if the other woman hadn't remembered it when I questioned her. At any rate, your wife did get up. Did leave the table. Did pass by their booth. Did refrain from mentioning this, either to you or to me the first time I questioned her. And seemed inordinately interested in what was going on in the booth when you returned from the bathroom.

"Now, can you point out any inconsistency in any of those statements?"

I blinked.

Groaned.

Rubbed my head.

TWENTY-ONE

"**THIS ISN'T SO** bad," Alice said.

I'm glad she thought so. We'd just careened around a hairpin turn. I don't know how it looked from Alice's side, but from where I sat, the outer wheels couldn't possibly have been on the road.

We were on our way up Mount Washington in the van. The Auto Road, as the narrow, winding road up the mountain was called, was open to private cars, but their use was discouraged by a vehicle-use fee of sixteen bucks per car and driver, plus six bucks per passenger. Since we'd come with Jean and Joan, it would have cost us thirty-four dollars just to drive up the road.

Instead, we were paying twenty-two bucks a head to take the van. Which might not seem very bright. But when we checked in at the Glen House visitors center at the base of the mountain, we were hit with a barrage of propaganda stressing the danger of the road and warning against private cars. I didn't think we needed any more tension just then—I voted for the van.

So, here we were, being driven up the mountain by a pimply faced young man, who looked as if he were probably driving on his learner's permit. Every time he turned a corner, I held my breath.

"I could have driven this," Alice said.

"I'm sure you could," I told her. And secretly wished she had, as our van lurched around another hairpin turn. I closed my eyes, wondered how much longer it could last.

The McInnernys weren't with us, by the way. Though the van was full, they were not among the present. This was, to the best I could determine, the sole benefit of Chief Pinehurst's lengthy questioning—by the time he was finished with us, the McInnernys were long gone.

Florence wasn't with us either. She begged off, saying Prince wouldn't have been allowed in the van. We were trying to talk her into leaving him behind, when the sad-sack cop showed up to say Chief Pinehurst wanted to talk to her again too. That had tipped the scale, and she told us to just go on ahead.

A noble sentiment.

On the other hand, as I viewed the narrow, curvy incline we were about to ascend, it occurred to me Chief Pinehurst might well have saved her life.

The young man who was piloting our van with such wild abandon accentuated the fact by keeping up a running commentary on the road, the conditions, the weather, the history, and what we could expect to see. Occasionally, he would spice this up by pointing out a place where people had been killed driving off the road. Somehow, this was more than I needed to know.

And the most disconcerting thing about what he was saying was the fact that his voice didn't appear to have changed.

"There's the timberline," he announced cheerily, pointing out the driver's side window to the left, while the van appeared about to launch itself off an embankment to the right. "I hope you dressed warm. It's cold on top."

That we knew. The summit temperature was almost as well publicized as the danger of the Auto Road. Alice had a sweater and I had a windbreaker. We were ready for anything.

"And to your right, down in the valley, that puff of smoke is the Cog Railway. We're gonna beat it up there, so you'll be able to watch it arrive."

"How long is the track?" Alice asked.

I had to stifle an impulse to elbow her to be quiet. No need to distract the man. Just let him drive.

"Three miles from the base station at Marshfield up to the summit. The train does it in about an hour and ten minutes."

"How come it's shorter than the road?"

"For one thing, it's more of a straight line. The road winds around."

It certainly did. And at each sickening bend, the driver was careful to note every point of interest. When we reached the summit, I practically leaped from the van in relief.

But what a view.

The McInnernys were right. There was not a cloud in the sky. The air was crystal clear.

You could see forever.

We poured out of the van, walked to the edge. Gawked like children.

It was wonderful. Below us, you could see the road on which we'd come, making its way down the mountain. At the very base was the highway, and across from it the parking lot where we'd left our car, and the Glen House visitors center where we'd signed up for the van.

Beyond it were mountains. And more mountains. And more mountains. And on and on, into the distance.

"Which way is which?" I said.

165

"What?" Alice said.

"I mean which way is north?"

Alice and Jean and Joan had a good deal of fun about that. I dug the binoculars out of the backpack, and we passed them around. And after determining which direction actually was north, I'd have been willing to bet it really *was* Canada we were seeing.

We were all having a perfectly good time until the McInnernys walked up.

"There you are," Johnny said. "Better late than never. Did I tell you, or what? Is this clear, or is this clear?"

"It's clear," I said.

"You'd better believe it's clear," Johnny said. He pointed. "You know, that's Canada up there. That last range of mountains is Canada."

Exactly what I thought. Though, somehow all the joy went out of it when he said so.

"You see," I said. "I told you that was Canada."

"That's right," Johnny said. "And over there's Vermont. And New York State as well. And over there's Connecticut and Massachusetts."

"Well, now you can't see Connecticut," Mrs. McInnerny said.

"You can today," Johnny said. "It's probably the only day of the year you can."

"Well, now how would you know?" his wife said. "It's not like they had borders on the states. Like here's Massachusetts, here's Connecticut. How would you know, Johnny McInnerny, which was which?"

"Didn't you hear what our driver said?"

"I heard what he said. And I also heard him say to get back in the van."

"They're not gonna leave without us."

"No, they're just gonna get mad. You want all the other passengers to get mad?"

"Oh, for goodness' sakes," Johnny said, but they were already walking back toward the parking lot.

"Check out the Summit Building," Johnny called over his shoulder. "Nifty souvenirs."

The Summit Building was a combination restaurant/souvenir shop, which also housed a publicly funded, nonprofit observatory, not to mention rest rooms and telephones. Jean and Joan went to check it out.

I forestalled Alice.

"Let's take a stroll around the summit first," I said. Alice looked at me quizzically. We had not been alone together since our talks with Pinehurst. "I think we'd better compare notes."

"Oh?"

"Yeah. Chief Pinehurst seems to have a new theory of the case."

"What's that?"

"You wouldn't believe."

I told Alice what Pinehurst had told me. She listened with an ironic deadpan.

"That's his theory of the case?" she said. "That I killed her in a fit of jealous rage?"

"Or coolly and deliberately to eliminate a rival."

"That's hardly any better."

"Actually, it's worse. It shows premeditation. The heat-of-passion defense doesn't work."

"But he's not serious."

"He sounds serious."

"Stanley, don't be dumb. The man's compulsive; he questions everything. That doesn't mean he believes it."

"Yes, but he does make good points."

"Like what?"

"Like you withheld it during your first interrogation."

"Withheld it? Talking to Jean and Joan? Would you mind telling me why I should have remembered that?"

"Didn't he ask you?"

"If I talked to Jean and Joan? He most certainly did not. He asked me if I left the room. I didn't leave the room. End of story."

"You didn't remember you got up?"

"Stanley, it wasn't important I got up. When he asked me if I got up, I told him I got up. It wasn't important until he asked me."

"Uh-huh. And the reason you went over to talk to Jean and Joan?"

"They're friends."

"Yes, but at that particular moment—why did you want to talk to them then?"

"Why are you asking me this?"

"Because Pinehurst did. Trying to make something of it."

"Well, that's stupid."

"But the man doesn't know you, so he's trying to make a case. His point is, the way he sees it, the reason you went over to talk to Jean and Joan was because of the girl."

"Oh, come on."

"No, it's true. Here's how he figures: You saw Randy serving them drinks. From where our table was, you couldn't see into the booth. You wanted to see into the booth. So you went over to talk to Jean and Joan so you'd pass by the booth and would be able to look in."

Alice frowned. "That's hardly fair."

"Fair? Alice, it's not a question of what's fair, it's a question of what's true."

"Yes, of course. But there's degrees of everything. I mean, how could I walk past that booth without seeing in?"

"What did you see?"

"Nothing. Randy was serving them drinks. Neither one of them was paying any particular attention to him."

"Which was interesting in itself, right? If she's involved with him and is elaborately pretending not to notice?"

"Uh-huh," Alice said. "Anyway, that's all it was. No big deal."

"What about on your way back?"

"What about it?"

"What did you see then?"

"Nothing. Randy was gone. The two of them were just sitting there together."

"Sipping their drinks?"

"Not when I went by."

"So what were they doing?"

"I think they were talking. But I couldn't really see. I couldn't hear, either. I told all this to the cop."

"The second time around."

"What's that supposed to mean?"

"It's given him a reason to suspect you."

"Oh, for goodness' sakes. He doesn't really suspect me. It's just the way he is."

"I know. But the problem is, you give him ammunition. He's able to say, Why didn't she tell me this the first time? And he's able to say, She got up to talk to the women because of what was going on in the booth. And when I ask you, it *was* because of what's going on in the booth. You wanted to talk to them about that, and you wanted to get a better look."

"Is that a crime?"

"Not at all. But this cop has an overactive imagination, and—"

"You want to discuss this with Jean and Joan?"

"No."

"Well, here they are."

"The train's coming," the plumper of the two said.

The thinner one pointed. "Around the other side."

We walked over to where we could see the train track. A puff of smoke was coming from the valley below. I took out my binoculars, located the train. It was a short little affair, with an engine and open passenger car. The car was full. I wondered if that was normal, or due to the exceptionally clear day.

I passed the binoculars around, but soon there was no need. The train came chuffing up the track, slow and steady, The Little Engine That Could. It clanked to a stop, and the passengers got out.

I scanned the faces getting off the train, looking for people I knew. Not expecting to find any, of course.

To my surprise I did. The family with the little girl, of TV-watching fame. She and her parents got off the train and went into the Summit House.

I continued to watch, though the chance of seeing someone else I knew seemed positively nil.

I didn't, but Alice did.

She nudged me in the ribs, said, "Look at that."

I looked at the man getting off the train, a large man in a parka and fur hat. The clothes were somewhat excessive—it wasn't *that* cold. Still, it hardly seemed worthy of notice.

"So?" I said.

"So?" Alice said. "You know who that is?"

"No."

"Take off the hat."

"Huh?"

"Imagine him without a hat."

I stared at him.

Blinked.

My eyes widened.

It was the bald, overweight hiker from Champney Falls.

TWENTY-TWO

I FOUND A pay phone in the Summit House, called the Blue Frog Ponds.

"Louise, it's Stanley Hastings. I need to talk to Chief Pinehurst."

"Oh, he left."

"Left?"

"Yeah. About a half hour ago. I saw him getting into his car."

"Where'd he go?"

"I have no idea. He didn't say anything, he just took off."

"I need to reach him. It's important."

"Well, he probably went back to the police station. You want the number?"

"Please."

Louise gave me the number. I didn't have a pencil to write it down, but I repeated it to Alice, who dialed it for me once I got off the phone with Louise.

I got a busy signal.

A busy signal?

No way.

The police station only has one line?

I hung up the phone.

"What's the matter?" Alice said.

"Busy," I said.

We gawked at each other. To New Yorkers, the concept of a police line being busy did not compute. Being put on hold would have been more in our realm of experience.

I retrieved the quarter from the coin return, dropped it in again.

"Still remember it?" I said.

Alice gave me a look and punched in the number.

Still busy.

"Maybe Louise gave it to me wrong."

"You wanna call information?"

"You call information. I'm gonna check on the train. See if I can get a seat."

I went out, inquired about the Cog Railway.

No luck. The return trip was sold out.

"When does it leave?" I asked.

"Forty-five minutes."

"And it takes an hour and ten minutes to go down?"

"More or less."

"Thanks."

I went back inside to find Alice. On the way I kept an eye out for our friend.

I spotted him sitting on a rock, one of a pile of rocks off to one side of the Summit House where people liked to climb. He was talking to a young man with long, blond hair, wearing jeans, work boots, and an army jacket. What the two of them had in common, I couldn't imagine.

But I sure meant to find out.

I went back inside to Alice. She'd been joined by Jean and Joan.

"Still busy," Alice said.

I raised my eyebrows.

"Oh, I told them," Alice said. "How could I not tell them?"

"We'll be discreet," Jean/Joan, the plumper one said.

"It's exciting, isn't it?" said the other.

I'm sure my smile was forced. The last thing I needed was people who found the whole thing exciting.

"Any luck?" Alice said.

"No. I can't get on the train. But it's all right. In fact, it's probably better."

"Why?"

"It doesn't leave for forty-five minutes, and it takes over an hour to get down. Our van takes half the time, and leaves before. So I can get the car, drive around, and be there when the train arrives."

"Terrific," Jean/Joan said. The thin one. "You mean we're gonna follow him?"

"I'm going to follow him. You can get a cab back."

"Don't be silly," Alice said. "You're not going to leave us."

"Well, you can't come along."

"Why not?"

"He'll spot us."

"How will he spot us? We'll be in the car."

"Exactly. He'll see the car following him."

"Stanley. You're not making sense. The car will be following him in any case. What difference does it make if we're in it?"

"If he see four people following him—"

"He will think we're out for a drive. Stanley, use your head. What is the man going to find more suspicious, a lone man tailing him in a car, or a man and three women out for a drive?"

As usual, there was no arguing with Alice. Much as I would have liked to. Not that I would have minded having her along, but I certainly could have dispensed with the presence of Jean and

Joan, who had never been involved in anything of the sort before, and found it fun, which was almost more than I could bear.

In the end I gave in with as good grace as possible, while stressing the need for being discreet and not discussing this in the van on the way down.

They didn't, but I did. Halfway down the mountain it occurred to me I had no idea where the base of the Cog Railway was. I was torn between not wanting to waste the time inquiring at the Glen House visitors center, and not wanting to distract our driver, who treated the journey down as if it were a roller-coaster ride, and seemed to get a kick out of freewheeling around the hairpin turns. I waited for a fairly straight and level stretch to ask directions.

"The Cog Railway," he said. "You're just comin' down, and you wanna go up again?"

"We just thought we'd like to take a look."

"It looks the same at the bottom as it does at the top. It's not like they change the train on you halfway down. You seen one train, you seen 'em all."

"Uh-huh. Well, could you tell us how to get there?"

"You meetin' someone on the train?"

"No. We'd just like to take a look."

"Well, if you wanna take a look, it's a free country, you gotta right to take a—Boy, that curve came up on us fast!"

Somehow we got to the parking lot with directions and without being killed, a long-shot parlay under the circumstances.

As soon as we got in our car, Alice was quick to find fault.

"So," she said. "You make us all promise to be discreet, and then you blow it yourself."

"I didn't blow it."

"Oh, no? Whaddya wanna bet that young man's in there calling the police right now?"

"In that case," I said. "They'll be on the lookout for a man and three women, and I'd better leave you behind."

"Here?" Alice looked at Jean and Joan, rolled her eyes. "Stanley, the driver is here. If you drive off and leave us, he'll wonder why. He might even ask. What would you suggest that we tell him then? The Cog Railway didn't really interest us, but you happen to be nuts for trains?"

"No, but—"

"Come on. Let's get out of here before they arrest us on the spot." Alice smiled. "Besides, you'd never find it alone."

While that wasn't exactly true, I did almost make one wrong turn before Alice pointed it out. Jean and Joan found that terribly amusing.

We got to the base of the Cog Railway, parked our car in the parking lot, and did not buy tickets. And then stood around and tried to blend in with the other people waiting for the Cog Railway, all of whom *had* bought tickets.

"Let's pretend ours are in my purse," Alice said. "What do you think, girls? Wouldn't that be a clever subterfuge, pretending the tickets are in my purse."

"I don't think that's fair," the plumper Jean/Joan said. "There's no reason to emasculate your husband. Let's let him pretend he has them in his jacket pocket."

And all three giggled.

The humor continued at about that level for the next forty-five minutes, until the train finally hoved into view. It was packed. As it came chuffing toward the station, Alice said, "Better get the car."

I blinked. Alice was right. The parking lot was nearly full. The minute passengers got off, there was going to be a monster traffic jam.

"Get the car, pull up to the front gate," Alice said.

She turned, headed for the platform the train was approaching. Jean and Joan tagged along, leaving me behind.

Great. Suddenly, they're the detectives, and I'm the chauffeur. I went and got the car, drove around the parking lot.

It was a good thing I did, because it took a while to get to the gate, even with the only traffic being cars circling looking for parking spaces. Once the train let out, it would be chaos. But I'd already be at the gate.

Or so I thought. It turned out other people had the same idea. Half a dozen cars were lined up at the exit with their motors idling. I had to either drive on out or get in line. If I drove out and waited on the highway, I'd be conspicuous on the one hand, and the women might not find me on the other. I got in line.

Or at least tried to. The end of the line turned out to coincide with an intersection of one of the rows of the parking lot. The minute I got in position, a car honked for me to let it through. I backed up, let the car go by. Wondered if I was close enough to the gate to do any good.

There was nothing I could do about it. I threw the car into park, turned, and looked out the back window for the train, which was still a good ways away. I sighed, settled back, tried to relax.

It was hard to do. Here I was, following my first solid lead of the investigation. One I was most eager to have pan out. Most eager.

It occurred to me, I was unduly anxious about what was going on. I mean, surely following this guy was not going to be that hard. Even with the women along. Even though I greatly would have preferred to be alone. If Alice hadn't insisted.

Alice. That was what was bothering me. Yes, it was rubbish what Chief Pinehurst suggested. But still. To have your wife a suspect in a murder case. And to have the facts laid out so carefully and logically in front of you.

All right, fine, so I'm getting to the age where a man's head is naturally turned by a younger woman. And his wife would certainly resent this and wish the woman ill. And Christine Cobb did turn up everywhere I went, and even asked me to share a secret with her. A secret I hadn't managed to tell Alice.

And Alice did get up from her table and pass by their booth. For an admittedly trumped-up reason. While I was out of the room.

I shook my head, smiled. On my way here it had occurred to me our real-life mystery involved a train, the Cog Railway, just like the Agatha Christie mystery I was reading, *The 4:50 from Paddington.* But what I was feeling right now came from another Agatha Christie novel, *Curtain,* the last case of Hercule Poirot, in which his trusted friend and my namesake, Hastings, comes to suspect a family member of having committed the crime.

No, I did not suspect Alice. It just made me very uncomfortable to think that someone else did.

I was roused from my musing by a car driving out. I glanced in the rearview mirror. Sure enough, the train had reached the platform, and people were streaming off.

So where was the man? I couldn't see him. Had he already left the train?

While I strained my eyes, three doors of the car opened simultaneously, and the women piled in.

"There's a blue Ford coming up from your left, be ready to pull out," Alice said. "Just be sure you have room to go."

"I have room," I said.

"He's gonna cut you off!" Jean/Joan screamed from the back— I couldn't see which one.

A Jeep wagon had just pulled in front of me from the right. Another car was inching along behind it.

"They're cutting you off," Alice said. "Don't let them cut you off."

"Coming up on the left," Jean/Joan said. "It's him, it's his car. Coming up on the left."

"Don't let 'em cut you off," the other Jean/Joan said.

"You're getting boxed in," Alice said. "Those cars are not gonna move."

"Pull out," Jean/Joan said. "Here he comes."

"He's passing us."

"He's going by."

"He's getting away."

The top of my head was coming off. I had the feeling if I attempted to drive in any direction, I was going to smash into the side of a car.

I took a breath, gritted my teeth, spun the wheel. Cut off a mother with two young boys and a kid in a car seat. She hit the horn and the brakes and gave me the evil eye.

I swerved into the outer lane, headed for the gate. Without the faintest idea of where our quarry was.

"Where is he?" I said.

For a second, no one knew.

Then Alice pointed. "He's behind you."

A glance in the rearview mirror told me Jean and Joan were pointing too.

"Could we all not point at the man we're trying to follow?" I said. I said it as nicely as possible, still I think the underlying irony shone through.

"He's two cars behind us," Alice said.

"Great," I said.

There was no easy way to get out of the lane of traffic. I drove out the gate, turned right, pulled up on the shoulder of the road. Popped the glove compartment, pulled out a map, and opened it up on the steering wheel.

"Good move," Alice said. "You look just like a man who's lost."

"I feel like a man who's lost," I said. "Just let me know which way he goes."

"He's turning left," Alice said.

"Figures," I muttered.

I passed the map to Alice, put the car in gear, and sized up my chances of a U-turn on this road. Actually, they weren't bad. With my quarry turning left, the same sort of traffic break that would work for him would work for me too.

Practically.

He hung a left by cutting off a truck coming up from the right. There was no way to get between them. I was lucky to make the U-turn and come up behind the truck.

"He's getting away!" Jean/Joan cried. "Look! He's getting away!"

The man was indeed speeding away from the truck. With a stream of cars coming from the other direction, there was no room to pass.

If I wasn't clear on what to do, it was not for lack of advice.

"Give 'em the horn!"

"Flash your lights!"

"Pass him on the right!"

Suggestions rang out in rapid succession. It was all I could do to separate out those that would not get me killed.

Luckily, as we rounded a turn, a passing zone appeared. There was a car bearing down on us, but from a fair distance. I pulled out, floored it, swept on by. The oncoming car was never really in danger, though the driver certainly had a good chance to test his brakes. I rocketed up the road after the blue Ford.

Which was nowhere to be seen.

"You lost him," Alice said.

Which seemed a pretty unfair assessment of the situation. *I* had lost him? This whole thing was my fault?

Around the next curve a car appeared in the distance. It was too far to tell, but it might well have been our blue Ford.

"There he is!"

"That's him!"

"Step on it!"

I already had the pedal to the floor. The ancient Toyota was giving its all. It seemed to me we were slowly gaining ground. As we whizzed around a particularly sharp curve, it occurred to me I was doing a fairly good impression of the pimply faced young man. It also dawned on me, after many years as a private detective, I was finally in a car chase.

With three backseat drivers.

"Look out!"

"Be careful!"

"Watch the road!"

Sound advice, that never would have occurred to me. I considered thanking the various parties involved. But sorting out just who had said what would probably take too much time. Particularly if I wanted to make the next curve.

I swung the car into a screeching left, wondering if there was any way the man we were following could possibly avoid spotting us. I mean, how often does a carload of sightseeing tourists cruise the road at ninety miles an hour?

The driver of the blue Ford was no slouch himself, because we didn't seem to be really gaining on him.

Until he hit the truck. I don't mean hit it. He didn't hit it. I mean, got stuck behind it. He evidently came up on it where there was no place to pass. Because we came around a curve and there he was. Smack-dab behind a tanker truck, crawling along at twenty miles an hour.

"There he is!"

"Slow down!"

"Don't get too close!"

Thanks to this advice, I was able to avoid driving straight up the back of the car in question. I slowed down, tagged along behind.

"He's gonna spot us," Jean/Joan said.

"I can't help that. At least he doesn't know who we are."

"But if he knows us from the inn . . ."

"Right," I said. "If he knows us from the inn. And if he knows

180

about the murder. And he *must* know about the murder. Particularly if he's a suspect. Particularly if he did it."

"Then he'll know why we're here."

"No, he won't," Alice said. "All he'll think is we're stuck behind the truck just like him."

That assessment seemed to satisfy everyone, and led to a debate over whether we should try to get close enough to get the license number. Before we could, we hit a straightaway, and the blue Ford pulled out to pass.

Jean/Joan split on what I should do next.

"Follow him!"

"No, stay put!"

"He's getting away!"

"He'll know we're after him."

"No, he won't," Alice said. "Who'd want to stay behind the truck?"

I sure didn't. I pulled out, zoomed on by. The question now was, how fast did I want to drive to keep up?

It turned out to be a moot point. Half a mile down the road, the blue Ford signaled a turn to the left.

For once, there was no dispute. All three women said, "Look, he's turning left."

I turned left, too, without putting it to a vote. If that alerted the guy, it was just too bad. If I'd kept going straight, I'd have lost him completely.

If the man was on to us, he gave no sign. He drove more slowly down the narrow side road, and after a mile and a half, turned into a driveway of a two-story red frame house.

I checked the mailbox as we went by. There was no name, just the number 154.

"Okay, gang," I said. "We did it. There's no car in the driveway but his, so we can assume he lives there. Number one five four. All we gotta do is find a street sign and phone it in."

Of course, there wasn't one. We drove three miles without finding any sign, at which point the road came to an end in front of a dilapidated farmhouse. I turned around, headed back to the highway, though I did not recall having seen a sign.

I hadn't. There was no sign whatsoever. Our quarry lived at a known address number on an unidentifiable street. To be truthful, I wasn't sure of the town, either.

"It doesn't matter," I said. "The point is, we could find it again."

The *we* was charitable and conciliatory, including them in the investigation. Not that it had much effect. Jean/Joan the thinner was all for staking out the place, and seemed to resent the fact that I was not. An offer to let her out of the car if she really felt that way was not met with good grace.

Aside from that, I was pleased. We'd actually accomplished something. Tracked down the man from Champney Falls. The man I'd been talking about from the beginning. Pinehurst would finally have to pay some attention to him. He couldn't ignore his existence now.

I stopped at the next gas station we came to, and called the police.

And got no answer.

I blinked.

A busy signal was bad enough, but no answer?

The police station does not answer.

We all had a good laugh over that. I must say, it was nice to have the women laughing with me instead of at me for a change.

We got in the car, drove back to the Blue Frog Ponds.

You could tell at once something had happened. There were people in the yard, standing, talking among themselves. True, it was a small community, and everyone could be reasonably expected to know everybody. But these conversations were not casual. The first impression I got was of neighbors observing a fire.

We headed for Louise, who was up near the porch. Unfortunately, the McInnernys cut us off.

"Isn't that something," Johnny McInnerny said. "Imagine, there we are up the mountain, with no idea."

"No idea of what?" I said. "What happened?"

"What do you mean, what happened? Didn't you see?"

"We just got here."

"Yeah, but didn't you see the police driving off?"

"Police?"

"Of course they didn't," Mrs. McInnerny said. "Johnny Mc-Innerny, when will you stop thinking of yourself? Just because you know something, doesn't mean everybody does. If they just got here, then they don't know."

"Know what?" Alice said.

Mrs. McInnerny tried to look stern. But her eyes were gleaming. "The police have made an arrest."

My first thought was Randy. I didn't want to voice it. Instead I said, "Was it the boyfriend? Was it Lars?"

"Nope," Johnny said.

My heart sunk. Poor Louise.

"So who was it?" I said.

Mrs McInnerny could not keep the note of triumph out of her voice. "It was her," she said.

"Her?"

"Yes." Mrs. McInnerny nodded. "The woman with that awful dog."

TWENTY-THREE

THE POLICE STATION was in the middle of the road. I'm not exaggerating. The road ran right up to the front door. Then turned ninety degrees to the right, ninety degrees to the left, ninety degrees to the left again, and ninety degrees to the right, continuing on where the road would have gone if the building hadn't been there.

The result was disconcerting. Park Avenue makes a square around Grand Central Station, but that's a big building. The police station was small. The road didn't have to aim at it, it easily could have gone by. But, no, it was a dead-on hit.

For my part, I was glad. I'd been given the usual kind of directions to the police station, that is, being told I couldn't miss it. For once, however, it turned out to be true. I braked to a stop, got out, went in the front door.

The sad-sack cop was sitting behind a desk. The one with the droopy mustache. The cop, not the desk.

"Where's Pinehurst?" I said.

"He's in the kitchen."

I blinked. "The kitchen."

"Yeah. He's making coffee."

"He's not with the prisoner, he's making coffee?"

Sad Sack tugged at his mustache. "You got a problem with that? We happen to be out of coffee."

"I need to see him."

"Sure thing." He pointed. "Right through there."

I went through the door indicated, down a short hallway, into a kitchen alcove on the left.

Pinehurst was pouring water into an electric drip perculator. He was bent over, squinting to make sure he filled it up to the line.

"I hate these things," Pinehurst said. "I don't mind making the coffee, it's washing the pot every time. And then, before you know it, you run out of filters, and what do you do then?"

I was in no mood for a lecture on coffee making. "You arrested Florence," I said.

"Yes, I did, and I'm glad you're here. She's been asking for you."

"Oh?"

"Yeah. I was going to have to send Henry to get you, but he wouldn't have wanted to go until he'd had his coffee. Now he won't have to."

"Why does she want to talk to me?"

"I have no idea. She wouldn't say. She just asked for you."

"I don't understand. Why is she under arrest?"

"For the murder of Christine Cobb."

"Yes, yes, of course," I said, impatiently. "*Why* is she under arrest for the murder of Christine Cobb?"

"Well, now," Pinehurst said. "I would rather not prejudice you until you've talked to the woman. Go have a talk, get her side of the story, then we can compare notes."

"You mean with what she told you?"

"I mean in general. But by all means, go have a talk with her."

"Fine, I'll do that," I said. "But that's not why I'm here."

"Oh?"

"I found the man I told you about. The hiker from Champney Falls. The one who was there that night."

"Well, that's interesting," Pinehurst said. "And I certainly want to hear about it. But since I have a suspect in custody, it's slightly less urgent. So why don't you hold that thought until you've talked to her. After that, it may not seem quite so important."

"Where is she?"

"Yes, do let me set you up," Pinehurst said. "Right this way."

He led me back down the hallway and through the police station proper, where Sad Sack gave us a sour look, probably because we did not come bearing coffee.

We went through another door to a lockup in the back, which consisted of four small cells. Two were empty. One housed what appeared to be a sleeping drunk.

In the fourth was Florence. She was sitting on the bed with her head in her hands. She looked up, saw us, got to her feet. Her eyes were red, her face was caked with tears. She looked at me, and her lip trembled.

We stood there, looking at each other, not knowing what to say.

"Well," Pinehurst said, "I'll leave you two together. I'm going to pat you down. I'm going to assume you're too intelligent to try to help her escape. When you're done, just come back down the hall."

Pinehurst left.

When the door closed behind him, I turned back and said, "Florence, what's going on?"

Her eyes were wide. "I have no idea."

"Why'd he arrest you?"

"I can't say."

"You don't know?"

"I'm not allowed to talk about it. My lawyer's on his way. He told me to be quiet."

"You called a lawyer?"

"Well, wouldn't you? They arrested me for murder. For *murder*, for goodness' sakes!"

"Yes, but why?"

"I can't talk about it. I called my lawyer in Boston. He's driving up. He made me promise not to talk. You know how frustrating that is, not to be able to talk?"

"Then why did you send for me?"

"Oh. The dog. Can you take care of Prince? He's got to be walked. He's got to be fed. He's in my room. They took me away and left him there. It's so awful. But he likes you, he'll go with you. Could you walk him, please?"

"Yes, of course."

"Thank you." She sighed. "At least I don't have to worry about that."

"But, Florence. What's this all about?"

She shook her head. "I can't talk. I can't. I'm sorry. I really am."

I went back to find Chief Pinehurst, who was sitting at a desk across from Sad Sack. The two of them were holding coffee mugs.

"Want some coffee?" Pinehurst said.

"No, thanks, I'm fine. You mind telling me what's going on?"

"You mean she didn't tell you?"

"Her lawyer advised her not to talk."

"That's a fine state of affairs," Pinehurst said. "You try to conduct a murder investigation, and the suspects decline to talk."

"You knew that when I went in there."

"So?"

"You sent me in anyway, hoping she'd spill something to me she wouldn't tell you."

"Did she?"

"That's hardly ethical."

"Ethical?" The coffee mug stopped on the way to Pinehurst's lips. "The woman asked to talk to you. I let her. If she told you anything interesting, then it would be your ethics whether you wish to withhold it from the police. Am I to gather she didn't?"

"That would be a good gather," I said. "The woman is sitting tight and waiting for her lawyer. She only wanted me to walk her dog."

"That's disappointing," Pinehurst said. "So, you want to tell me why you're here? Some other suspect you'd like me to run down?"

"I told you what other suspect. The man from Champney Falls. The one who's not staying at the inn, but keeps showing up there."

"Uh-huh. What about him?"

"I saw him today on the Cog Railway. I followed him to where he lives."

"And where is that?"

"I don't know."

"You don't know?"

"I don't know the address. I can find it, though."

"You don't know the address?"

"It's one five four something road. Only there's no sign for the road."

"In what town?"

"I'm not sure."

"What about the license plate?"

"I couldn't get close enough to see."

"This is an excellent lead you're bringing me."

"I can show you the house. You will know the street and town."

"That's very interesting. You will understand why I'm not as thrilled as I would have been had I not made an arrest?"

"What if you're wrong?"

"Then I will apologize. And probably get slapped with a suit for false arrest. Though that will be just a gesture, and won't hold up when the lawyer fails to establish malice."

"What I meant was, if you're wrong, this man could be the answer you're looking for."

"He could, and I will certainly check him out. At the moment, I'm more concerned with my prisoner's request. She would like you to walk her dog?"

"That's right."

"So would I. Like you to walk her dog, I mean. We have a warrant to search the room. I'm reluctant to do so while the dog is there. Perhaps if we were to take a run over, we might kill two birds with one stone."

"Could we stop by my friend's on the way?"

"Your hiker suspect? Does it happen to be on the way?"

"More or less."

"Then I suppose we could swing by. Not to talk with the gentleman, you understand, just to verify the address." He looked at me. "Would that satisfy you?"

"I don't think *satisfy* is the right word. But I'd certainly like you to do that."

"Then I'd be happy to," Pinehurst said. "Just let me finish my coffee, we'll take a run over. How's that?"

"Wonderful," I said. "Now that we've got that out of the way, would you mind telling me why you've arrested this woman? Surely it wasn't on a whim."

"I assure you it was not. I arrested her on the basis of the evidence."

"What evidence?"

"Unfortunately, it is not physical evidence, merely circumstantial. That's why I want to search her room. I don't think she'd be stupid enough to hang on to the poison, but if it had been in some container, there might be a trace left. That would certainly nail it down."

"Nail what down? What do you have on her?"

"Well, you will admit she had the opportunity, won't you? Because just before the murder, she got up and went out to walk her dog. At exactly the critical time. The drinks had already been served and were sitting there on the table. Including the fatal one. And, yes, it *was* the fatal one—that's come back from the lab. Christine Cobb died of cyanide poisoning. The poison was administered in her drink. The drink was a stinger, which is some god-awful sweet-tasting concoction young people seem to like. Ideal for disguising the poison.

"Anyway, she went out and came back during the time of optimal access. When Lars was presumably not in the booth. Which, we all agree, is when it probably happened."

"So what? So she went out to walk the dog. Anyone actually see her at the booth?"

"So far, no one did."

"So far?"

"In the first round of questioning, we didn't know what we were after. So some things slipped by. Such as your wife getting up from the table, which she didn't mention the first time around. But we hear about later on. Prompted, the witness' recollection improves. So it's entirely possible someone saw her and failed to mention the fact."

"Fine. It's entirely possible, but so what? So far, no one did. So what have you got? Yes, she was up from the table, but so was everyone else. I was. My wife was. Half a dozen other people were. And the waitresses, the busboy, and even Louise. So why pick on her?"

"Well, there's the motive."

"The motive?"

"Yes. She's the one with the motive. It took a little doing, but

I finally ran it down. Not that easy to do over the phone, but sometimes you get lucky."

"Florence had a motive? Are you kidding? She didn't even know Christine Cobb."

"Maybe not, but her husband did."

"What?"

"Florence's husband. He knew Christine. Knew her well." Pinehurst shrugged. "As a matter of fact, they had an affair."

TWENTY-FOUR

PRINCE NEARLY KNOCKED me down. He came bounding out the door, leaped up, put his paws on my shoulders, and licked my face. Before I could grab him he hopped down and took off, his paws skidding a mile a minute on the wooden floor like a cartoon dog, before finally gaining traction and rocketing around the corner and down the stairs.

"Better get him," Pinehurst said.

"Leash. I need the leash."

"Yes, yes. Get the leash."

It was hanging on the inside doorknob. Pinehurst found it first, thrust it at me before I had a chance to look around. I caught a glimpse of a bare room not dissimilar to mine, before Pinehurst shoved me out and slammed the door in my face.

I had no time to take offense. The dog was on the loose. I turned, hurried down the steps.

Prince was cavorting downstairs. He came out of the TV room and shot by me, heading for the front desk. By the time I got there he was in the dining room, where dinner was not yet being served—thank goodness for small favors. Prince circled the room once, then went through the swinging kitchen door. I heard a yowl and a spat, followed by furious barking. I gritted my teeth, sprinted through the kitchen door.

It was quite a tableau.

Max the cat, up on the windowsill, appeared twice his normal size. His back was arched, his teeth were bared. His orange fur was standing straight up all over his body. He looked like malevolent marmalade.

Prince the dog was barking at him ferociously. Yet there was a somewhat plaintive, hurt, surprised quality to his bark. And on closer look, his nose appeared to be scratched.

Between the two of them, and protecting the cat, stood Louise's nameless husband, the cook. He was dressed in his chef's apron and hat, and stood, meat cleaver in hand, poised and ready, if need be, to behead the dog on behalf of the cat.

I didn't want that to happen. I slipped up behind Prince, snapped the leash on, turned and pulled him away. It took all my strength to get him out the kitchen door. Fortunately, Prince seemed to believe in "out of sight, out of mind." Once we were in the dining room he gave up tugging, his tail began to wag, and in no time at all he was leading me outside.

Alice was waiting on the front lawn. She'd seen us drive up and tried to tag along. Pinehurst hadn't let her, which, in terms of endearing himself to her, probably ranked right up there with being willing to consider her a murder suspect.

"What's happening?" Alice said.

"I have to walk Prince."

"I know you have to walk Prince. What's happening with Florence?"

"Let's take a walk." The McInnernys were on the porch, along with the two businessmen who might be gay—it occurred to me I had to learn their names so I could stop thinking of them like that. "Let's get out of earshot, shall we?"

"Is it that bad?"

"Worse."

I dropped the bombshell on her. Alice took it about as hard as I'd expected.

"Florence's husband had an affair with Christine Cobb?" she said, incredulously.

"That's right. Before the divorce too. The way Pinehurst tells it, Christine Cobb was responsible for breaking up the marriage."

"It doesn't mean she killed her."

"No, but it sure looks bad. I mean, here she is, following the woman around."

"That has yet to be proved."

"Alice, what's to prove? She follows them to New Hampshire, checks in at the same bed-and-breakfast."

"You don't *know* she followed them," Alice said. I could tell she was upset because she didn't issue her usual disclaimer that the Blue Frog Ponds was really an inn.

"What do you mean, I don't know she followed them? She's *here*."

"Yes, but she didn't have to follow them. Maybe she's just here."

"You mean it's coincidence?"

"Why not?"

"Because it's too much coincidence. If two people happen to vacation in the same place, that's coincidence. When one of them hates the other, and the other one dies, that's too much coincidence. You see what I mean?"

"I suppose."

"You'll recall she was also at Champney Falls."

"So?"

"So? Here she is, dogging the woman's footsteps, following her everywhere she went."

"But she didn't follow her to Champney Falls. Don't you remember? When we got to the top, she was already there."

"Yes, but so were they."

"Yes, but they passed us on the way up. Florence didn't pass us on the way up. She and Prince were already there. Now, you have to admit that. Bad as you are with faces, you would have noticed if a woman had passed us with a dog."

"Fine. She didn't pass us on the way up. But that doesn't prove anything. Say Florence is following them. The minute they drive into the parking lot, she knows where they're going. So she parks the car, and she and Prince go up the mountain. While they're fussing with their gear. Or packing their backpacks. She goes on up and waits for them at the top."

"Why?"

"Huh?"

"Why would she do that. I mean, what does she plan to do to them at the top of Champney Falls?"

"She didn't have to have anything planned. If she's an obsessive stalker, she just wants to be there. She can follow them for days before taking action."

"I think that's stretching."

"Stretching? Alice. Pinehurst found the motive. Just who is stretching things here?"

"Pinehurst found the connection. It doesn't have to be the motive."

"So now we're into semantics? Alice, look how far you have to go even to plead your case."

We had reached the road. Two figures coming back from the direction of town called out and waved their arms.

"Uh-oh," Alice said. "Jean and Joan. They're gonna want to hear."

I knew they would. And I didn't feel like going through it again. "You tell 'em," I said. "I gotta put the dog away."

I headed for the Blue Frog Ponds. The McInnernys came down off the porch and cut me off.

"What's going on?" Mrs. McInnerny demanded.

I was in no mood for them, either. "You know as much as I do," I said.

"Well, now, that can't be true," Johnny said. "We don't know about the affair."

"The affair?"

"Yeah. From what I hear, that woman was having an affair, and—Hey, watch that dog, willya?"

Prince had started to sniff Johnny McInnerny's crotch. A bad move if ever I saw one. I tugged him away, and he aimed at Mrs. McInnerny, with an unexpectedly fortuitous result. When she said, "Get that animal away from me," I was happy to comply, and guided Prince in the front door.

Lars was coming down the stairs. I had to admit, I'd forgotten all about him. The fact that he was there, I mean. The grieving boyfriend, former suspect. Living right there in the main building. But seeing him come down the stairs reminded me that, not only was Florence staying at the same bed-and-breakfast, she was right there on the same floor. The odds of winning the lottery began to appear *better* than the odds that this was just coincidence.

While I was thinking that, Prince took off for the kitchen. He was still on his leash, but it didn't mean anything except that he pulled me right through the dining room door. I stopped him, turned him around, and walked back out, just in time to see Lars leave by the front door.

Prince and I went on up the stairs. When we reached the landing, I realized I didn't have Florence's room key. Pinehurst was gone, the door was closed, and I couldn't get in. A fine state of affairs.

Just on the off chance, I tried the knob, but of course it was locked.

I looked ruefully at the door. Looking back at me was Fenwick Frog. Fenwick was a happy-go-lucky sort, depicted flipping a coin in the air, à la Cyd Charisse and Gene Kelly in the "Gotta Dance" number from *Singin' in the Rain*. Looking at Fenwick Frog, one wouldn't expect the occupant of his room to be in jail for murder.

Florence's room was number three. The door across from it was number four. They were the only two doors on the landing. So rooms one and two must have had a separate staircase.

And room four must have been Christine Cobb's.

I looked at the door for no other reason than to check out her frog. Silly, I know, but I was curious. I wanted to know who the decedent's frog was.

It was Felicity.

Felicity was a decidedly female frog, with a pink bow on her head, and long eyelashes. If you've never seen a frog with long eyelashes, it's impossible to describe the effect. But trust me, this was one attractive frog.

I swear I had not had the intention, and I don't know what it was that possessed me, but I had just tried Florence's doorknob and found it locked, and now unconsciously I found myself trying Christine's.

It was locked. Thank goodness. I mean, what was I thinking? Had it clicked open, what would I have done? Taken the dog in and let him sniff around? Somehow, I don't think so. It had been a long day, I was tired, I was not thinking clearly, I needed to put the dog away and get out of there.

I went downstairs, found Louise, asked her for the key. Tried to forestall the barrage of questions she wanted to ask me. Louise was naturally excited by the arrest. Not that she had anything against Florence, I'm sure, it was just the thrill of having her son in the clear.

"It's a relief," she said. "You can't imagine what a relief."

"I know how you feel."

"Do you? I don't think so. Unless it's your son, you just can't know."

"Maybe not, but I'm glad it's off your mind. Anyway, could I have the key?"

"Yes, of course," Louise said. She popped behind the desk, checked the board. "Let's see, room three? No, it's not here. That's funny. There should be one here."

"There has to be," I said. "The police were just there. I took out the dog."

"And they're not still here?"

"No. They're gone. I was just up there. The door is locked."

"Then they must have the key," Louise said. "They must have forgotten to turn it in."

"There's only one key?"

"No, there's two. Florence has one."

"You mean both keys are at the police station? Great. So what do I do with the dog?"

"Don't worry. I'll give you a passkey."

"You have a passkey?"

"Sure. For emergencies like this. Let's see. Here it is. Just don't lose it. And be sure to bring it back."

"Thank goodness," I said. "He's a nice dog and all that, but we hadn't planned on keeping a dog, and he doesn't really get along with the cat."

"No, Max isn't big on dogs," Louise said.

I took the passkey upstairs, unlocked Florence's door, and let Prince in.

And remembered I had to feed him.

His water and his bowl were on a newspaper near the bathroom door. Dry and canned dog food was on the floor beside it.

Florence hadn't told me how much to give him. I guess she must have had other things on her mind. I put dry food in the bowl, opened one of the cans, scooped about half of it out on top. Looked critically at Prince, added the other half.

Prince was not one to stand on ceremony. While I was still filling the bowl he nosed his way in, and began chomping the dog food down.

I stood up, looked for a place to get rid of the can. I rinsed it out in the sink, and put it in the wastebasket. I washed the spoon, put it back next to the canned food. Prince was still merrily chomping. I stood there and surveyed the room.

What, if anything, had the police found? I had no idea. The room looked exactly as it had when we'd first entered it. There was no indication anyone had even been there.

Oh, well.

I told myself it was for Florence's own good. I went over to the dresser, began pulling out drawers.

Found nothing. Just clothes.

The closet yielded only more clothes and an empty suitcase.

The bathroom only cosmetics.

Nothing in the end table. Nothing under the bed. Nothing under the chair.

Nothing.

Had the police taken it?

Taken what?

The vial with the poison?

Had I been reading too many mystery stories?

No, there was nothing here. It was time to go.

I debated turning out the light. Would Florence leave Prince in the dark? I figured she wouldn't sleep with the light on. But she wouldn't turn it off this early, either. I finally compromised by turning off the overhead light and leaving the bedside light on.

Prince was still eating. Had I overfed him? The least of my worries.

I let myself out, took out the passkey, and locked the door. Turned and looked.

Across from me was Felicity Frog. She of the long eyelashes. She whose occupant was dead. One of whose occupants was dead. The other I'd seen going down the stairs.

Had Lars come back? No, surely I would have heard him. Surely he was still gone. Surely the room was empty.

The passkey. I held it in my hands. What Louise had described as a passkey.

Uh-oh.

Don't be a fool.

I walked to the door, put the passkey in the lock.

It fit.

Of course it fit. It was the passkey. That's what they do.

I turned it. The lock clicked back. I turned the doorknob, and the door opened. Had a moment of absolute panic that I hadn't heard Lars come back, and when I opened the door he would be standing there.

He wasn't. The room was empty. I hesitated a moment, and stepped in.

Next decision—did I close the door for privacy, or leave it open so I could hear him coming? I decided to leave it open. So I'd at least have a chance of getting out. Short of diving out of the second-story window.

All right, enough thinking. This had to be done fast.

I marched to the closet door, threw it open.

Felt a pang. The clothes in the closet were largely hers. There were a jacket and pants that belonged to Lars, as well as a dress shirt. But mostly there were dresses, skirts, shirts, sunsuits, pullovers, and shorts that had belonged to Christine. Lars hadn't packed them up, and why would he? Why would he want to, why would he care, and how could he bring himself to do it?

Poor man.

I realized it was the first time since the murder I had thought of him in that way. As a poor man. Whether it was the sound of the slap, or the tears on her face, or the look in his eyes when I'd passed the booth, or whether I was just projecting all that, but up till now I had never once felt sorry for Lars.

And it bothered me. Not that I hadn't felt sorry for him. But that I did now. Because it occurred to me the only reason I did now was because mentally I had taken him off my list of murder suspects. And the only reason I would have done that was if I thought I knew who did it. And in the present state of the evidence, the only one I could possibly make a case for thinking they might have done it would be Florence.

And I had *not* let myself believe that. Despite the evidence. Despite what I'd said to Alice. Despite everything else, I still clung to the hope that Florence, the woman with the dog, was not guilty. Was not the one who had done it.

My sudden feeling for Lars showed me just how hollow was that particular hope. How much I had been deluding myself.

I shook my head angrily. *Get a grip. You're in here, risking discovery, for a purpose. Go to it.*

I went through the clothes in the closet, searching the pockets. Christine's held nothing. Indeed, her clothes had few pockets to search.

Lars' jacket was another story. I found a comb, a pen, a handkerchief, and a half-dozen business cards from an insurance firm in Boston. In the lower right hand corner it read LARS HEINRICK, SALES EXECUTIVE. A fancy name, to be sure.

I put one of the cards in my pocket. I don't know why, I just found it interesting. Maybe the fact he was from Boston. Of course, they had to be from Boston for Christine and Florence's husband to have gotten involved.

Or maybe it was the fact Lars sold insurance for a living. I wondered what that meant. Was a sales executive just someone who ran around trying to sell people insurance? Did he work on commission and, if so, just how successful was Lars?

Believe me, I hadn't been standing there thinking all that. I, in fact, had moved on to the dresser, was pulling open drawers.

The top one held her underwear. It was sheer. I felt a number of conflicting emotions. Here I was, snooping through the lingerie of this very attractive woman, who had appealed to me for help before becoming the centerpiece in this murder I felt I now had to solve.

Second drawer, more clothes. Of the T-shirt variety. Plus the bathing suit she'd been wearing by the pool. Another disturbing mental image.

Bottom drawer, just a couple of pairs of pants.

I started to close the drawer, noticed a bulge.

Stopped.

Lifted the pants.

A case. A small leather case. The size a man might use to carry his toiletries.

Oh, boy.

I cocked my ear to the door.

Heard nothing.

Looked at the case.

It had a zipper that went three quarters of the way around.

Enough hesitation. I pulled the zipper, lifted the top.

Inside was just what I'd expected. A comb. A hairbrush. A safety razor. A toothbrush.

Perfectly normal.

Except.

Even from where I stood, I could see all those items laid out on the shelf over the bathroom sink.

So why the case?

There was a zippered compartment in the lid. I unzipped it, pulled out a nail clipper. Some Q-tips. Some Band-Aids. Some Tylenol.

And . . .

A small, glass, screw-top bottle half full of white powder.

Good lord.

The poison?

Had I actually found the poison?

I was beginning to sweat. Too many things were open. The open door. The open drawer. The open case. The open compartment.

The open vial?

I felt in my pocket for a piece of paper. Found a stick of gum. Wrigley's Doublemint. Double your pleasure, double your fun. I pulled the wrapper off, unfolded it. Set it on the floor. Unscrewed the top from the little glass bottle, tilted it over the gum wrapper, tapped some powder out.

And heard a step on the stair!

What a chill.

What a rush of adrenaline.

What a moment of sheer, unadulterated panic.

I screwed the top on the bottle, zipped the bottle in the compartment, zipped the case shut, slid the case in the drawer, flipped the pants over it, closed the drawer, bolted out of the room.

Before I could slam the door, a voice demanded, "What are you doing?"

I turned around to find Lars Heinrick. He'd stopped a few steps from the top of the stairs. He was looking up at me, a scowl on his face.

I blinked at him. Said the first thing that came to mind. Which turned out to be, "Huh?"

Lars Heinrick came up the last few steps. "Just what do you think you're doing?"

"Walking the dog."

He blinked at me. "Huh?"

"The woman's in jail. They asked me to walk the dog."

Lars Heinrick blinked again. I could practically see his mind struggling its way through the non-sequitur. "That's my room."

"I beg your pardon?"

Lars pointed. "That's *my* room."

I pointed too. "That's *your* room?"

"Yes."

"I was wondering where the dog was."

"How did you get in my room?"

"I wasn't going in your room. I was just gonna walk the dog."

"How did you open the door?"

"Oh. I have a key." I held it up.

"You have the key to my room?"

"No. I have the passkey. They gave me a passkey to walk the dog. So, this is the wrong room." I pointed across the hall. "Is that room hers?"

"Yes, of course."

"Oh. My mistake. Sorry to bother you."

I crossed the hallway, put the key in the lock, unlocked the door.

"Here, Prince," I called.

I was afraid Prince would be too busy eating to care, but he came bounding right up. I grabbed him by the collar, pretended to find the leash on the inside doorknob.

"Right where she said it would be," I said, although it was actually right where I'd left it.

I snapped the leash on the collar, closed the door, smiled at Lars, said, "Come on, Prince," and followed the dog down the stairs.

My heart was pounding. Had I really gotten away with it? Had Lars bought the story? Or had he seen me with Prince earlier, when he was coming down the stairs? And even if he hadn't, would something else trigger his memory? Make him suddenly realize I'd already walked the dog?

Well, there was nothing I could do about it, but thanks to Lars, Prince was getting a double dip. I took him out on the front lawn, ran him around a while. Just long enough to seem reasonable, in case Lars noticed me bringing him back.

He didn't. At least, as far as I know, he didn't. He might have been listening just inside the door. But, in that case, I realized, it made little difference, since his suspicions would be already aroused.

At any rate, I didn't see him. I put the dog back in the room, went downstairs, and returned the passkey to Louise.

"You walked him twice," Louise said.

I was afraid she'd noticed. "Yeah. After I fed him, he needed to go again."

"Maybe you should feed him first."

I nodded. "Now I know."

Moments later I was out the front door.

With the evidence in my pocket.

TWENTY-FIVE

PINEHURST WASN'T IMPRESSED.

"You stole this from his room?"

"I uncovered some evidence."

"Is that what you call this?"

"You think this isn't evidence?"

"It doesn't matter what I think. It matters what a judge does."

"A judge, Chief? Let's not get sidetracked here. The point is not whether this evidence will stand up in court. The point is what it means."

"It means you're guilty of criminal trespass."

"Fine. Arrest me. Put me in jail. But that's another tangent. The point is, if this is poison, you've got your killer."

"I've already got my killer."

"You just think you do. But what if you're wrong?"

"Then I will need to catch another killer. Which I can only do by legal means."

"Fine. Do it by legal means. Just do it."

"Unfortunately, you've rendered that impossible. By an illegal search and seizure."

"Wrong. Absolutely wrong. I am not a policeman. I'm a private citizen. I cannot violate Lars Heinrick's rights. I might lay myself open to criminal prosecution or a civil suit, but that's another matter. And that's way off the subject. The point is, Lars Heinrick had this powder. It might be poison. Now, you want to analyze it or not?"

"Of course I want to analyze it. Otherwise I won't know what it is."

"Fine. Then we have no problem."

"That will depend on what it is. If it's poison, we have a big problem."

"No, we don't. If it's poison, you know who the killer is. So you get a warrant, you search his room, end of case."

"And if it turns out that warrant was obtained on the basis of information found during an illegal search, any evidence I find during my own search is contaminated and cannot be used in court."

"Fine, Chief. Split hairs all you want." I pointed to the Doublemint gum wrapper full of powder I had laid on Pinehurst's desk. "If this is poison, never mind what it means legally, at least you'll know who did it."

"But I won't."

"What?"

"I won't know. You give me this powder. You say it's from his room. It could be. But I have only your word for it."

"So you search his room and find the vial."

"That wouldn't change a thing. For all the same reasons. If you're making the story up, the question then is how much of your story is true. The part that sounds true is the part about you getting a passkey. If you did, what's to stop you from planting the poison in his room?"

"Oh, come on."

"Come on? Why is that any different than you lying in the first place?"

"Why would I lie?"

"Are you kidding? If the woman is innocent, as you maintain, then you yourself are a suspect. Not to mention your wife. You'd have every reason to lie."

I looked at him narrowly. "You know, Chief, it occurs to me the way you're belittling this, maybe you got something better. You find anything in Florence's room?"

"I was not aware that you were a party to this investigation."

"I'm not. I'm that insufferable amateur detective that's always messing around with the evidence. However, if you want me to go away, your best bet is to give me what you've got. Because I'm not inclined to fly in the face of logic. If you found something that nails down the case against Florence, I'll feel stupid about my gum wrapper full of powder."

"And it would be worth telling you just for that," Pinehurst said. "Unfortunately, I can tell you nothing. Because we found nothing. Not that we expected to. And not that it weakens our case. I wouldn't expect her to hang on to the murder weapon. If she had, I would have found it suspicious." He pointed to the Doublemint wrapper. "Just as I find this somewhat suspicious."

"Beware of Greeks bearing gifts, Chief?" I said. "Anyway, when you get this analyzed, you mind telling me what it is?"

"You'll be one of the first to know. If it's poison, you'll probably be under arrest."

"I beg your pardon?"

"For trying to frame Lars Heinrick. And that's just for starters. You might be under arrest for murder."

"What?"

"Well, why not? If you had the murder weapon in your possession."

"Which I brought to you."

"Yes, of course. The colossal double bluff. The killer, arrogantly overconfident, walks into the police station and hands over the murder weapon to the poor, bumbling investigator, all the time laughing in his sleeve."

"I think that's a misplaced modifier, Chief."

"Huh?"

"Wasn't it the *murderer* who was laughing in his sleeve?"

Pinehurst frowned. "You think I'm kidding?"

I exhaled, shook my head.

"I sure hope you're kidding."

TWENTY-SIX

WE HAD DINNER with Jean and Joan. After the events of the day, I suppose that was inevitable. They were eager to pump me for information.

So were the McInnernys. They descended on our table before Louise could stop them, and demanded to know what was going on. I was torn between wanting to be rid of them, and not wanting to be outright rude. Fortunately, they didn't know how much I knew. In fact, they didn't know much at all.

"An affair, that's the rumor," Mrs. McInnerny said. "That's the story going around."

"Well, let's not spread it any further," I said. "If we could at least keep our voices down."

"As if everyone didn't know," Mrs. McInnerny said. "That woman was having an affair right under her boyfriend's nose."

Ah. That affair. The one with Randy. The McInnernys knew nothing about Florence's husband. In terms of the murder investigation, they were a good two steps behind.

"One shouldn't speak ill of the dead," Jean or Joan said. The plumper one. It occurred to me I had to ask Alice which was which again.

"Don't be silly," Mrs. McInnerny said. "It's a murder case, and the facts are the facts. But they have to make sense. What could this possibly have to do with your friend with the dog?"

"Absolutely nothing," I said. "It's my opinion the police made a mistake."

"But they must have *some* reason," Johnny said. "You spoke to them, what did they say?"

"Florence isn't talking on the advice of her attorney."

Anyone wondering about the actual effectiveness of the concept of innocent until proven guilty and the right to remain silent should have seen the look on the McInnernys' faces. From their reaction, I might as well have told them Florence had confessed.

"I can't believe it," Mrs. McInnerny said. "She seemed like such a nice woman."

I resisted adding, "With an awful dog."

"She *is* a nice woman," Jean/Joan the thinner said. "The police made a mistake."

It was nice to see her standing up for Florence. Particularly since she was better informed than the McInnernys. Jean and Joan knew about Florence's husband's affair.

As I sat there, trying to figure our how to get rid of the McInnernys, it occurred to me what a complicated dynamic there was at the table, in terms of levels of information.

The McInnernys were at the bottom of the food chain. They knew about Christine's affair with Randy, and not much else.

Jean and Joan, on the other hand, knew about Christine's affair with Florence's husband. But they didn't know about my discovery in Lars Heinrick's room.

Alice knew that. I told her as soon as I got back. Actually, I told her before I left. What I'd found and was talking to Pinehurst about. Then when I got back, I told her Pinehurst's reaction. Which was frustrating as hell. And not just his reaction. But her reaction to it. Because Alice, in her infinite contrariness, saw nothing wrong with Pinehurst's point of view.

"But I *didn't* plant the evidence," I told her.

"Of course not," Alice said. "You don't have to convince me. But I can see why it wouldn't convince him."

See? Totally exasperating. Anyway, there I was, sitting at the table, dealing with a who-knew-what-when scenario potentially more complicated than Watergate. So it was a relief when Louise showed up to guide the McInnernys away.

When she did, it seemed to me they were regarding her differently. I wondered if that was because they had identified her as the mother of the person with whom they had heard Christine had had the affair.

The minute they were gone, Jean/Joan the thinner took up the attack.

"So, what's the story?" Jean/Joan the thinner said. "Has he traced him yet?"

The *he* and the *him* had been gone over before the McInnernys' interruption. Jean/Joan was asking if Pinehurst had found out who the hiker was. Jean and Joan knew I'd gone back to the police station. They did not know I'd gone back there to deliver evidence that might be poison. They had assumed—and Alice and I had not contradicted the assumption—that I had gone there to follow up on the investigation we'd begun. To see if the police had traced down our man.

"Not yet," I said. "He assures me it's being done, but claims he hasn't had the time."

"How long could it take?" Jean/Joan the plumper.

"Longer than usual, because he doesn't know what road it is, either."

"What?"

"He doesn't know the name of the road, any more than we do. There's no signpost, so he doesn't know."

"What about the license plate number?"

"He doesn't have it."

"Why not?"

"Because there's no way to get it without tipping the man off."

See what I mean about complicated? What I was telling Jean and Joan now was a complete fabrication. What I *assumed* was Pinehurst's assessment of the situation. In actual point of fact, Pinehurst and I hadn't discussed the hiker from Champney Falls at all. At least not when I'd gone there to give him the poison.

It was long about then that Lucy passed by and slipped a piece of paper under Alice's coffee cup. I couldn't quite believe she'd done that. I snatched it out, opened it up, read:

CHICKEN DIJONNAISE

> *2½–3 pound whole free range chicken*
> *sprigs of fresh tarragon*
> *2 tablespoons Dijon mustard*
> *1 cup dry white wine*
> *2 tablespoons olive oil*
> *2 tablespoons crème fraîche*
> *1 teaspoon lemon juice*
> *kosher salt and pepper*

Preheat oven to 375°. Wash and dry chicken thoroughly.

Prepare the chicken by rubbing kosher salt and pepper on the skin and in the cavity. Stuff the cavity with fresh tarragon sprigs. Coat the chicken with Dijon mustard and let sit at room temperature for 1 hour.

On top of the stove in a heavy Dutch oven, brown the chicken on all sides in 2 tablespoons of olive oil. Add 1 cup of dry white wine. Bring to boil. Cover with a lid and place in the oven for 1¼ to 1½ hours.

Remove the chicken from the pot. Skim fat from cooking liquid. Remove the tarragon, chop and return to the pot liquid. Add the crème fraîche, stir in lemon juice and simmer 1–2 minutes until thickened slightly.

Divide the chicken into serving pieces and top with sauce. Serve with small steamed new potatoes.

Serves 4.

"Alice," I said.

Alice looked somewhat defensive. After all, a friend of hers was in jail. "I couldn't help it," she said. "That chicken was to die for."

Jean and Joan were in complete agreement that Alice's actions were totally justified. What a surprise. I wondered cynically if their support had been purchased by the promise of Xerox copies.

While we were bantering about the recipe a hush fell over the dining room. It was sudden and unmistakable. I knew without looking that Lars Heinrick had walked in.

I took a sip of water, which allowed me a sideways glance over my shoulder. Lars Heinrick was plodding along behind Louise. He was taking no apparent notice of his surrounding. If I'd aroused his suspicions by searching his room, you wouldn't have known it. He followed Louise to a table on the far side of the dining room and sat down.

"I don't know why he's here," Jean/Joan the thinner said.

"Who?"

"Lars. I don't how he can stand to be here."

"The man has to eat."

"Yes, but here? With everyone staring at him? You think he doesn't notice everyone stops talking when he enters the room?"

"Well, he can't leave," I said. "The police ordered everyone to stay."

"That was before they made an arrest," Jean/Joan the plumper said. "Do they really expect us to stay now?"

"I hadn't thought of it."

"Then you must be staying the week. Jean and I were checking out tomorrow."

Aha. Jean and I. Thank you, Joan the plumper, for that valuable bit of information.

"Are you going to make an issue of it?" I said.

"We would," Jean said. "Except . . ."

"Except what?"

She shrugged. "Well, how could we leave now?"

"Yes," Joan said. "With poor Florence in jail."

I stifled a grin. So that was how they had worked it out in their minds. Poor Florence, indeed. Jean and Joan weren't checking out, and it had nothing to do with Florence or Pinehurst's instructions. They couldn't bear not to see how this turned out. Jean and Joan had signed on for the duration.

As if on cue, Louise arrived at the table. I had a premonition—she somehow knew what we'd been discussing and was about to inform us that, in light of Florence's arrest, the police were now allowing the guests to leave. This, of course, proved to be entirely wrong.

"Excuse me, Mr. Hastings," she said. "You have a phone call."

"Oh?"

"Yes. You can take it at the front desk."

"Who is it?"

Louise lowered her voice. "The police."

I got up and left the room, leaving three very curious women at my table.

The receiver was lying next to the phone on the front desk. I picked it up, said, "Hello?"

"Stanley Hastings?"

"Yes. Chief Pinehurst?"

"Yes. Sorry to drag you away from dinner, but I thought you'd want to know. I got the results back from the lab."

"So soon?"

"You'd like them to take longer?"

"No, no, Chief. I'm glad. Just surprised. So, what was it?" I lowered my voice. "Was it poison?"

"No."

"No?"

"No. At least, not officially. It's poison in my book. But it isn't cyanide."

"So what is it?"

"Cocaine."

"What?"

"Cocaine. Evidently you stumbled upon a stash of drugs."

"Oh."

"Disappointed?"

"Well, it's not what I was hoping."

"I understand. But the facts are the facts. The sample is cocaine. Now, however you may feel about that, it is *not* what killed Christine Cobb."

"So what are you going to do about it?"

"Me? Absolutely nothing. I'm not about to make a drug bust on the basis of an illegal search and seizure. Life is too short. That type of aggravation one simply does not need."

"Oh, good lord."

"Well, now, don't be too upset. We follow lots of leads. Not all of them pan out."

"No kidding. So, I don't suppose you got anything on our friend?"

"Who?"

"The hiker from Champney Falls. You get anywhere with him?"

"Why do you ask?"

"Why do I ask? What kind of question is that?"

"I'm just wondering why you chose to ask that now."

I took a breath. "I'll tell you why, Chief. You just had me paged in the dining room. I've got three women at my table dying to know why the police wanted to talk to me. What could possibly be so urgent. When I get back to the table, I am going to have to answer questions. My wife knows about the sample I gave you, but the other women don't. And I don't particularly want to tell them. So when they ask me what you had to say, I have to come with something else."

"And that's the reason for your interest?"

"Frankly, yes. I'm grasping at straws. I didn't expect you to have anything by now."

"Oh, but I do."

"I beg your pardon?"

"I have the information you've been bugging me about. That's partly why I called."

My patience with Pinehurst was wearing awfully thin. "Then why couldn't you just say so?"

"I *am* saying so. I wasn't withholding anything. I was merely curious why you would be asking now."

"I'm asking now because I've been asking all along. What are you talking about?"

"I'm talking about the connection."

"Connection?"

"Exactly. No pun intended. But there you are. The man you refer to as the hiker from Champney Falls is Delmar Hobart. That is confirmed both by his address and the registration of his car. The license plate number of which I have still not gotten close enough to read. But which I now possess. And it was issued to a blue Ford that matches the description of the car in the gentle-man's driveway."

"And what has this man got to do with the case?"

"Absolutely nothing. However, he happens to have a record. Guess what for."

I blinked. "Drugs?"

"Very good, Mr. Hastings. Very good, indeed. Of course, this is just circumstantial, but putting two and two together, and con-sidering the fact that Delmar Hobart came to the Blue Frog Ponds but did not eat there, I would think we can conclude why he was there."

"I see," I said.

"I know you're not happy to hear that. You would have pre-ferred some bizarre murder plot. And not just to get your friend off the hook, either. You strike me as the type of man whose taste gravitates toward bizarre murder plots. If that's an unfair assess-ment, I can only say I'm sorry."

I sighed. "What about Florence?"

"What about her?"

"Has her lawyer showed up yet?"

"No, but don't hold your breath. If you were expecting her back, I mean. Because it isn't going to happen. I know the judge. He's not about to set bail in a case like this. No matter what some smart city lawyer says."

"Smart city lawyer? Chief, did a prejudiced observation just cross your lips?"

"Prejudiced? Don't be silly. Which word were you objecting to? Smart, city, or lawyer? I assure you, all three apply."

"Never mind, Chief," I said. "Nice talking to you."

"My pleasure," Pinehurst said, and hung up the phone.

The line did not immediately go dead. After the click of Pine-hurst hanging up, the line stayed open.

A moment later there was another click.

The sound of someone hanging up a phone.

TWENTY-SEVEN

I STOPPED IN the door of the dining room, looked around.

Alice and Jean and Joan were at our table.

At the next table was the family with the little girl, all of whom were present.

Behind them was the McInnernys' table. Johnny McInnerny was there, but his wife was gone.

Next to them was a table at which sat one of the two possibly gay businessmen. The other was nowhere to be seen.

Neither was Lars. I wasn't sure exactly what table Louise had shown him to, but wherever it was, he wasn't there.

I strode back to my table, sat down, leaned in, and lowered my voice. "Who went out right after I did?"

"Huh?" Alice said.

"Someone listened in on the call. Keep your voice down, don't spread it around, and don't point. But who went out right after me?"

"Lars Heinrick," Jean said.

"Are you sure?"

"Sure. He left right after he placed his order."

"Anybody else?"

"Mrs. McInnerny," Alice said. "She left right after you did."

"Before Lars?"

"Absolutely. She left right after you."

"Anyone else?"

"No."

"How about the businessman over there?"

"He came in after you went out. I haven't seen his brother."

I blinked. "His brother?"

"Yes, of course," Alice said. "Didn't you know they were brothers?"

"It never occurred to me."

Alice rolled her eyes. "You're hopeless. You can't see the resemblance?"

I was in no mood for a lecture on my powers of observation. I spotted Louise in the doorway, got up, intercepted her, led her outside.

"Anything wrong, Mr. Hastings?" she said.

"No, not really," I said. "I was just wondering."

"What?"

"About the phone. The one at the desk. Where I just took the call. Is there any extension to that phone?"

"Extension?"

"Yes. Could I have taken that call in another room?"

"Yes, if it was important. Is anything wrong?"

"I'm just trying to understand the mechanics. Where is the extension?"

"Actually, there are two. One in the kitchen, and one in the den."

"The den?"

"Yes. Just off the living room. There's a small reading room we call the den."

"With an extension phone?"

"That's right."

"I don't understand. You mean any guest could go in there and make a call?"

"No. It's locked."

"Locked?"

"Yes."

"The room?"

"No. The phone."

"The phone?"

"Yes."

"Show me."

"Now?"

"Please."

I followed Louise down the hall through the living room into the den. It was a small room, boasting a bookcase, a desk, and two overstuffed chairs.

There was a phone on the desk. A black rotary phone. Almost an anachronism in the day and age of Touch-Tones.

A metal lock protruded from one of the holes in the dial.

"See," Louise said. "It's locked. You can't dial it. There's no way to call out from here."

"But I could have taken my phone call?"

"Of course. That's why it's here. I'm not always at the desk. If I'm working on this side of the house, I'll answer the phone here."

"And if you're not?"

"They'll get it in the kitchen. Though I prefer that not to happen."

"Uh-huh," I said. I noticed she'd said *they*, rather than referring to her husband.

Louise was looking at me closely. "Can you tell me why you're so interested?"

I smiled enigmatically. "Just getting the lay of the land."

I reached for the phone. And felt a thrill. It was stupid, I know, but it occurred to me if this were a mystery story, the phone would be warm, so the detective could tell it had been used. Or cold, so he could tell that it hadn't.

I picked up the receiver.

It didn't tell me a thing.

TWENTY-EIGHT

"WHAT'S THE REAL story?" Alice asked.

"Real story?"

"Don't be dumb," she said as we went out the front door. "I heard what you told Jean and Joan. Now what really went on?"

"Let's take a walk," I said.

"Where?"

"Down by the swimming pool."

"I thought it was closed after dinner."

"It is."

We went down to the pool, sat in deck chairs. As expected, we were the only ones there. We watched the sunset and discussed the crime.

I had told Jean and Joan that Pinehurst had identified the hiker, but not as a drug dealer. I told Alice now.

"Interesting," she said. "So the man was Lars' connection. I wonder if he appreciated having a rendezvous at Champney Falls."

"He certainly didn't look like it," I said.

"No, he didn't," Alice said. "And I apologize."

"You do? For what?"

"What I said. When we saw him on the path. You pointed him out as a hiker grumpier than you. I said, maybe so, but at least he was a volunteer. No one was forcing him to do it. It now appears that wasn't the case."

"If Lars did indeed set it up. Which would seem likely. On the other hand, the guy shows up on the top of Mount Washington. Where I saw him talking to a young man. Who, in all likelihood, was buying drugs. At least, that would seem a reasonable assumption. So, maybe it's the hiker who had a penchant for conducting drug deals outdoors."

"A penchant?"

"I used the word wrong?"

"No. You just used it. Do people really say penchant?"

"Alice, I've had it up to here with Pinehurst. Don't you start digressing on me too."

"Okay. Sorry. Say the man did like to deal in the great outdoors. How come he shows up here?"

"The first time he ate here. Which might have been coincidence. I don't like coincidence, but you can't rule it out. The second night he popped in and out, undoubtedly a sale. I would imagine Lars had gone through his stash."

"So, he leaves the dining room, buys some dope, and then what?" Alice said. "Hides it in his room?"

"I would tend to think so," I said. "One, because that's where I found it. And, two, because the cops didn't. After the murder, I mean. I didn't ask Pinehurst, but I would assume the police searched Lars. In which case, he could not have been carrying drugs."

"Does that make sense?" Alice said. "That he would buy the stuff, and immediately hide it in his room?"

"Why not?"

"He's in the middle of dinner. Why wouldn't he just put it in his pocket?"

"I don't know," I said. "I'm not sure where this transaction took place. Say it was in or around the men's room. That's right near the stairs. It would only take a minute to pop up to his room, stash the stuff, and return to the booth. Which he might do if he were at all uneasy about making the buy in a semipublic place. Just in case he was seen, he might feel better not having it on him."

"Thin," Alice said. "But, since you found it there, you're probably right. So, what do we do now?"

"What do you mean?"

"We have a major problem here. The click on the phone line— if that was Lars, listening in on the conversation, then he knows you found the cocaine." She looked at me. "He *would* know that, wouldn't he? Did you discuss that with Pinehurst—the fact it was your sample he was testing?"

"I'm not sure. I would tend to think so."

"So would I. And, even if you didn't, he can put two and two together. The drugs came from his room. He caught you opening his door. So, even if he doesn't remember seeing you earlier on the stairs—and you don't think he did?"

"He looked totally oblivious. And if he *had* seen me with the dog, he would have *known* what I was telling him couldn't be true."

"Right. So we have to assume he didn't. But he knows you opened his door. So, if he overheard the conversation, that would give him enough. So, if it was him listening in on the line, what's his first move?"

"To get rid of the drugs."

"Or to get rid of you."

"I beg your pardon?"

"We can't be too careful here. Christine Cobb was killed. You have got to be very careful here not to fall into a trap."

"What do you mean?"

"You're used to big-city crime. Now you're here on vacation. This is not all fun and games. You've got to be sure you don't take this too lightly just because you're in a New England bed-and-breakfast."

"You realize you just said bed-and-breakfast?"

"Stanley, I'm not kidding. I don't like the idea this man may have seen you going into his room."

"So, whaddya wanna do, follow him? We shouldn't be here now, we should be back at the inn, waiting for him to come out of the dining room?"

"You realize you just called it an inn?"

"Alice, I'm very upset I got caught in his room. I said the first thing that came to mind, which was a very stupid thing to say if he had seen me earlier with the dog. But I don't think he did. He came down the stairs walking like a zombie. And the dog took off for the kitchen. So we didn't pass him. I saw him from a distance, and I don't think he saw me.

"And it really didn't register when I told him I was going to walk the dog. Yes, he was skeptical. Yes, he thought my behavior was strange. But that's what he was reacting to—the fact it was odd. *Not* the fact it was a complete fabrication, an absolute, obvious falsehood. *That* did not register."

"I'll keep an eye on him," Alice said.

"I don't think we should follow him."

"I'm not going to follow him. I'm just going to see where he goes."

"Most likely, it will be back to his room."

"Okay, what are you gonna do?"

"When dinner's over, I thought I'd check up on the kitchen phone."

"Sounds good. Let's go back inside, see if anything's happening."

Nothing was.

In the dining room, Lars was still at his table, waiting for coffee and dessert. The McInnernys were on their way out, and were arguing about the evening movie. Johnny McInnerny wanted to see it, and his wife didn't.

"You can see it if you want to," she said. "I've seen it a million times."

"So have I," Johnny said. "But it's always good."

"What's the movie?" I said.

"Arsenic and Old Lace," Mrs. McInnerny said.

"The old Cary Grant version," Johnny said. "You know, with Peter Lorre."

"Oh, so there's a new version?" Mrs. McInnerny said.

"What new version?" Johnny said.

"Exactly," Mrs. McInnerny said. "If there's a new version, I never heard of it. And neither did you. So what sense does it make to say the old Cary Grant version? That's the only version there is."

"Well, these people might not know that," Johnny said. "It doesn't hurt to say who's in a movie. Now how could that hurt?"

"Well, it's a questionable choice, if you ask me," Mrs. McInnerny said. "What with everything that's going on. To show a movie about poison."

"Well, let's not give away the plot," Johnny said.

"Now, Johnny McInnerny, you think these people don't know *Arsenic and Old Lace* is about poison?"

"Oh, well, I suppose."

"Come along now. You can see the movie if you want. It doesn't mean I have to."

The McInnernys went out the front door. A moment later I heard, *Pssst!*

Alice and I looked around.

Jean and Joan were gesturing to us from the direction of the TV room. Alice and I went over and joined them.

"What are you doing?" I said.

"Waiting for Lars to get finished," Jean said. Then looked around to see who might be overhearing us, though we were alone.

"Now, look," I said. "You can't follow Lars."

"You said to keep our eyes open," Joan said.

"Yes, I did. And that's fine. Go about your business, keep your eyes open, see what happens. But don't hide in corners and spy on people. Because if someone sees you doing it, the result could be very bad."

"So what should we do?" Jean said.

"I don't know. The movie tonight is *Arsenic and Old Lace*."

"Oh, I love that movie," Joan said.

"Then maybe you should check it out. See who's there. You might try to sit where you can watch their reactions."

"Why?" Jean said.

"Because it's a movie about poisoning people. Someone might be uneasy about the subject."

"Gotcha."

"Meanwhile, leave Lars alone. There's no need to put him on his guard."

Jean and Joan gave in, though with somewhat bad grace.

"I feel like the Grinch Who Stole Christmas," I said as they went out the door.

"They'll get over it," Alice said. "Besides, I can't wait to hear their reports on how Johnny McInnerny reacted to the poison in *Arsenic and Old Lace*."

"It will make my day," I said. "Let's see how dinner's coming."

We strolled back past the dining room. Lars Heinrick was the only one left. He sat sipping his coffee, his back to the door.

Most of the other tables had been cleared. Randy the busboy was working on the last one.

"I think I'll try the kitchen," I said.

"Fine. I'll hang out here," Alice said. When I raised my eyes, she added, "Discreetly."

"Just be careful," I said. I turned toward the kitchen, turned back. "What's the chef's name?"

The look Alice gave me might have been appropriate if I had asked her for *her* name. "Charlie," she said.

"Right. Charlie. Thanks."

I pushed through the swinging doors into the kitchen.

The chef, Louise's husband and Randy's father, was at the sink.

He heard me, turned his head, did a double-take, wheeled around and said, "Oh! You don't have the dog?"

"No."

"I don't want him in here, that dog."

"I got that impression."

He seemed surprised when I didn't turn and go. "Did you want something?"

"I'd like to ask you a couple of questions."

"I don't give out recipes."

"Yes, I know. Not that the food isn't very good. But that wasn't it. I have some questions about the girl."

"The girl?"

"The dead girl. Christine Cobb."

"I don't know anything about that."

"I know. But I'm looking into it, and there are some things I need to ask."

"You're looking into it?"

"Yes."

"Why?"

"Actually, your wife asked me to. On account of your son."

As if on cue, Randy came through the swinging door with a tray of dishes. He carried them over to the dishwasher, began loading them into racks to go into the machine.

His father and I stood there looking at him. As if we couldn't talk while he was in the room.

Randy finished unloading the tray into the rack, went back out through the swinging door.

His father turned to me. "You're not making any sense. My son has nothing to do with this. The police made an arrest."

Yes, they did. Your wife asked me to help before that happened. Because she did, certain things were set in motion. Now they need to be tied up."

"What things?"

"Nothing that should concern you. You, or your son. When you hear my questions, you'll see what I mean."

"What questions?"

"You have a phone in the kitchen?"

"I beg your pardon?"

"Your wife said there was a phone."

"Sure. Over there on the wall."

I could see it from where we stood. In a small alcove with shelves of canned goods. A black wall phone with a rotary dial. This one did not appear to have a lock.

"I see," I said. "So you can call out from here?"

"Or take calls, sure. What's the idea?"

"Did anyone use that phone tonight?"

"Tonight?"

"Yeah. During dinner. Did anyone use the phone?"

"I have no idea. I didn't. Randy didn't. The waitresses, I'm not sure."

"The waitresses?"

"Well, they're in and out all the time. I can't pay attention, I'm cooking the food. They're not supposed to make phone calls when dinner's being served. But if one of them did, just a short call, how could I possibly notice?"

"And you didn't notice?"

"No. If I did, I would say so. But the fact is, I didn't."

"And you didn't notice anyone else in the kitchen tonight?"

"Anyone else?"

"Yeah. Who wouldn't normally be here. Like one of the guests."

"Now, *that* I would notice."

"You're saying it's impossible one of the guests slipped in here and made a phone call?"

"Without being seen? I would say so. Sure, I'm busy cooking. But it's not just me. There's the waitresses. Any guest who comes through that door's gonna be asked what they're doing here."

"And no one was?"

"As far as I know."

"Where are the waitresses now?"

"On their way home. They don't have to clear. Last dessert served, and they're gone."

Randy came back through the swinging door with a coffee cup and a dessert plate. He took them over to the dishwasher, put them in the racks, began feeding the racks into the machine.

Which meant Lars was done.

I wondered where he'd gone.

I wondered where Alice was.

Randy fed the last rack into the machine, took a broom and dustpan, and went back out the swinging door.

"What's this got to do with the crime?" the chef said. "I thought it was solved."

"The police made an arrest. It's not the same thing. The case is yet to be proved."

"And you're looking for proof?"

"In a manner of speaking."

"What does that mean?"

"I'm looking for evidence."

"That this woman committed the crime?"

"Or that she didn't."

"I'm not sure I like that."

"I can see why you wouldn't. But please understand. I was doing this on behalf of your son. That job doesn't end just because the police made an arrest. In the event that they're wrong, they'll come looking for someone else. It would be nice if the facts indicated it wasn't him."

"And do they indicate that?"

"That's what I'm working on now."

The sweeping up either wasn't that big a job, or Randy wasn't very careful about it, because he came back through the swinging door, dumped the dustpan, put the broom away, and, without a word to his father, went out the door to the back.

When Randy went out, Max came in. He hopped up on the kitchen table, strolled between the pots and pans, climbed up onto the butcher block right next to the carving knife, and meowed loudly.

"Hello, Max," the chef said. For the first time his eyes lit up.

It was kind of sad. He showed only minimal interest in his wife and son. But he seemed to care about the cat.

"Hungry, Max?" he said. "Want some fish? Is that what you'd like?"

Max meowed loudly, which was disconcerting. It was as if he'd answered the question.

The chef certainly took it that way. He said, "Sure you do. Well, look what I've got here."

He went to the refrigerator, took out a tin wrapped in a plastic sandwich bag. He slid the bag off the tin, held it up.

"Sardines," he said. "His favorite. Drives him nuts."

He looked at me and his eyes were bright. "Watch this," he said. "A Stupid Pet Trick. Like on the Letterman show. Here. I'll show you."

Near the coffee urn was a stack of foam cups. He took three cups off the stack, brought them over to the butcher block, where Max was waiting impatiently, licking his lips and swishing his tail.

"Ready, Max?" he said. "Let's do your trick."

As if on cue, Max yawned and stretched, as if to show his complete indifference in the proceedings.

The chef knew better. He smiled, took the three Styrofoam cups, turned them over, and set them in a row upside down in front of the cat.

"There you are," he said. "The old shell game. Guess which cup the pea is under. Ever see it played by a cat? Watch this."

He took a sardine out of the tin, put it under the center cup. Then, he began switching the cups around, sliding them on the butcher block, faster, faster, faster, just like a con man playing the old shell game.

The cat never moved a muscle. He sat there, staring at the cups.

The chef finished. The three cups sat in a row. He'd gone so fast I had no idea which was the right one.

But Max did. He stretched out a paw, tipped the cup over, grabbed the fish.

The chef smiled, did a *ta-da!* gesture. "And there you are. A Stupid Pet Trick." He shrugged. "It's the smell, of course. He can't watch the cup. He goes by the smell. But people don't think of that. A dog, they credit with a sense of smell. But not a cat. Well, Max smells just fine. He can find the fish."

"I see that," I said.

We watched the cat tear apart the small fish.

The chef nodded in agreement with himself. "It's like catnip to him," he said. "Drives him wild."

He nodded again. Then his face sobered. "About what you said."

"I beg your pardon?"

"What you said before. If they let the woman out."

"Yes?"

"Protect my boy." He exhaled, looked at me. "That's what you said you were doing, right? That's what she asked you to do?

Well, can you do it? Will you promise me that? Will you protect my boy?"

He looked at me with anxious eyes. A father, concerned for his son. It occurred to me I knew his name. For all the good it did me. I wasn't about to call him Charlie.

I took a breath. "I'll do my best."

TWENTY-NINE

I FOUND ALICE in the living room. She was sitting in an overstuffed chair reading a magazine. Or at least pretending to. If the latter, it was for the benefit of the two brothers formerly known as the businessmen I wondered if might be gay, who were drinking at the bar.

I sat in a chair next to Alice. "What's up?" I said.

"Nothing. Lars finished his meal, went back to his room."

"That's boring."

"I'll say. Whaddya wanna do now?"

"Shall we check out the movie?"

"When's it start?"

"About five minutes ago."

"Why not."

Alice and I went up to the game room. The lights were out,

and on the big-screen TV Cary Grant was finding out the neighbors had been complaining about Teddy blowing his bugle again.

Enjoying the movie were Jean and Joan, Johnny McInnerny, the family with the little girl, and a man and woman I hadn't seen before, who must have just checked in today and for some reason dined somewhere else.

And Lucy.

Our waitress sat in the dark, watching the movie. I nudged Alice with my elbow, pointed to her.

Alice nodded.

Gratefully.

I leaned close, whispered, "This is not a chance to buy recipes, this is a chance to find out if anyone used the kitchen phone."

Alice nodded impatiently, as if the idea of obtaining recipes had never crossed her mind.

While this was going on, the two brothers from the bar came in and sat down. That left Alice and me as the only people still standing.

I gave Alice a look.

"I'll stay," Alice whispered.

I had a feeling recipes had more to do with her decision than she would like to pretend. Still, that was fine with me.

I said, "Okay, I may be back," and slipped out the door.

I stood outside of the recreation room and looked around. It was dark out, and lights were on in all the buildings. East Pond. West Pond. The main house. And there was a light over the sign by the road.

Across the road, I could see the path into the woods, the path I'd taken on another night just like this, when I'd decided not to see the movie and wound up spying on Christine. I wondered how much it mattered—if it did at all—the fact that I had seen them, and that I had told people. Had that not happened, would she be alive?

I didn't think so. I didn't want to think so. I mean, surely it couldn't be all me. If I hadn't seen them, we might not know about Randy. But what would that mean in the general scheme of things? What I mean is, had someone else known? Would the police have known? Would Randy have even been a suspect then?

I had no idea. And it occurred to me, the more I learned in this particular case, the less idea I had. Because the only thing that made sense, the only thing that was logical at all, much as I hated to admit it, was that Florence had done it, that Florence was guilty, that the killer was indeed the woman with the dog.

I roused myself from this melancholy musing, went for a walk around the grounds. East Pond and West Pond seemed quiet enough. So did the main house, for that matter. I walked around it, looking at the lights. That light there, for instance—was that Lars' room? No, his room was on the other side. That must be someone else's room. The McInnernys', perhaps. Or perhaps the family with the little girl.

How about Jean and Joan? Were they in West Pond? Did Alice say that? Why did I think that?

It occurred to me, aside from Lars and Florence, I had not sorted out where anybody lived.

I wondered if that mattered.

I continued walking around the inn. Reached the back. I could see a light on in the kitchen window. I wondered if that meant the cook was still there. Surely he would turn the lights out at night, and—

I froze.

Randy's door was open. And someone was standing in it. I could see the person's back. Not clearly, just a shadow, a silhouette.

Who could be calling on Randy at this time of night? Did he have a girlfriend? A lover? Someone who might be jealous of Christine?

I shrunk back into the shadows, began to creep around to where I could get a better look.

There. I could see the light from the door, and there was Randy standing there, talking to the woman. Yes, it was a woman. So why didn't he invite her in? If it was a lover, surely he'd invite her in.

Unless there was friction.

Tension.

Caused by Christine.

Could that be it?

I had to move a little farther. I was only seeing the woman's back. I crept through the shadows and—

Felt like a total fool.

The woman calling on Randy was Mrs. McInnerny.

But of course. The gossip. The snoop. Who had only just heard of the affair. The wrong affair. The affair with Randy. Not the affair with Florence's husband. Yes, it was poor old Mrs. McInnerny, a good two steps behind. No wonder she'd begged off the movie. She was all gung-ho to go detecting.

With yesterday's clues.

I'm sure Randy'd had many lectures about not being disrespectful to the guests, still, I wondered how long it would be before he slammed the door in her face.

I didn't stay to find out. I continued around the building.

On the far side there were two lights on on the second floor. The one on the right would be Florence's room. I'd left the bedside light on for Prince.

The one on the left would be Lars. Who should be there now, since Alice told me he'd gone back to his room.

What was he doing, I wondered? Was he lying in bed with his thoughts? Was he reading a book? I knew he didn't have TV.

TV.

I wondered if anyone was in the TV room. What with *Arsenic and Old Lace* being so popular and all.

I completed my circuit of the building, went inside. There was no sign of Louise or her husband. In fact, there was no one there.

The bar was unattended. It was also open and unlocked. Anyone could walk right up and pour themselves a drink. In New York City that would happen. A bar like this wouldn't last a day. But in New Hampshire, no one gave it a thought.

I glanced into the dining room. The lights were out, and the moonlight coming in the window cast dark shadows on the walls.

I looked over at the booth where it had happened. I couldn't see it clearly. Because of the darkness and the angle.

An impulse seized me. I walked over to the booth and sat in it. In her seat. Sat where she sat. Looked to see what she could see.

Not much. Her back was to half the dining room. As to the other half, Lars' side of the booth cut off her view of most of it.

She could see the door. The angle was just right for that. She could see anyone who walked in. She would have seen the hiker. Lars' connection. The man from Champney Falls. She would have seen him come in, and Lars wouldn't have. Because his back was to the door. She would have had to tell him he was there. Otherwise, the man would have had to find them. Stop at their booth. Which I didn't think he'd done. So she must have told him.

Did that matter?

I had no idea.

I got up from the booth, looked around.

There was light coming from under the bottom of the kitchen door. No surprise there. I'd seen the kitchen light was on from outside. Did that mean the chef was still there, or was the light left on all night? For Max, perhaps?

I went to the swinging door. It wasn't locked. I pushed it open, looked into the kitchen.

There was no one there. Just the ovens and refrigerators and hanging pots and pans. There was the dishwasher Randy had filled, silent now, the trays having emerged from the other side. And there was the butcher block where Max had done his Stupid Pet Trick.

And there was the phone in the alcove. With no lock on the dial, and no lock on the kitchen door. A phone any guest could use in the dead of night to call Australia, if they saw fit. Apparently, that was not a problem.

I left the kitchen and the dining room, went by the front desk, which was unmanned. Anyone could use that phone, too, right after fixing themselves a free drink at the bar.

Well, it wasn't my concern. I went into the TV room. As expected, there was no one there. I sat down on the couch, picked up the remote control. Clicked the TV on. Flipped through the channels.

And found the Red Sox game.

All right, I admit, I'd had it in mind when I'd seen everyone watching the movie. And there didn't seem to be much I could do in the way of detection. There really didn't. And this vacation had just been one disappointment after another—I realize that's an insensitive word to use under the circumstances. But still, could you blame me for taking time out to enjoy a baseball game?

Go ahead and blame me, because that's what I did.

The Red Sox were playing the White Sox, and it was the top of the first inning, and there were runners on first and second, and Nomar Garciaparra was up, and on a three and one count he hit the ball up the gap in right center, driving them both home, and I for one could not have been happier at finally getting to watch my game.

It got rained out in the top of the third. The Red Sox were leading seven to one. If play ever resumed, they had the game well in hand. But this wasn't a shower, it was an absolute gale, and despite the announcers' attempts to be upbeat, it was easy to tell that there wasn't a prayer.

I switched off the TV and went out.

The place was still deserted. I saw no one inside, no one outside.

I walked by the rec room. The movie was still going on. I considered going in, catching the end. Decided against it. There was no one I really wanted to talk to. Alice could give me a report. It had been a long day, and I was tired. I went back to my room. Kicked off my shoes, got in bed, and began reading *4:50 From Paddington*. Or, *What Mrs. McGillicuddy Saw!*

I had trouble finding my place. I hadn't used a bookmark, and I wasn't sure of the page. I kept reading stuff I'd read before. Which didn't always register, because, of course, I'd read the book years ago, so all of it was vaguely familiar. It was a question of separating what was *recently* familiar.

Which was difficult with what had happened lately. Too much input. I mean, which crime are we dealing with, the real one or the fictional one? What the woman saw on the train, that's the train in the book, not the Cog Railway. What we saw on the Cog Railway was the drug dealer, who may have had nothing to do with the murder. So just what is it I'm reading here?

I wasn't sure. So I was glad ten minutes later to hear voices in the hallway and footsteps on the stairs.

One voice was Alice's. I wondered who she was talking to. I got up, opened the door.

Just my luck. She was talking to Johnny McInnerny about *Arsenic and Old Lace*.

"Oh, and there's my stick-in-the-mud husband," she said, "who missed the whole show."

I groaned. I didn't want to go through the seen-it-before routine again with Johnny McInnerny. I had also hoped Alice would have something interesting to report. Obviously not, if she'd wound up discussing the movie with Johnny McInnerny. I was certainly glad I'd been spared that, and—

Good lord.

Johnny McInnerny?

I have to admit, what with everything that had happened, I was so stressed out that things were slow kicking in.

Johnny McInnerny had come upstairs with Alice.

Johnny McInnerny was standing in front of the room with Freddy Frog on the door.

Johnny McInnerny and his wife were the couple whose amorous adventures I'd envied through the paper-thin wall.

The McInnernys?

The mind boggled.

That revelation having hit me, I found myself incapable of speech. I stood there like a lump, grinning moronically.

However, Johnny needed no prompting. "Well, you missed a good show. And it's so much better with an audience. I must have seen that movie on TV a dozen times. But it's not the same thing, watching it alone. It's so much better with an audience laughing at it."

I quite agreed. I just had no wish to prolong the conversation. "Absolutely," I said. "Wish I'd been there. Well, good night, now."

I took Alice by the hand and practically pulled her into the room.

"Are you kidding me?" I whispered the minute the door closed. "The McInnernys live next door?"

"So it seems."

"The McInnernys are the reason we've been keeping quiet?"

"Stanley," Alice said, reprovingly.

From next door came a horrifying scream. We would have heard it even if the walls hadn't been paper-thin. As it was, it might as well have been in the same room.

Alice and I looked at each other, bolted for the door. Alice, who was closer, got there first, ripped it open, dashed out into the hall. I followed.

The McInnernys' door was open. Inside, Johnny McInnerny was kneeling next to his wife.

Mrs. McInnerny lay sprawled out on the floor.

A large carving knife protruded from her chest.

THIRTY

PINEHURST SEEMED IRRITATED. Which didn't seem quite right. Don't get me wrong. I'm not saying he should have been pleased. Still, his reaction went beyond what one would expect. The man was definitely annoyed.

Alice and I were outside, where access to East Pond was being denied by the cop with the droopy mustache. Aside from the police, the only one allowed inside was the medical examiner, who was currently plying his trade. I, for one, was not holding my breath waiting for his report. There was really nothing the man could tell me. Mrs. McInnerny had been stabbed in the heart with a knife somewhere between eight and ten o'clock. I doubt if the doctor could do better than that.

Also outside on the lawn was practically everybody from Blue Frog Ponds. Pinehurst had come whipping in with his siren. By then everyone was already outside, but just in case anyone was inclined to sleep through the action, that sort of sealed the deal. They were all out here now, even the six-year-old girl, who wore a pink flowery nightgown, and was yawning and rubbing her eyes as she snuggled up in her father's arms.

I knew how she felt. With Pinehurst in charge of the operation, it was going to be a long night.

He came out of East Pond, looked around, spotted me standing with Alice and Jean and Joan. He strode over to us and addressed Alice.

"You were with Mr. McInnerny when he found the body?"

"We both were," I said.

"Yes, yes," Pinehurst said. "But you were with him before, at the movie. You came back from the movie together and were there when he found his wife."

"That's right," Alice said.

"Mr. McInnerny was at the movie the whole time?"

"Yes, he was," Alice said. "I can vouch for his whereabouts from eight o'clock on."

"So can we," Jean said.

"Oh?"

"Joan and I were at the movie too. And she's absolutely right. The man never left."

"And you didn't either?"

"No, of course not."

"None of you?"

Jean frowned. "What do you mean, none of us?"

"Mrs. Hastings too?"

"We were all there the whole time," Jean said.

"Uh-huh," Pinehurst said. He turned to me. "But you were not?"

"No."

"Why not?"

"I'd seen the movie before."

"Who hasn't?" Pinehurst said. "Everyone's seen that movie before. Most people decided to see it again. Why not you?"

"You want me to discuss this in front of everyone?"

Pinehurst frowned.

So did Alice.

So did Jean and Joan.

I realized I had suddenly made myself unpopular with everyone.

"If you'll excuse us," Pinehurst said.

He led me off in the direction of the road.

"Now then," he said, when we were presumably out of earshot, "what was so all-fired important that you decided to miss the movie?"

"It wasn't like that. I wanted to look around, and I wanted to watch the game."

"The game?"

"There was a Red Sox game on television. With everyone in the rec room, I figured the TV room might be free."

"Was it?"

"It was. I saw three innings of the Red Sox–White Sox."

"Three innings?"

"It rained in Chicago."

"Oh." Pinehurst cocked his head. "You didn't feel you could tell me this in front of the others?"

I almost said, "Don't be dumb." I took a breath, exhaled. "Before I watched TV, I went for a walk. I happened to see the victim."

"Mrs. McInnerny? Where?"

"In back of the main house. In the door to Randy's room."

"Randy?"

"Randy the busboy. Louise's son. The one who was having an affair with Christine Cobb." I looked at Pinehurst. "Is this an interrogation technique? Or have you *really* forgotten who these people are?"

247

"It was conversational, merely," Pinehurst said. "So, you saw Mrs. McInnerny in the busboy Randy's room?"

"Not in his room. In the doorway."

"In the doorway?"

"Yes. Like she'd knocked on the door and he'd opened it."

"But had not invited her in?"

"Well, would you?"

"And he didn't?"

"As far as I know."

"You didn't stay to see?"

"No. It was old news. Mrs. McInnerny had just found out about the affair. Between Randy and Christine Cobb. She told me so this afternoon. I knew that's why she was talking to him."

"You didn't think it was important?"

"It was yesterday's news. My only interest in Mrs. McInnerny was she was out of the room when I got the call."

"The call?"

"From you. Telling me about the cocaine. She was out of the dining room at the time."

"What's that got to do with it?"

I told him about the click on the line.

"Interesting," Pinehurst said. "So you think someone may have overheard the call?"

"It's the obvious explanation."

"And you thought it was her?"

"She was one possibility. Another was Lars Heinrick. Then there's the cook, the waitresses, and the busboy."

"Why them?"

"Because there's an extension in the kitchen. As well as one in the reading room."

"Uh-huh," Pinehurst said. "Well, that's certainly something to take into consideration. For the time being, I'd like to concentrate on this murder. What time was it you saw Mrs. McInnerny talking to the busboy?"

"Around eight-fifteen, eight-twenty."

"How do you fix the time?"

"The movie started around eight. Alice and I got there late, after it had started. Say between five and ten after. She decided to stay, I decided not to. I left there, walked around the grounds. By the time I got to the back of the main house it was probably eight-fifteen to eight-twenty. Somewhere along in there. I saw Mrs. McInnerny, but did not stay to watch. I finished checking out the building and went inside."

"To watch TV?"

"That's right. I watched three innings of the ball game."

"When you turned on the TV, was the game already on?"

"Yes. It was in the first inning, with two on and nobody out."

"The first inning?"

"Yes."

"The game was only in the first inning?"

"They're playing in Chicago. The game had an eight-thirty start."

"Eight-thirty?"

"Yes."

"And the game was already in the first inning and there were two runners on?"

"Yes. Why?"

Pinehurst shrugged. "Well, I'm not a huge baseball fan, but I do watch the game. And you know, they start five minutes late. An eight-thirty game starts at eight-thirty-five. Some papers even list them that way. A seven-thirty-five start. A seven-o-five start. That's when the first pitch is thrown, as opposed to when the broadcast starts."

"So?"

"So, if you turn on the game and there's two men on base, it's gotta be around eight-forty. And you just saw Mrs. McInnerny around eight-fifteen."

"I said eight-fifteen to eight-twenty."

"It's still a good twenty minutes. If you went inside to watch TV, there's no way you'd miss the beginning of the game."

"I didn't go straight to the TV room."

"No? What did you do?"

"I circled the house. I remember seeing the lights on in Lars' and Florence's room. I knew he'd gone back to his room, and I wondered what he was doing. And I remembered I'd left the light on in her room for the dog.

"Anyway, I did that. Then when I went inside, I didn't go to the TV room, I went to check out the dining room first."

"Why?"

"I don't know. It was there. It was dark. Everyone had left. It was quiet. I went and sat in the booth, where Christine Cobb had sat, and tried to put it all together in my mind."

"Any luck?"

"The only thing I came up with was from where she was sitting she would have seen the drug connection come in the door. And Lars wouldn't. So she would have had to tell him he was there."

"Uh-huh," Pinehurst said, without enthusiasm. "And that took twenty minutes?"

"I also checked out the kitchen."

"The kitchen?"

"Yes."

"Why?"

"Like I said. One of the extension phones was there."

"And what did you hope to learn from the kitchen?"

"I don't know. But there was a light on. I could see it under the door. I wondered if anyone was there. I also wondered if I could get in."

"Could you?"

"Sure. The door was unlocked. I pushed it open, went right in."

"The door was unlocked at that time?"

"Yes. Why?" My eyes widened. "The knife?"

"It appears to have been from the kitchen, yes."

"Oh, no."

"Oh, no, what?"

"I think I saw it."

"The knife?"

"Yes."

"Then?"

"No. Earlier this evening."

"How is that?"

I told him about talking to the chef and seeing Max's Stupid Pet Trick.

"The knife was on the butcher block then?"

"Yes. I remember seeing it."

"And when you checked out the kitchen later, somewhere around eight-thirty?"

"I don't know."

"You don't remember seeing it?"

"No."

"But you don't remember *not* seeing it?"

"No, I don't."

"It's somewhat important."

"I'm aware of that."

"Are you? Good. Then should anything jog your memory, please be so kind as to let me know. Anyway, you went in and watched the ball game. Or at least three innings of it."

"Until it started to rain."

"And what time was that?"

"Around nine-thirty."

"An hour later. That figures. That's how slow ball games are these days. At which point you went back to your room."

"That's right."

"You got back to your room some time around nine-thirty?"

"Say nine-thirty, nine-thirty-five."

"And what did you do?"

"I got in bed and read a book."

"Until your wife came home with Johnny McInnerny?"

"That's right."

"And during the time you were reading, did you hear anything, anything at all?"

"Not a peep."

"Is it possible that the murder happened then, during that time while you were reading—that someone came up the stairs, knocked on the door, stabbed Mrs. McInnerny dead?"

"Not at all. The walls are paper-thin. I would have heard the footsteps, I would have heard the knock on the door, I would have heard the body fall."

"So that pins it down. The murder had to happen between eight-fifteen and nine-thirty. Which is probably better than the doctor can do. Fine. Thanks for your help."

Pinehurst turned, strode away.

I was puzzled by Pinehurst. Not only did he seem peculiarly annoyed, somehow he had become practically animated. Unlike his ponderous questionings in the Christine Cobb affair, his interrogations now were far less formal. As I watched, he descended on the clump of people clustered outside East Pond, buttonholed Randy, and led him away from the group, very much in the manner of a sheep dog, singling out a lamb from the flock.

As I walked back to the others, Louise came rushing up.

"What did you tell him? What have you done? Now he's after my boy."

"It's all right. He's only concerned with the time element."

"What?"

"Mrs. McInnerny saw Randy tonight. In his room."

Her eyes widened. "You told him that?"

"Relax. He's not a suspect. The fact is Mrs. McInnerny was snooping around. She'd heard your boy was involved with Christine Cobb. She wanted to know if it was true."

Louise looked even more distressed. "That sounds like a motive."

"Not at all. It's old news. Trust me, all Pinehurst wants to know is when she left."

Louise didn't look convinced, but at that moment Pinehurst left Randy and headed back our way. He veered off, however, to intercept Sad Sack, who was coming back from the direction of the main house. Sad Sack spread his arms, shook his head. "Still no luck," he said.

Pinehurst frowned, turned, surveyed the group.

Lars Heinrick was standing off to one side, alone as usual. He appeared absorbed in his thoughts. Pinehurst swooped down on him, attracted his attention, led him aside.

"See," I said. "There's your real suspect. No one really thinks it's your boy."

"No one *did*," Louise said. "They arrested that woman. And everything was all right. I know that's a terrible thing to say, but that's how I saw it." She spread her arms. "And then this. It's awful. They know *she* didn't do it now."

Of course. Louise had just put into words what I myself had known, but hadn't quite processed. No wonder Pinehurst was so upset. His whole theory of the case had just blown up in his face.

Florence was in jail. Florence hadn't killed Mrs. McInnerny. And unless these were separate crimes committed by two separate murderers—the probability of which I figured somewhere around a million to one—Florence hadn't killed Christine Cobb.

So Pinehurst's bad mood was suddenly quite understandable indeed.

The medical examiner came out of East Pond. Pinehurst went to meet him, and the two of them conversed in low tones.

Louise swooped down on Randy. He brushed her off, walked away. I wondered if Sad Sack would let him go, or head him off and herd him back to the group. However, Randy stopped of his own accord, circled away from his mother, and hung out on the edge of the crowd.

I felt a hand on my shoulder, looked around to find Alice. She didn't look pleased.

"So," Alice said, "what was so important you couldn't talk about it in front of me?"

"Not you," I said. "Jean and Joan. We haven't told them everything, and I'm going nuts keeping straight who knows what. All I was telling him about was Mrs. McInnerny calling on Randy. But other stuff came up. About the cocaine. That I didn't want to go into in front of them."

"Fine. But you cut me out."

"I'm sorry."

"And I have something to say."

"I beg your pardon?"

"About the movie. He was asking if Johnny left the movie. Which he didn't. Or if I left it. Or Jean and Joan. Which we didn't."

"So?"

"Someone else did."

I looked at her in surprise. "Who?"

"Lucy."

"Lucy?"

"I know," Alice said. "I don't suspect her for a moment. But she's a waitress. She did have access to the kitchen phone. And she left in the middle of the movie."

"You mean she went home?"

"She's here now. Didn't you see her?"

"Yes, I did. So what do you mean?"

"She went out and came back. She left the movie in the middle, came back and saw the end."

"Maybe she went to the bathroom."

"Not for that long," Alice said. "She was gone long enough

that I assumed she'd gone home. It was a surprise when she came back."

"You should tell Pinehurst."

"I was about to when you led him away."

"I'm sorry. How was I to know?"

"Not that I suspect Lucy, you understand. I don't for a minute think she did this. But we do have to report the facts. The police are never going to get anywhere without the facts."

It occurred to me Chief Pinehurst was unlikely to get anywhere, even *with* the facts. So far all he'd managed to do was arrest an innocent woman.

"So you think I should tell him about Lucy?" Alice said.

"In good time. I don't think it's particularly urgent. The woman's here, he can question her if he likes."

When I said that I naturally looked over to where Lucy was standing.

And she wasn't there. Right where she'd been a moment before. It was like a magic trick. As if talking about her had made her disappear.

I glanced around, spotted Lucy heading in the direction of the inn.

I turned back to Alice. "There goes Lucy now. I wanna see where she's going. If you get a chance, tell Pinehurst. I should be right back."

I walked hurriedly across the lawn after Lucy. She was already in the driveway, heading for the front door of the main house. I hung back, not wanting her to hear my feet crunch in the gravel. I circled around in the grass, waiting for her to go up on the porch. As she did, I was across the driveway on little cat feet, heading up the steps the minute she went through the front door.

The lights were on in the building. Through the glass door I could see her pass by the front desk heading for the dining room. I waited a few seconds, slipped in the door. Tiptoed swiftly past the front desk. Reached the door to the dining room.

The room was dark, but the light in the kitchen was still on. It was flickering through the swinging kitchen door. I crept to the door, pushed it open a crack, peered in.

Sure enough, Lucy was headed for the phone.

I tried to tell myself it didn't have to mean anything. It was late, and she was calling her husband, her brother, her mother, her friend, or whatever to say she'd been detained.

Nonetheless, I couldn't help feeling excited. I had caught her sneaking off to the phone.

Only she wasn't. She stopped right next to the phone and opened a cabinet in the cupboard beside it. She reached in, took something down, brought it over to the kitchen table, right next to the butcher block where Max had done his Stupid Pet Trick. When she brought it into the light, I could see what it was.

It was a file. A brown cardboard accordion file. The type with alphabetical divisions. The type you might use to file important papers if you didn't have an actual file cabinet.

Lucy set the file on the table. Then opened her purse and proceeded to rummage through it. It was a large, drawstring purse, wide enough that she was able to take out a stack of unfolded sheets of paper.

Lucy took one page from the top of the stack and set it aside. She took the rest of the stack, straightened the edges, fished a paper clip from the bottom of the file folder, and clipped them together. She then took the stack of papers, riffled through the file for the right alphabetical listing, and inserted them into the file folder.

From the same space in the file folder she extracted a single sheet of paper, looked at it, put it down on the table. She rummaged through her purse, found a pen, marked something on the paper, and returned the paper to the file. She put the pen back in her purse, closed the file, and returned the file to the cabinet.

And headed for the door.

I had a moment of panic. There was no way I could get out

the dining room door before she came through the kitchen one. She was going to catch me spying on her.

I was not standing there thinking this. Futile or not, I was fleeing as quick as I could.

Halfway across the room I was seized by inspiration. Prompted largely by the kitchen door starting to swing open. Quick like a bunny, I slipped into the booth.

And suddenly, there I sat, heart pounding fiercely, right in the seat where Christine Cobb had died.

From where I sat I could not see the kitchen door, which was good, because it meant Lucy couldn't see me. But I could see the dining room door. I could see when she went out.

Which she did.

Without seeing me.

I heaved a sigh of relief, then waited in the booth until I heard the outside door bang. Even so, I went to the door of the dining room to look out to make sure she was gone.

She was. There was no one there.

As soon as I had assured myself of that fact, I went back to the kitchen. I went straight to the cabinet and took out the file.

It was too dark in the alcove by the phone to examine it. Like Lucy, I found myself bringing it over to the butcher block. Where I would have no way to hide it if someone came in. Well, it couldn't be helped. This was a murder investigation.

The file was tied shut with string. I untied it, pulled the file open.

It was, as I'd assumed, an alphabetical file, with compartments for each letter.

I tried to judge which compartment Lucy had used. It seemed to me it was about two thirds of the way through.

I tried the compartment marked *R*. Pulled out a stack of papers.

The one on top was a chart of some kind. In the form of a grid. Like an accountant might use.

Down the left side was what proved to be a vaguely alphabetical listing. Reading down the row I found such entries as "Raisin Cake," "Raspberry Tart," "Ratatouille," "Relish—Antoine's," "Relish—Carl's," "Relish—Victor's."

Across the top of the grid were the months of the year. There was a total column after each month. Under the months, and after the names, were check marks, which were then totaled up. For instance, in January, under "Relish—Victor's," were four check marks. In the total column was the figure *$40*. "Ratatouille" had two check marks for twenty dollars. The "Raspberry Tart" had seven for seventy.

I pulled the top sheet off the pile. Underneath was a recipe for ratatouille. At the top of the recipe was a paper clip. Taking the paper off the stack, I saw that the paper clip held three of four pages together. I flipped through them. They were all Xerox copies of the same recipe for ratatouille.

Beneath them, attached together by a paper clip, were a number of copies of the recipe for the raspberry tart.

I riffled through the rest of the stack, found nothing but Xerox copies of recipes.

I took the stack of papers, squared it up, and started to put it back in the proper slot in the file. To do so, I spread the slot open with my left hand.

Something yellow near the bottom caught my eye. I reached in, pulled it out.

It was a small, crumpled piece of paper. I unfolded it, smoothed it out. It was a yellow Post-it, the type people use to write short messages on.

There was a message on this one, scrawled in pen. It was almost illegible. I held it up to the light, tried to make it out. It began *L—*, which made sense, since I assumed it was a note to Lucy.

I squinted at the note.

Blinked.

The first word appeared to be *cop*.

Cop?

What had I stumbled on?

What cop?

The next word was hard to make out. I deciphered it as *restart*.

The next two words were easy. *Check others*.

It was signed *C—*.

That made the whole message: *L—Cop restart check others C—*.

Obviously a note to Lucy from the cook, who signed it *C* either for *cook, chef,* or because his name began with *C*. Alice had told me his name. Charlie. Which clinched it. Clearly a note to Lucy from the chef.

Cop restart check others? What sort of warning was that?

I peered closer. Discerned a squiggle after *cop*. And a slight break in *restart*. I also realized what I had thought was an *e* was really an *a*.

Which allowed me to revise my translation of the message to: *L—Copy ras. tart Check others C—*.

Undoubtedly instructions from the chef to have Lucy Xerox more copies of the raspberry tart recipe and check the other recipes to see if anything else needed duplicating.

So I had not indeed cracked the murder. Instead, I had learned the chef was not at all reluctant to give out his recipes, he just wasn't giving them out for free.

I wondered how Alice would take that news.

I folded up the file and put it back in the cabinet. It occurred to me, every investigation I'd undertaken in this case had led to a dead end. Or at least a lesser crime. First I'd unmasked a cocaine dealer. Now I'd penetrated a phony blackmarket recipe ring.

I wondered if Pinehurst had to hear about this. I realized if Alice had told him about Lucy leaving the movie he probably would.

I was not a happy camper as I left the main house. From up on the porch I could see the people gathered around East Pond. I had no real wish to return to them. In particular, I was not eager to report my findings to Alice. Not that she wouldn't find it fascinating, it was just there was no way I was going to be able to tell her without seeming to gloat.

I felt like I needed to clear my head. Just relax and not talk to anyone for a few minutes. So instead of joining the group around East Pond, I walked down to the road.

It was dark. The moon was behind some clouds, and the street light was burned out. I could barely see the outline of the fence around the swimming pool.

I stood there a few moments, letting my eyes grow accustomed to the dark. Shapes became slightly more distinct. I walked down to the pool, unhooked the gate, went inside, and sat in one of the chairs.

I had to think it out. Somehow or other, I had to think it out. Because, as Louise said, with Florence out of it, the cops would pick on someone else. And while Lars seemed the likely suspect, Randy wasn't a bad guess. But, aside from him and Lars, who else was there?

Of course, one name loomed larger than the rest. Johnny McInnerny. The husband is always the prime suspect in a case like this. Only Alice said he never left the movie. And Alice was surely right. So Johnny McInnerny could not have done it. He had an ironclad alibi.

So did Florence. That was the other given. Florence was off the hook, because Florence was in jail.

So who could have done it? Lars. Randy. Louise. The chef. Lucy. The other waitress, who wasn't there, and had presumably gone home.

And . . .

The man from Champney Falls.

What if that was it? What if it had been about drugs all along? Granted, the man from Champney Falls hadn't been here tonight. But that was just as far as I knew. All I really knew was that no one had seen him. But if everyone was in the movie, no one would have seen him. He could have driven up, approached Mrs. Mc-Innerny.

Why?

Small stumbling block there. Somehow putting Mrs. Mc-Innerny together with a drug dealer just didn't compute.

Except for the phone call. If she'd overheard the phone call, it could work just fine.

Had it?

I had no idea.

Across the road in the distance, I could see the activity around East Pond. Not clearly, just indistinct shapes milling around in the light flickering through the windows.

As I watched, two of the shapes detached themselves from the general mess, and headed in the direction of the main house. As they drew nearer, I could see it was Louise and Sad Sack. I wondered what they were after. It occurred to me, most likely coffee. They came up on the porch and went in the front door.

I could have used a cup of coffee just then. I wondered if they were making it for everyone, or just for the cops. I had to laugh at myself. There was no reason at all to assume they were making coffee. In all likelihood, they weren't. I just thought they were because I wanted some.

I heaved a sigh and got to my feet. It was time to take the bull by the horns and go back and join the group. I was also curious as to what was going on. Though, with Pinehurst in charge, that was very likely nothing. It occurred to me this was the only murder investigation I could imagine that, with the police on the scene and the body not yet removed, I could take ten minutes out to sit down, kick back, and collect my thoughts.

That thought amused me. Made me decide, perversely, to give it one more minute. I lay back down in the deck chair, gazed up at the stars. Which I couldn't see for the clouds. Which didn't mean they weren't there. Just like the solution to this crime.

How profound.

Maybe I'll solve this yet.

A door banged. I looked up to see Sad Sack and Louise come out on the porch. They looked animated, and Sad Sack had something in his hand. They came down the steps, hurried off in the direction of East Pond.

I sprang from the deck chair, went out the gate and across the road. I was walking briskly across the lawn when I heard a jangling sound behind me. The next thing I knew something banged into me and knocked me down.

I instinctively rolled over, and put up my hands to protect myself from my assailant.

And felt something wet on my face.

Licking me.

A voice said, "Prince! Stop it, now!"

I blinked.

Reached up, grabbed his collar, pushed him off. Struggled to my feet.

It was Prince, all right.

And the person whose voice I'd heard, the woman who'd just stooped down to retrieve the leash, was Florence.

"I'm sorry," she said. "He's just so excited to be out at night. And he really does take to you."

I gawked at her, incapable of speech.

I was dimly aware of people approaching us. I looked around, saw Pinehurst and Sad Sack, followed by what appeared to be practically everyone.

Sad Sack was holding a plastic evidence bag. Inside was something white and bloody.

They marched straight up to Florence.

"Florence Baker," Pinehurst said. "You're under arrest for the murder of Clara McInnerny."

THIRTY-ONE

"WE HAVE HER dead to rights," Pinehurst said. He didn't seem particularly happy about it. He leaned back in his desk chair, took a sip of coffee.

Pinehurst and I were in the police station. Florence was in her jail cell, waiting for her lawyer to drive up from Boston. Or rather from someplace halfway between here and Boston—the lawyer had a car phone, and Florence had reached him on his way home. The lawyer had driven up earlier in the day and arranged for bail. Which was, of course, the real reason Pinehurst looked so grim. He'd fought vigorously against her release, only to have another murder occur not two hours later.

"There must be some mistake," I said.

Pinehurst grimaced. "Yes, you would think that."

"Can you tell me what you've got?"

"Might as well," Pinehurst said. "She's not talking until the lawyer gets here, and I doubt if she will even then."

He jerked open his desk drawer, took out a plastic evidence bag. "What we've got are these. A pair of bloody gloves. We can match the blood type to the victim's, then nail it down with DNA."

"You've done that?"

"No, but we will. And it will match. Why? Because Christine Cobb was poisoned, and there is no other bloody crime it could be."

"Which doesn't mean it couldn't be something else."

Pinehurst put up his hand. "I don't want to argue it. Odds are it will match. Even if it doesn't, the woman gets out of jail, silences the prime witness against her."

"*What* prime witness? Mrs. McInnerny didn't know anything."

"Ah, but she did."

"How do you know?"

"Because she's dead."

"That's circular logic, Chief. It doesn't mean anything."

"Maybe not to you, but it does to me. Anyway, she was snooping around. According to the busboy, Randy. She came around asking prying questions."

"Indicating she was way off base."

"Not really. Randy and Christine Cobb *were* having an affair. That information was accurate."

"But irrelevant. And shows the woman was on the wrong track."

"Yes, but she must have gotten on the right one, because she's dead."

"Fine," I said. "You wanna tell me about the gloves."

"I thought I did."

"No, you just showed them to me. Where did you get them?"

"Oh, well, that's the thing. They were in her wastebasket."

"You're kidding."

264

"Not at all."

"You arrested her on the basis of a pair of bloody gloves found in her wastebasket?"

"Why not?"

"Why not? Give me a break. Your theory is this woman went out and killed Mrs. McInnerny. She was smart enough to wear white gloves so she wouldn't get blood on her hands. Then she's dumb enough to leave the white gloves in her room?"

"Undoubtedly what her lawyer will argue."

"That doesn't bother you?"

"Everything bothers me. The stupidity defense—which is what you're arguing—how could the woman be that stupid?—I don't go for it. Criminals always do something stupid. I can't go around apologizing for them."

"Uh-huh," I said. "And the time element?"

"What about it?"

"How does that work out? Did Florence have time to kill this woman?"

"Absolutely," Pinehurst said. "Her lawyer showed up right after I talked to you. He called ahead, had a judge waiting. Slapped me with a habeas corpus, told me release her or take her before a magistrate. The judge in question is off my Christmas list. He grants her bail, and she commits another murder."

"Is there any possibility of an overlap?"

"What do you mean?"

"Any possibility Mrs. McInnerny was killed before Florence was released?"

"Not according to you."

"Huh?"

"By your own statement you saw Mrs. McInnerny alive as late as eight-fifteen. She was out of here by then."

"This works for you?"

"It works just fine. The McInnerny woman was a snoop. She stumbles on something that's dangerous to the killer."

"What about the murder weapon?"

"What about it?"

"Was it from the kitchen like you thought?"

"It appears to be. The chef admits it looks like his. Rather reluctantly, I might add. Of course, he still thinks he's protecting his son. Plus, no one's ever too eager to claim ownership of a murder weapon."

"So your theory is the killer took the knife from the kitchen, which was unlocked?"

"Yes, of course."

"Then this might interest you."

I told him about following Lucy and discovering the recipes.

"Interesting," Pinehurst said. "Your wife told me she left during the movie. Your theory is she went out to make copies?"

"I think so. There's a copier behind the front desk. I figure she went to the kitchen, got the things she needed to copy, went to the front desk, copied them, and went back to the movie."

"And returned later to put them back?"

"Exactly."

"Why would she do that?"

"I assume because of the crime."

"I beg your pardon?"

"I mean because Mrs. McInnerny was killed."

"Oh, really?" Pinehurst said. "I was going to point out it seemed strange to me she'd bother to put them back with all that going on."

"I can give you a theory."

"By all means do."

"I would say Lucy had no intention of putting the recipes back, and she would have gone home after the movie and brought them in tomorrow. When the body's discovered, she hangs around like everybody else. So she's hanging around with the copies in her purse. And she knows there's going to be a police investigation.

She doesn't want to have to explain the copies, so she puts them back."

Pinehurst frowned. "I suppose that could be it."

"I can only think of one other explanation."

"What's that?"

"That she's guilty of the crime. Of the murder, I mean. She left the movie, not to make copies, but to go to the kitchen, get the knife, and kill Mrs. McInnerny." I shrugged. "Either that or it's both."

"Both?"

"Yes. Lucy goes to the kitchen to make copies. Mrs. McInnerny finds her, demands to know what she's doing. She kills her to shut her up."

"Over a bunch of recipes?"

"Stranger things have happened."

"Not in my lifetime. Not if you tie it in to the murder of Christine Cobb. Then you have two, separate, unrelated murders in one week at the Blue Frog Ponds, which I cannot credit. Or, Christine Cobb was also killed over these recipes. Which I credit even less. I'm very glad you told me this, however."

"Why?"

"It makes talking to Lucy my next order of business. It wasn't important when your wife told me. Not with Florence on the loose. Now she's important, not as a suspect, but as a witness. If she really went to the kitchen when she left the movie, there are only three possibilities. The knife was taken before she got there. After she left there. Or while she was there. It becomes very important whether she saw that knife."

"It's also possible she saw the killer."

"Maybe, but I don't think so."

"Why not?"

"Because she didn't mention it. Everyone thought Florence was in jail. If Lucy had seen her, she'd have said so."

"You're assuming the killer is Florence."

"Yes, I am."

"If you're wrong, and the killer was someone else, Lucy might have seen them and not have mentioned it."

"I'll certainly ask her. Not that a response is likely to vindicate the suspect. Still, if anyone was prowling around, I would certainly like to know."

"I'm glad to hear it. Might I ask if you've pursued any *other* avenues that might tend to vindicate the suspect?"

"Such as?"

"How about the phone call?"

"The phone call?"

"Yes. Your phone call to me. Someone listened in on the line. That person obviously wasn't Florence, because she was in jail at the time. So, are you assuming that was Mrs. McInnerny?"

"It would seem likely."

"Maybe so, but have you any positive indication that it was?"

"Only that after dinner she began snooping around."

"By that you mean talking to Randy. Aside from that, the only indication she was snooping around is the fact she wound up dead. Or is there something you're not telling me?"

"No, that's really all I have."

"What did Randy say?"

"Just what you'd expect. Mrs. McInnerny wanted to know about him and Christine Cobb."

"And that's all?"

"What do you mean?"

"Did she ask about anything else?"

"Not according to him. Of course, the boy's not particularly forthcoming. Just getting him to admit she was there at all was like pulling teeth."

"But he admits she was asking about him and Christine Cobb?"

"Rather grudgingly. And only when specifically asked."

"Did you specifically ask about anything else?"

"Like what?"

"Did you ask him about drugs?"

"Drugs?"

"Yes."

"No."

"Well, wouldn't that be a logical question? I mean, if we're taking the premise Mrs. McInnerny began snooping because of the phone call, the phone call was about drugs."

"True."

"You didn't ask him about that?"

"It's a side issue."

I smiled. "You'll pardon me, but that's never stopped you before."

"I admit to taking great pains to see which suspect to arrest. Having made that determination, I do not hesitate to act on it."

"I suppose that's commendable. But just on the off chance that you're wrong, you want to follow this thought process through? If Mrs. McInnerny overheard our conversation, and started snooping because of it, then we both agree Randy was the wrong track. She got on the right track and she got killed. Well, that conversation she overheard was about drugs. They were Lars Heinrick's drugs. So, if she got on the right track, it would lead to Lars Heinrick, and not Florence."

"Yes, but how would she know?"

"I beg your pardon?"

"How would she know that? About Lars Heinrick, I mean. She didn't find out from our phone conversation. I am rather careful talking on the phone. I am sure I didn't mention his name."

"You mentioned Delmar Hobart's."

"That I did. And if you would like to point out to me how Mrs. McInnerny could trace the drugs from Delmar Hobart to Lars Heinrick, I would be delighted to listen. She overheard the phone call during dinner, right after dinner she's out talking to

Randy, right after that she gets killed. Now, how did she manage to track this down? Even if Delmar Hobart is listed in the phone book—I'm not sure he is, but let's say so just for the sake of argument—well, then she gets him on the phone, says, 'Excuse me, I'm sorry to bother you, but could you tell me just who you sold drugs to at the Blue Frog Ponds?' " Pinehurst shook his head. "I'm sorry, but it just doesn't fly."

"You wanna make the connection to Florence work?"

"I don't have to. The connection is there. The woman's a busybody, she's snooping around. In the course of her investigations what does she find? The person the police have accused of the crime. You think she's not going to ask some probing questions? Maybe insinuate she knows something the police might like to know?"

"That's all speculation. You're making it up."

"Yes, but it's certainly logical."

"Maybe so. Tell me something, Chief. Aside from the bloody gloves, is there anything to connect Florence to the crime?"

"You mean aside from the fact it was committed to cover up *another* crime I have her dead to rights on?" Pinehurst's smile managed to seem both smug and pained. "No, probably not."

THIRTY-TWO

THE NEXT MORNING we did not hike. Alice woke up with a severe headache, and right after breakfast she went back to bed. Not that we would have hiked in any case. What with everything that had happened, no one was in the mood. Nonetheless, there I was, on a beautiful sunny morning, with a sick wife, and nothing to do.

Except walk the dog. With Florence back in jail, that duty had once again fallen on me. After breakfast I got the passkey from the desk, went up to the room, and let him out.

He nearly knocked me down again, but this time I saw him coming. I was able to sidestep him, grab his collar, and attach the leash. He actually pulled me down the stairs in his eagerness to get out the door.

We walked everywhere. Around the grounds, along the road, and down to the stream.

Randy was there, sitting on a rock. I gave Prince his head, let him pull me along. He bounded to the rock, dog tags jangling, looked up at the boy.

"Hi," I said. "How you doing?"

As usual, Randy didn't answer.

"It must be rough," I said, "to have this happen on top of everything else."

"A lot you care," Randy said.

"Huh?"

"You're the one who told him. Again. You told him again."

Randy was right, of course. I'd told Pinehurst about seeing him with Mrs. McInnerny. Just like I'd told Pinehurst about seeing him with Christine. I'd seen him with both of the victims. Reported it to the police. It was a little much.

But totally irrelevant.

"Don't be silly," I said. "No one thinks you did it. No one suspects you of either crime. It's just you happen to be the last person to see Mrs. McInnerny alive. Usually that's suspicious to a cop, but not in this case, because he's already made an arrest. Yes, you're important, but as a witness, not a suspect. Don't you understand?"

"Sure, I understand. They let that woman out of jail. The woman who killed Christine. And what does she do, she kills someone else. Is that supposed to make me happy, that it wasn't me? Well, guess what? This is not big news. I *knew* it wasn't me."

"What if it wasn't her?"

"What?"

"What if it wasn't her, either? What if the woman happens to be innocent?"

"You trying to pin this on me?"

"Not at all. I'm trying to keep you out of it. But if the case against Florence blows up, the police will pick on you. I'd like to head that off. I promised your mother. Besides, the person who did this should pay. The police think they know who did it. They're not going to look any further. I am. So I put it to you. Do you want the killer caught?"

"Don't be silly."

"That's not silly. You might have reasons to want the killer to get away."

"Oh, yeah? Why would I want that?"

"What if it was someone you knew?"

"It isn't."

"Are you sure?"

"Yes, of course."

"Then you must want the killer caught."

Randy refused to dignify that with an answer.

"If you do, help me."

He didn't answer that either. I let it lay there, waited him out. After a while he said, "How?"

"Tell me about Mrs. McInnerny. When she called on you last night, what did she want?"

"What do you think?"

"Yes, I know. You and Christine. I don't care about that. I mean aside from that. Did she mention anything else?"

"Like what?"

"You tell me. What did she ask about?"

"Nothing," Randy said.

But his eyes shifted.

I shook my head. "Randy, you're no good at this. Every time you lie, I can tell. And if I can tell, the police can tell. Did you lie to Chief Pinehurst when he asked you?"

Randy looked away, refused to answer. I could see him set his jaw.

"Right. You didn't tell him anything. Because he didn't ask you. He asked you about Christine Cobb. And that's what you told him. Mrs. McInnerny wanted to know about Christine Cobb.

273

So that's all you talked about. With Pinehurst, I mean. The other subject never came up.

"And you weren't going to bring it up, were you?" I smiled, lobbed it out there. "It's hard to talk to a policeman about drugs."

Bingo.

Bull's-eye.

Randy's eyes widened, and his mouth fell open. He turned and stared at me as if I were some weirdo psychic who could read his mind.

"She asked you about drugs, didn't she? Specifically, she asked you about cocaine. That must have freaked you out, particularly if you've ever done any."

Randy's lip quivered. His eyes blinked rapidly. "Who are you?" he said.

"And there," I said, "is another indication of your being poor at this. You *know* who I am. Asking that question is the same as saying, 'How did you know that?' Which confirms that it's true. But, to answer your question—the one you didn't ask—Mrs. McInnerny was a snoop. She found out cocaine was involved in the case. But she didn't know whose cocaine. So she was asking around. That's why she asked you. Not that she had anything to go on. But that's why she asked about drugs. Maybe even asked about Delmar Hobart."

He frowned. "Who?"

I raised my finger. "Now, there's where it's good to be bad. I can tell from your reaction you've never heard the name."

"What are you talking about?"

"I'm trying to get your story. It would be easier if you just told it. You wanna fill me in?"

Randy looked away, set his jaw again. "I have nothing to say."

Maybe not, but it didn't matter. He'd already confirmed what I wanted to know. Mrs. McInnerny had asked him about drugs. Mrs. McInnerny had listened in on the phone line.

I walked Prince back to the inn. I didn't run into anyone on the way. I took him upstairs, put him back in his room.

When I came out, I looked over at Lars' door. Felicity Frog smiled back at me, she of the long eyelashes. She seemed to be batting them at me. Enticing me. Luring me in,

I resisted manfully. Which wasn't easy. Had Mrs. McInnerny been up here last night? Somehow followed the trail to Lars? Or had she, as Pinehurst assumed, followed the trail to Florence?

I stood there, the passkey clutched in my hand.

Then, like a good boy, I walked down the stairs and returned the key to the front desk.

Louise wasn't there, so I went behind the desk and hung the passkey on its hook.

I stood there a moment, looked around. There was the Xerox machine, where Lucy had presumably made the copies. And there was the register, where Jean or Joan had snuck a peek and found out Lars and Christine weren't married, not that hard to do with the front desk so seldom manned.

I looked around some more. In the corner was a tall plastic wastebasket, from the top of which protruded the handles of several golf clubs. I walked over, looked in. Discovered it was putters and golf balls for the putting green.

Why not? That was just the sort of mindless activity I needed to clear my head. I took a putter and ball and went outside.

The putting green was next to the swimming pool. It wasn't that big, but it was gently sloped, and featured nine numbered holes, the numbers on the nine metal flags sticking up from them. Which allowed me to play it as a nine-hole miniature golf course. I figured each hole was a par two. So par for nine holes was eighteen. That was the score I was trying to beat.

I am not a good golfer, but I had beginner's luck. My first putt, a twenty footer, stopped inches from the hole. I tapped it in for a two.

The second hole, about as long with a sharp break to the left, I ran the ball three and a half feet by, and sank the return putt.

The third hole, maybe fifteen feet with a slight break to the right, I started the ball wide to the left and watched it curl neatly into the cup.

Unbelievable. I had done the first three holes in five strokes. One under par. With that kind of a start, I was on my way to a record round.

I fished the ball out of the hole, lined up my putt on four. Took back my putter.

A ball rolled across the hole. Just as I swung. Whether it was that or the high-pitched giggle that accompanied it, I couldn't quite say, but for a moment I was completely unnerved. My hands tensed on the putter, my arms jerked forward, and I nearly lost my balance. The ball, struck with far more force than I'd intended, shot by the hole and rolled right off the green into a clump of tall grass.

So much for my record round.

I turned my gaze from the hopeless lie to the one who had caused it.

Smiling up at me was the six-year-old girl. That figured. First she rained on my Red Sox, then she ruined my golf.

Not only that, from the look on her face, she had finally concluded I wasn't the enemy. I had become, instead, another grown-up she felt free to annoy.

"Hi," she said. She couldn't have been more chipper if she'd been auditioning for *Sesame Street*.

I took a breath, smiled, and said, "Hi."

She giggled, pointed at my ball. "You missed."

I smiled, ruefully. "Yes, I believe I did."

I looked around for the girl's parents, but didn't see them. I couldn't help wondering what they were thinking, letting her out alone like this. After all, there'd been two murders at the inn. For all they knew, I could be the killer.

The girl didn't seem to think so. In her mind I had somehow made the transition from loathsome stranger to her best friend. "I bet I can get closer than you can," she said.

I didn't doubt it. Her ball had rolled a good twenty feet by the hole, but it was still on the green. If one were making odds, she would have been an overwhelming favorite.

Not that she really meant to play. With another giggle, she ran across the green to her ball, and then, wielding her putter like a hockey stick, dribbled it toward the hole with a series of short swings, pushes, and pokes. With a final squeal of delight, she stopped it next to the hole and tapped it in.

Had it been possible to count her strokes, they probably would have numbered around nine or ten.

Which was still likely to beat me.

With another squeal of delight, the girl grabbed the metal flag and pulled it up, flipping her ball out of the hole. She rammed the flag back in the hole, looked up, smiled, and declared, "My name's Margie."

"Margie?"

"Yes. What's your name?"

"Stanley."

She burst into hysterical laughter. Then waggled her finger at me. "No. What's your *real* name?"

"Stanley."

She burst into laughter again.

It was somewhat disconcerting. As a stand-up comedian, I had never played to a better audience. Still, I was not that happy with the punch line.

"What's your name?" she demanded.

"George Washington," I told her.

Her face twisted into a happy pout. "No, it's not," she said.

"It's not?"

"No."

"What is it?"

"Stanley."

I don't know why it wasn't funny when she said it.

"Stanley?" I said.

She laughed hysterically.

Maybe it was my delivery.

When she stopped laughing, I said, "Stanley," again.

And she started again.

I don't know how long we might have kept it up. I, for one, found it more promising than attempting to hit my golf ball. But after a while she looked at me and said, "I feel sorry for the man. Do you feel sorry for the man?"

If the little girl, who I had to remind myself was named Margie—I almost couldn't remember, having repeated Stanley so many times—really felt sorry for the man, you would not have known it from her face. Still, I was willing to give her the benefit of the doubt.

"Yes," I said. "I feel sorry for the man."

"Me too. It's so sad. He lost his wife."

I nodded. A forgivable euphemism, I suppose, for a six-year-old. Lost his wife, as if Mrs. McInnerny had somehow been mislaid, instead of been stabbed in the heart with a carving knife.

"Yes," I said. "Poor Mr. McInnerny."

She wrinkled up her nose. "Who?"

"Mr. McInnerny. You were saying it was sad about his wife."

"No, I wasn't."

I almost said, "Yes, you were." I stopped myself. Just because you're dealing with a child, doesn't mean you have to get into a childish argument.

"You weren't talking about Mr. McInnerny?" I said.

"No, not him," she said. Then added, as if in complete explanation, "He's old."

If Mr. McInnerny was old, I wondered what that made me.

"Who were you talking about?" I said.

"The *young* man. I was talking about the young man."

Oh. Lars Heinrick. I wondered if she just assumed he was married, or if her parents had told her that to account for Lars and Christine living together. In any event, if she was feeling bad about it, it seemed kinder to disillusion her.

"If you mean Lars Heinrick," I said, "she wasn't his wife. They weren't married."

"Yes, they were," she said.

She seemed quite positive. So her parents must have told her. I can't say I approved of the practice, lying to children in an effort to make things easier to comprehend. It occurred to me male-female relationships were hard enough for the young to understand without an underlying layer of deceit.

"Oh," I said. "Is that what your parents told you?"

"No."

"So how do you know they're married?"

"I just know."

So. The other possibility. The six-year-old mind simply decides something is true.

"So," I said, "no one told you that?"

"Yes, they did."

"Oh, is that right? Someone told you Lars and Christine were married?"

"Uh-huh."

"Oh?" I said. "And who told you that?"

"She did."

THIRTY-THREE

PINEHURST WASN'T CONVINCED. No surprise there. Chief Pinehurst was *never* convinced.

Which was totally frustrating. He had started off with a completely open mind. Then he'd arrested Florence. And his mind had closed. It would admit no information other than that relating to her guilt.

"You're not listening," I told him.

"I'm listening," Pinehurst said. "I'm just not hearing anything."

"Oh, no? Randy confirms Mrs. McInnerny was asking about drugs."

"So you say."

"Ask him yourself."

"I most certainly will. Not that it will prove anything."

"Oh, no? It proves she heard the phone call."

"So what?"

"So what? How can you say so what? She overheard the phone call, found out about the drugs. She was asking Randy about the drugs. Trying to find out whose they were. And the next thing you know she gets killed. Wouldn't that make the person who owned the drugs a likely suspect?"

"The case is not about drugs. That's a tangent. It's coincidental. The woman may have been asking about drugs, but you and I both know she was investigating a murder."

I took a breath. "Yes, of course. She was investigating a murder. And when she started asking about drugs, it got her killed."

"That has yet to be proved."

I exhaled sharply. "Fine. Will you at least concede it can be shown by inference?"

Pinehurst pushed back his chair, got up from his desk. "I don't know why we wind up arguing about these petty issues."

"Going somewhere, Chief?"

"I need a cup of coffee. Couldn't you use a cup of coffee?"

"I suppose it couldn't hurt."

I followed Pinehurst into the pantry. The coffeemaker was still on, heating the remnants in the pot. Pinehurst took two cups, divided the coffee. It poured like mud. I added milk and sugar. Pinehurst took his black.

"How is it?" he said.

"Dreadful."

He took a sip, nodded. "Yeah. Pretty bad. But better than nothing."

He switched off the coffeemaker, and we carried the coffee back to his desk.

"Now," I said, "we've stalled and made coffee, had a chance to think it over. Would you care to consider the information I've brought you?"

Pinehurst took a sip and grimaced. I wasn't sure if it was the coffee or what I said. "I've thought over what you've brought me.

282

I continue to think over what you have brought me. I assure you I will not discard it. It just happens to be relatively minor in the general scheme of things."

"Lars Heinrick and Christine Cobb were married."

"According to a six-year-old girl."

"Here again, Chief, this is something that could be checked."

"And I assure you I will. It just doesn't mean as much as you think it does."

"Oh, no? You have a secret marriage. One they carefully refrained from telling anyone about. Even after her death. Does Lars Heinrick pine for his murdered wife? No. He keeps up the pretense of merely being the boyfriend."

"Oh, but he doesn't. If you'll recall, he refused to answer questions. Withdrew his cooperation. He never denied they were married. The subject never came up."

"He never brought it up, and never would. Not until someone else got hooked for the murder. Then he would quietly assert his rights.

"What rights?"

"To inherit her estate."

"What estate?"

"Again, I have no idea. But you could find out."

"Anything else you'd like me to find out?"

"Yes. How much money did the McInnernys have? Does Mr. McInnerny inherit under his wife's will? And did he have an outside interest?"

"Are you serious?"

"Absolutely." I held up my finger. "We have two separate but interrelated crimes. Your present theory is the same person committed both."

"Isn't yours?"

"I'm trying to keep an open mind. But, assuming that theory, that one person committed both, you have two suspects looming larger than the rest. Lars Heinrick and Johnny McInnerny."

Pinehurst winced. "Oh, please."

I put up my hands. "Yes, yes. I understand, Florence is your chief suspect. But, aside from that, you've got Johnny and Lars. In which case, possibility number one is Lars Heinrick kills Christine Cobb, and to cover it up, he has to silence a snooping Mrs. McInnerny.

"Possibility number two, Johnny McInnerny is the killer, the killing of Mrs. McInnerny is the main crime, and the killing of Christine Cobb is merely a ploy to divert suspicion from himself."

"Oh, for goodness' sakes."

"You don't like that?"

"Like it? Your theory is the man kills a woman he never met?"

"Exactly. In order to draw suspicion from himself. Suppose Christine Cobb hadn't died. Then Mrs. McInnerny is killed. Who is the chief suspect? Johnny McInnerny, cut and dried. No doubt about it. On the other hand, if he kills Christine Cobb first, what a master stroke. Now he can kill his wife, and no one will suspect him at all. Which is exactly what's happened. Not only do you not suspect him, you ridicule the suggestion."

"And for good reason," Pinehurst said. "*Arsenic and Old Lace.* Johnny McInnerny never left the movie. According to your wife. He returned with her and found the body. He has a perfect alibi for the crime."

"Yes, and isn't that suspicious?"

"I beg your pardon?"

"When a suspect has a perfect alibi, doesn't that raise a red flag? Like maybe he *meant* to have a perfect alibi?"

"Whether he meant to or not, the fact is he does. You can't get away from that."

"Oh, no? I'm thinking of another movie. *Strangers on a Train.*"

Pinehurst's eyes widened. "Are you saying . . . ?"

"Suppose Johnny McInnerny and Lars Heinrick have a pact. You do my murder, I'll do yours. Johnny McInnerny poisons Christine Cobb. Lars Heinrick stabs Mrs. McInnerny."

Pinehurst stared at me. Blinked twice. Then shook his head. "No, it doesn't work."

"Why not?"

"Johnny McInnerny has an alibi for killing his wife. Lars Heinrick doesn't. If your theory was right, he would. Christine Cobb would have been killed in a way he could not possibly have done it. Because otherwise there is no point."

"So what if Johnny McInnerny was inept?"

Pinehurst rubbed his forehead, put up his hands. "Stop, stop, stop. Good lord. Do you have any idea how convoluted this is? How far you are stretching things, to try to make your theory hold water? The two men have a pact to kill each other's wives, so as to give each other alibis. Johnny McInnerny kills Christine Cobb, but is so stupid he *fails* to give Lars Heinrick an alibi. Lars Heinrick, being a man of his word, feels morally obligated to kill Mrs. McInnerny, even though the murder of Christine Cobb has been bungled to such a degree he might as well have done it himself."

"I admit it's not the best theory in the world."

"No kidding. Particularly since I have the killer dead to rights." Pinehurst took a sip of coffee, grimaced. "Not to put too fine a point on it, but all of these theories are somewhat irrelevant, since they happen to ignore the person who actually committed the crime. Can you give me any theory, any theory at all, to account for the fact that Christine Cobb had an affair with Florence's husband and broke up her marriage, after which Florence followed Christine Cobb to New Hampshire, registered at the same inn, and dogged her footsteps everywhere she went? You got any explanation for that?"

"Sure."

THIRTY-FOUR

PINEHURST LOOKED AROUND the dining room. "Is that everybody?"

Sad Sack referred to a list, nodded yes.

"Good," Pinehurst said. "Then let us begin."

We were once again back in our original positions where we had been sitting on the night of the murder of Christine Cobb.

With a few exceptions.

Mrs. McInnerny, of course, was no longer with us. Johnny McInnerny sat alone.

And the dinner crowd was not included. That is, those who were not staying at the inn.

That left:

Lars Heinrick.

Jean and Joan.

The two businessmen who had turned out to be brothers.

The family with the little girl.

And Alice and me.

Florence was not at our table. She sat at another table with her attorney, a rather sour-looking man in a brown suit, who gave the impression he was not at all happy to be there. Indeed, I gathered he was a divorce lawyer, and found the criminal practice somewhat distasteful.

Florence wasn't in handcuffs, which was something of a concession. She'd arrived in handcuffs, but was being allowed to sit at a table without them. Her lawyer had argued for the right.

At another table sat Louise, Randy, and the chef. I realized it was the first time I'd ever seen them together. They did not look like a harmonious family unit.

Randy looked aggrieved, among other things. Those included cocky, arrogant, sulky, sullen, insolent, and on edge. In short, your typical teenager. I had to remind myself he was actually a young man in his twenties.

His mother was a picture of concern. Louise looked as if her world was crashing down on her. Whatever relief she must have felt at learning Florence was free when Mrs. McInnerny was killed, and had been arrested for the crime, had apparently been undone when Pinehurst had called and instructed her to assemble everyone in the dining room at five o'clock. Canceling dinner was surely the least of her worries.

Evidently, she had done so at the last moment. The chef, sitting on the other side of Randy, was still wearing his apron. At least he had taken off his hat. His hair was brown, flecked with gray, and was quite full. For the first time I could see a resemblance to his son.

The two waitresses sat together. The young one looked somewhat nervous, but Lucy looked positively miffed. I wondered if that was due to missing out on the possibility of selling recipes at dinner, or if it was the defensive look of someone who expected to be accused. In any event, her expression recalled my first impression of her, my concentration-camp-commandant assessment.

As for the rest, Jean and Joan seemed positively thrilled; the two businessmen who might be brothers seemed slightly bored; and the mother and father seemed concerned for and protective of the six-year-old girl, who looked as bright-eyed and bushy-tailed as if she were on line for a ride at Disney World.

Johnny McInnerny and Lars Heinrick sat in their respective seats, Johnny at his table, and Lars in the booth. They looked dull, vague, numb, as if they could not believe this thing that had happened to them.

And then there was Alice, sweet Alice, sick this morning, recovered this afternoon, or at least feigning recovery, bundling up in sweater and slacks, clutching a box of tissues, and venturing stoically forth, despite sniffles and sneezes and a fever of 102. She sat at the table, watery-eyed, sweating, determined not to miss a thing.

Pinehurst took a breath, looked around the dining room, and said, "I'd like to go over this one more time."

There were audible groans.

"Yes, I know," Pinehurst said. "It would seem as if we've been over the ground enough. And yet, each day there are new developments, new matters that come to our attention. Matters that must be addressed.

"We are all aware of what happened last night. Mrs. McInnerny was killed. Florence Baker was arrested for the crime." He held up one finger. "However, this must not prejudice us. There is in this country a system of justice that maintains that a person is considered innocent until proven guilty. Which is why she is with us today, sitting here among us."

"Is she out on bail?" Louise demanded.

If Pinehurst was annoyed by the interruption, he didn't show it. He considered a moment, then said, "Actually, she is not. Since we are here to share information, I suppose I should tell you. In point of fact, bail was asked for and denied in this case. The judge who had previously granted bail ordered it revoked. In light of the subsequent crime."

Pinehurst put up his hand. "But that's a side issue. Florence is here today because I asked that she be here. She is here with her attorney's consent, and in his presence. So that she may hear some of the things that we are going to hear."

"Are you going to make a statement?" Louise said.

"No, I am not. As the arresting officer in the case, I feel it would be inappropriate for me to do so at this time. For that reason, I am going to turn the floor over to another type of investigator. That is, Mr. Stanley Hastings, a private detective from New York, who has been looking into the matter. Mr. Hastings?"

All eyes turned to our table.

Alice sneezed.

I handed her the box of tissues. She pulled out two and blew her nose.

I got up, walked to where Pinehurst was standing. He gave way, sat at an empty table. I stood there, surveyed the room.

I felt a sudden, overpowering urge to say, "Let's go over this one more time." I stifled it.

"Thanks for your attention. I am, as Chief Pinehurst said, a private detective. I have no official standing in this case. What I am about to tell you does not bind anyone to anything. I am merely presenting some facts and/or theories for your consideration. In an effort to clear up the crime. Or, rather, crimes.

"Let us take them one at a time. To begin with, the murder of Christine Cobb. By now, you are all aware of the background. Christine Cobb had an affair with Florence Baker's husband, who subsequently divorced her. Florence became embittered, fixated on revenge. Followed Christine Cobb on vacation, observed her in the company of a young man."

I turned, gestured to Lars in the booth. "Lars Heinrick. Young, handsome, romantic. In every way, they are the perfect couple.

"She spies on the young couple, and what does she see?" I raised one finger. "Christine Cobb does it again. She leaves the young man to run after another."

I gestured to Randy.

"As far as Florence is concerned, this is the last straw. She has brought poison with her. She uses it."

I paused, looked around the room.

"At least that is how the police construct the case. And how do they construct the second one? Mrs. McInnerny was interested in the crime. As are we all. But she was interested enough to do something about it. She began her own amateur detective work. She had learned of the affair between Randy and Christine Cobb. She questioned him about it last night. Visited him at approximately eight-fifteen, when almost everybody else was in the movie. She called on him in his room behind the kitchen."

I pointed at the boy. "Now, Randy had been admonished many times not to be rude to the guests. Just how well he took that to heart remains to be seen. The fact is, he gave Mrs. McInnerny no satisfaction and got rid of her as quickly as possible.

"Then sometime between eight-fifteen and ten o'clock, Mrs. McInnerny was killed. And we can narrow that down a bit more. Because I returned to my room at nine-thirty. And I heard nothing. And the walls in East Pond are paper-thin. Not only would I have heard the murder, I would have heard Mrs. McInnerny return to her room. So she *had* to have been killed before that.

"What is the police theory of the case? Florence, released from jail, returns to the inn. She encounters Mrs. McInnerny, who has just been rebuffed by the busboy, Randy. Mrs. McInnerny accosts Florence, springs on her some fact she has managed to dig up with her detective work.

"In all likelihood, Mrs. McInnerny did not know how devastating this information was. But Florence did. She hears it, and panics. She swears Mrs. McInnerny to silence. She tells her that though the facts look black, she can explain everything. In fact, she has evidence. She can *prove* she's not guilty. If Mrs. McInnerny will just give her the benefit of the doubt, she will show it to her. She will bring it to her room.

"So, Mrs. McInnerny goes to her room and waits. But Florence doesn't go to get the evidence, she goes to the kitchen to get the carving knife. She goes to Mrs. McInnerny's room, stabs her, rushes back to her room to get Prince, and takes him out, so if anyone asks her what she was doing at the time of the murder, she can say she was walking the dog. Her only mistake is leaving the gloves she wore to commit the crime in her room."

I paused, spread my arms. "Is there any problem with this police theory of the case? Anything about it that doesn't quite seem right?"

After a few moments, I said, "No, there is not. It's a perfectly logical interpretation of the facts. It could have happened just that way.

"So, the thing we have to ask ourselves now is, is there any *other* logical explanation. Anything else that might have happened. Or, in legal terms, can these facts be explained away by any reasonable hypothesis other than that of guilt? Or, more simply, could anyone else have committed the crimes?

"In order to consider that, we have to throw in a few more facts."

I looked around the room. "I assume you are all familiar with Agatha Christie? Even if you haven't read the books. You've heard of her Belgian detective Hercule Poirot, and Miss Marple, the little old lady who solves crimes in a small English village. Well, in one of Miss Marple's books she finds a clue at Somerset House." I looked around at utterly blank faces. "Yes, I know, it means nothing to you. But in England, that is where the marriage records are kept.

"Which brings us to fact number one. Lars Heinrick and Christine Cobb were married."

I looked over to see the sheer astonishment on the faces of Jean and Joan.

"That's right. I know you all made the assumption that they were not, as they had registered under both of their names. But, in point of fact, they were man and wife.

"Does this change things? Well, yes, it does, if you throw in fact number two. Christine Cobb had some money. Which Lars now stands to inherit. Money is always a motive for murder."

I glanced over at Lars. His face betrayed nothing. If I'd been playing poker with him, I wouldn't have known whether to raise or fold.

"Does that mean he did it? Not necessarily. But it certainly gives him a motive."

I turned to the other side of the room.

"Just as it gives Johnny McInnerny."

Mr. McInnerny, on the other hand, was transparent as glass. His face, already a picture of grief, twisted into one of horror and surprise. He gawked at me, as if unable to believe I'd said such a thing.

"I'm sorry if that upsets you, Mr. McInnerny. But it happens to be a fact. You and your wife had some money. With her death, it now comes to you."

I turned back to the room at large.

"But would he kill for it? And, if so, why would he also kill Christine? Because that is the situation here. We have two crimes. And the first question is, are they separate, or are they connected?

"That is the easiest question to answer. They are connected. Why? Because if they were separate, it would defy the laws of logic, the law of averages, and the name of reason. For the murders to be unrelated is just too fantastic to be considered.

"There is one small possibility I would grant. That the one murder was *inspired* by the other. For instance, Lars Heinrick kills his wife, Johnny McInnerny says, 'That's a good idea,' and does the same.

I put up my hands. "I am not saying that happened. I am using it as an example. But I believe it is one we can discard. It is my personal opinion the same person killed both women.

"So, let us look at our potential killers. First off, Lars Heinrick. Because his wife died first. It is what the police would call the primary crime.

"The first question is, could Lars Heinrick have committed it?"

I spread my arms.

"Absolutely. He was sitting in the booth with Christine. During the course of dinner he drops the poison in her glass. He leaves the dining room before she drinks it, does not return until he hears the screams. As far as murders go, it's easy as pie. In terms of opportunity, clearly Lars Heinrick had the best.

"Next best would be the busboy, Randy."

Louise sprang to her feet. "Now see here, I'm not going to let you accuse my son."

I put up my hands. "No one's accusing anyone of anything. I am merely laying out facts. Some of them will involve your son, just as others will involve other people. Could we all take that for granted? I am going to lay out facts involving several people in this room. There is no reason for us to take offense each time someone's name is mentioned."

Louise sat back down.

"Now, as I was saying, the person with the next best opportunity is Randy, who served them the drinks. He could easily have put the poison in the glass. Why he would *want* to is hard to comprehend, unless you are willing to grant the youthful obsessive love of the if-I-can't-have-her-no-one-can mentality."

Since both Randy and Louise seemed on the verge of springing up, I went on quickly.

"But I am not claiming that happened. I am presenting all these theories for what they're worth. Granted, some of them are not worth much.

"Where was I? Oh, yes. Who had opportunities to poison the glass? Well, the next best would be Florence. She had an opportunity to poison the glass when she left the dining room to walk the dog. What gives her a good opportunity is the timing. She left the dining room after Lars Heinrick went out. At a time when Christine Cobb would have been alone in the booth. So no one but Christine would know that she stopped there.

"Also—and this is an important point that I happen to know because she was sitting at my table—she left the table just as Mr. and Mrs. McInnerny stopped to talk to us. When the McInnernys stopped by our table, she excused herself to walk the dog."

I raised my finger. "Why is that important? It is important because the McInnernys were a distraction. To Alice and me. Ordinarily, when a person gets up and leaves your table, you would watch them go. At least to some extent. And look where our table is."

I pointed to our table, where Alice was blowing her nose. She looked out from under the tissue with pink eyes, like a little white mouse.

"If you get up from our table and go out the door, you walk by the booth. But you reach it rather quickly. It's actually quite close. So, without the distraction of the McInnernys, either Alice or I would have been likely to notice if she'd stopped at the booth. By carefully timing her exit, Florence is able to insure that that does not happen. She stops by the booth when the only witness to see her there will shortly be dead."

I raised one finger. "And what of Johnny McInnerny? Did *he* have an opportunity to poison the drink? Remember, he came in with his wife, he came in late, and he came directly to my table. This was after the drinks had been served, and after Lars Heinrick had already left. Johnny McInnerny is at my table, with his wife, talking to Alice and me, just as Florence is leaving to walk the dog."

I pointed. "After which, Louise escorts him to a table on the other side of the room. But could he, at any time, have stopped by the booth?"

I paused, looked all around the room.

Smiled.

"I can see the answer on all of your faces. You . . . don't . . . know. Not one of you can tell me whether Johnny McInnerny had an opportunity to go to the booth. And why is that? Because you never once considered him a suspect. Ever. Not until the murder of his wife. That is the first thing that involves him in any way in the crimes. Johnny McInnerny is a perfectly ordinary middle-aged man that there is no particular reason to notice at all."

I looked at him. "No offense meant, Mr. McInnerny, but you are not memorable. Not like a Lars Heinrick, who is a young, handsome man traveling with a drop-dead gorgeous woman whom everyone notices at once. So, for that reason, and that reason alone, you could get up from your table, walk over to the booth, tell Christine Cobb some innocuous fact about some hiking trail or other, drop poison in her glass, and no one would particularly notice.

"So the answer is yes, Johnny McInnerny could have committed the crime. Why would he do so?" I smiled. "Well, I explained this to Chief Pinehurst, and I can't say he liked it. But, of course, he thinks he has his killer in jail. If Johnny McInnerny planned to kill his wife, if that was the point all along, if he were to simply do so he would be the number-one suspect. But if he kills someone else first, someone he has absolutely nothing to do with—and the police investigation has shown that there is no connection whatsoever between Johnny McInnerny and Christine Cobb—well, if he can make the murder of his wife look like it's tied in to the murder of this other woman, then no one in the world will seriously suspect he did it."

I looked around the room. "Pretty clever, huh? When you think about it, it is an absolutely brilliant crime."

I paused. Frowned. "There is only one problem. Johnny McInnerny was at the movie *Arsenic and Old Lace*. And he never left. That fact is verified by several of you, including my wife."

I tried to avoid looking at Alice, though I could see several heads swiveling in her direction.

"So, Johnny McInnerny would seem to have a perfect alibi for the murder. So does that mean he couldn't have done it?" I smiled. "Well, not if my reading of crime fiction is any guide. The person with the perfect alibi is always suspect. For, while an innocent man may have an alibi, a guilty man usually goes out of his way to see he has one. So the very fact that Johnny McInnerny's alibi is so good is in itself suspicious."

I turned, pointed to the booth. "On the other hand, Lars Heinrick has no alibi at all. He was alone in his room. While almost everyone else was in the movie. Could he have left his room and killed Mrs. McInnerny? Absolutely. Particularly if she came and found him. We know she was snooping around about the crime. She had already called on Randy. Suppose she calls on Lars? Now we have the same scenario as with Florence. Mrs. McInnerny drops some information that alerts Lars to the fact she knows he committed the crime. Lars arranges to meet her in her room, goes to the kitchen, gets the carving knife, and kills her. No problem at all. Piece of cake.

"And, of course, Randy was not at the movie. Randy was in his room. Mrs. McInnerny called on him there at eight-fifteen. By his own admission, he is the last person to see Mrs. McInnerny alive. And no one can vouch for *his* whereabouts. He says he sent her away. He could also have accompanied her up to her room, and killed her."

I held up my hand. "And, thank you, Louise, I don't need you to point out that he didn't. I am merely saying he *could*. And he, of all people, would have had access to the knife.

"As would his father and mother. Neither of whom were at the movie. Either of whom could have taken the knife. Indeed, who would have had more access than the chef? As to motive, a parent will often kill to protect a child. Either one of them could have struck Mrs. McInnerny down if they saw her as a threat to their son.

"And here again we have the exception that proves the rule. I said there had to be one killer. Well, yes and no. If the killer was their son—if Randy killed Christine Cobb—well, they could kill to cover up that fact."

I spread my arms. "Well, you see, we suddenly have several suspects. Can we narrow it down? Let's go at it from another angle. Let's see who could have taken the knife."

I turned, pointed to another table. "I'm going to ask you, Lucy, if you saw it there when you went to the kitchen during the time you were gone from the movie?"

Lucy's eyes widened, and her face drained of color. "I . . . I . . ." she sputtered.

"There are many witnesses to the fact you left the movie. At approximately the time Mrs. McInnerny was killed. It becomes very important whether you saw that knife."

Lucy had regained her composure. Her face was hard. "Are you accusing me of this crime?"

"Not at all. You certainly had the opportunity. But your motive's a little thin. Even if Mrs. McInnerny had accosted you in the kitchen and wanted to know what you were doing, when all you doing was copying a recipe, well, I can't see you killing her over that."

Murmurs of "recipe" could be heard around the room.

I smiled. "I see that rings a bell. I gather some of you are aware of Lucy's sideline." I turned back to Lucy. "But so what? Even if she caught you at it, it wasn't as if she could turn you in." I smiled again, gestured to the chef. "Particularly since your employer knew you were doing it. There was nothing illegal about it. A chef has every right to sell his recipes, even if his manner of doing so is somewhat bizarre."

The murmurs this time featured both surprise and grumbling. I avoided looking at Alice.

"But that's a side issue. The point is, did you see the knife?"

Lucy's jaw had been set, but now her face showed her dismay. "No. I didn't notice."

"That's a shame, but I didn't really expect you did. And, of course, if you had seen anyone you would have said so. I take it you did not?"

"No."

"Then we must move on. One more fact is known. At the time of her death, Mrs. McInnerny was inquiring about drugs. She asked Randy about them. Specifically, she asked about cocaine. I know that's news to most of you, but it is also a significant fact.

"Oh, one more significant fact. The bloody gloves. The evidence against Florence includes a pair of bloody gloves that were found in her room. This, I must say, is the one thing that most strongly convinced me of her innocence. I don't care how stupid a murderer is, they do not leave the bloody gloves in their room.

"On the other hand, the murderer is happy to leave the bloody gloves in someone else's room. Could someone have planted the gloves in Florence's room? Absolutely. There's a passkey hanging on a hook behind the front desk. All the murderer had to do was take the passkey, open Florence's door, and plant the gloves. I happen to know this key opens Florence's door because while she was in jail I used it in order to walk her dog.

"And that's another thing. The dog. Florence got out of jail, came home, and went right out to walk Prince.

"And that's when the murderer planted the gloves. That's the only time the murderer could have planted the gloves. Because the murderer couldn't have done it while the dog was there.

"So. A picture is beginning to take shape. The murder had something to do with money. Something to do with drugs. The murderer was connected in some way to at least one of the two victims. And the crimes are related.

"Do we have a suspect? Yes. Unfortunately, we have several. The first one we must set aside. That would be Florence. I admit the evidence against her is grim. Her husband had an affair with Christine Cobb. She came to New Hampshire, registered at the inn, and appeared to dog Christine Cobb's footsteps until her death. Is there an explanation for her behavior other than guilt?"

I paused, looked around. "Unfortunately, we do not know. And the reason we do not know is because Florence has not told us. Nor has Florence told the police. Nor has Florence told her lawyer."

I paused, let that sink in. "And why not?"

I shrugged. "Because, point of fact, Florence doesn't know. Florence's biggest problem in defending herself is the fact that she is totally ignorant of all aspects of the crime. So we must take her for a moment and set her aside.

"So, what are we left with? Of the remaining suspects, we have three. Lars Heinrick. Johnny McInnerny. And Randy Winthrop. Is there any way to choose among them? Actually, there is not. Any one of them might have done it. And while we can raise inferences through deductive reasoning, there is nothing that can be proved."

I paused, looked around the dining room.

"So how can we know who did it?"

I smiled.

"Actually, it's rather easy."

I paused again, then spoke softly.

"We have a witness."

I waited for the reaction, the murmur of whispers through the room.

I smiled again.

"That's right. Ironic, isn't it? Here we drive ourselves crazy trying to develop theories of the case, and all the time there is an eyewitness. No need for guesswork, we can solve the crime.

"I'm going to solve it now. To do so, we need a lineup. That's how identifications are made. The suspect is picked out of a lineup."

I went to an unoccupied table, took three chairs, placed them in a row in the front of the room.

"I realize in a police lineup there's usually six. In our case there are only three. Randy, come here."

Randy looked up, sullen and unwilling. I walked over to his table.

"You want the killer caught, Randy? Help me out here."

Louise looked about to protest, but her husband said quietly, "Do it, Randy."

Randy looked at his father. Then got up, followed me over to the chairs. I sat him in the one on the left, then went and got Johnny McInnerny. He didn't protest, just followed me blindly to the front of the room. I sat him in the chair in the middle.

I walked over to the booth. "Come on, Lars," I said.

I took his arm, helped him out of the booth. Guided him over to the chairs, sat him in the one on the right.

"And there you have it," I said. "Our three suspects, all in a row. Your basic lineup.

"And now the witness."

I went through the swinging door into the kitchen.

I returned a minute later with Max the cat. I cradled him in my arms, stroking him, keeping him calm, a tough job, with so many people around.

"Here's your witness," I said. "Max the cat. Max lives in the kitchen, but he also hangs out in East Pond. He was there last

301

night, and he saw the murder. He saw the killing, and he was absolutely traumatized by it. I'm trying to calm him down. I'm going to ask you all to be very quiet and not scare him. But the fact is, Max saw the murderer, and Max is going to identify him now."

I looked around. Everyone in the dining room was staring at me as if I'd lost my mind. I ignored them, talked to the cat.

"Are you ready, Max? Here we go."

I set Max on the floor in front of the three chairs.

No one moved. You could have heard a pin drop.

Max looked toward Randy.

Then toward Johnny McInnerny.

Then toward Lars.

He lashed his tail back and forth. Licked his lips.

Looked at Randy again.

Then his head swiveled around. His body followed. He padded over to Lars, dropped his hindquarters, and suddenly sprang into his lap, landing with his full weight, and digging in with his claws.

Lars sprang to his feet, hurling the cat to the floor. He glared at me, his face contorted with rage.

"You devil!" he cried. "How did you get it?"

I smiled.

A quote from Agatha Christie.

Perfect.

THIRTY-FIVE

"I CAN'T THANK you enough," Louise said.

"Don't be silly."

We were sitting on the porch of the Blue Frog Ponds. There we were, at long last, the owner and I having the dreaded bed-and-breakfast conversation. Though at least it didn't seem to be running to "how we came to buy the inn."

"It's not silly," Louise said. "I mean, look what happened. The police made a mistake. Arrested the wrong person. What if she'd gone to trial, and the case had fallen apart. And the evidence had gotten mixed up, and nothing was ever proved. All his life, there would have been a stigma on my boy."

"I'm glad there's not, but I don't think anyone ever seriously suspected him."

"It doesn't matter. There'd be talk. There still will. Particularly if they can't convict that young man."

"I think they can. Of course, I don't want to talk out of turn."

Jean and Joan came out on the porch.

"Oh, good, you're up," the thinner one said. A mental cross-reference reminded me that would be Jean. "We're checking out this morning, but we have to know. Is it over? Did he confess?"

I shrugged. "You know as much as I do. I haven't heard a word since they took him away."

"And you," Joan said, accusingly. "We looked for you last night, and you were gone."

"I'm sorry. I had to take care of my wife."

Which was true. While the police were taking Lars into custody, I had bundled Alice off to bed. Which was one of the reasons Pinehurst and I hadn't spoken.

"Oh, how is she?" Jean asked.

"Much better, thanks. Twenty-four-hour bug." I jerked my thumb. "She's calling the camp now, trying to see how our son is doing."

Jean and Joan sat down at the table.

"So, tell us," Jean said. "What's the story? How did you know it was Lars?"

"Because it wasn't Florence."

Joan made a face. "Don't be like that, or I'll strangle you. Tell us how you knew."

"I would rather not be strangled, but that happens to be the answer. Florence looked guilty. Florence had the motive and the opportunity. Her husband had an affair with Christine Cobb, and she followed her here and dogged her footsteps. Those are facts that you could not get away from. If Florence is not guilty, how could they possibly be true?"

I shrugged. "They could only be true if they were carefully engineered by someone else. In which case, there was only one person that someone else could be.

"Forget Florence for a minute, and think about what really happened. Lars Heinrick is an unscrupulous young man who wants money. So he marries a young woman and kills her for it. A perfectly simple crime. Of course, I don't know if it was that premeditated. He might have married her, and then decided to kill her, or he might have been planning on doing it all along. I would assume the latter, since he kept the marriage a secret. And this secret was a major factor in obscuring his motive. Not that it wouldn't have come out eventually, but, in the meantime, their ignorance of this made it all too easy for the police to develop a case against a different suspect."

"What's that got to do with Florence?" Joan said.

"I'm getting there. But it's important to understand the background. Lars Heinrick has married Christine Cobb. She has money. He wants it. His problem is how to kill her without suspicion attaching itself to him. The concealed marriage is a step in that direction. As I say, it will give the police time to suspect someone else. He has to make sure that happens. How does he do that? He frames them.

"And how does that work? Let's go back to the original problem. Christine Cobb is a attractive young woman who happens to be a bit of a flirt."

Jean snorted. "That's one way of describing her."

"Right," I said. "Some people would say she was downright promiscuous. At any rate, she's had her share of affairs, some with married men. Lars pokes around, finds a case of one man she's had an affair with who subsequently divorced his wife. That wife is Florence Baker. So Lars proceeds to find out what he can about her. Which is probably not that hard. Christine Cobb knew Florence's husband. She met him somehow. So they must have had some acquaintances in common. Through them, Lars learns about Florence Baker. Keeps tabs on her, to see what she's going to do. And what does he learn? He learns she's going on vacation in New Hampshire. He finds out where and when, and makes a reservation for the same day at the same bed-and-breakfast."

"It's an inn," Louise said.

"Of course," I said. I was glad Alice was still on the phone. "Anyway, he books a vacation at the Blue Frog Ponds. On the day in question, he leaves early, to be sure he checks in *ahead* of Florence. So it will look as if she followed him there."

I held up one finger. "Here we have a flaw in his plan, and one that will come back to haunt him. He had a reservation. And so did she. So it's not like she followed him up here. The rooms were booked in advance."

"Right," Joan said. "So how could that work?"

"The only way would be if she found out where he was going, and then made a reservation there. But in point of fact, her reservation was made first. Now, granted, it *could* have happened that way. She could have learned where Lars and Christine were *planning* to go, and made a reservation at that place before they did. But that's pretty thin. It's not the type of argument I'd be happy to make. And I'm sure Lars' attorney will not be particularly pleased, either.

"On the other hand, thin as it is, it probably would have been sufficient to convict Florence. Since everything else damning was in place, or seemed to be. As long as you take the facts at face value, here's Florence following the woman around who had the affair with her husband. It's hard to see beyond it.

"Anyway, that's what Lars did. That's why he wound up at Champney Falls." I smiled. "Here again, we overlook the obvious. Florence got there first. When Alice and I went to Champney Falls, Lars and Christine passed us on the way up. When we got to the top, Florence was there eating lunch with her dog. Obviously, she'd gone up ahead of them. The police explain it away—she overheard them at breakfast saying that where they were going, so she simply went there first.

"Actually, it was the other way around."

Louise frowned. "What do you mean?"

306

"Actually, it was Lars who overheard Florence saying she was climbing Champney Falls and arranged to go there too."

"How do you know he didn't just follow her there?" Joan said.

"Because Christine isn't in on it. *She* doesn't know Lars is following Florence. Lars can't get in the car with her and say, 'Let's follow the woman with the dog.' He has to say, 'Hey, I've got an idea, let's go to Champney Falls.' And if Christine isn't ready to go when Florence leaves, he has no reasonable explanation for hurrying her. Not that he can tell her. Which is why he gets there after Florence, much as he would prefer to have gotten there before."

A police car pulled up, and Chief Pinehurst got out. As he came up on the porch the women all began talking at once.

"What happened?"

"Is it over?"

"Did he do it?"

"Did he confess?"

Pinehurst put up his hands. "Please, please," he said. "I'll tell you all about it, but not so fast. I don't suppose I could get a cup of coffee?"

Jean and Joan looked at him in total exasperation, but Louise said, "Anything you want, Chief," and went in the front door.

Pinehurst pulled up a chair, sat down at the table, and deflected any questions until Louise returned. As he accepted the coffee and took a sip, it occurred to me the case was ending just as it had begun, with Pinehurst stalling and dragging things out.

"So," he said, "in point of fact, Lars Heinrick has not confessed, nor do I expect him to. But that shouldn't concern us, because we should have no problem building a case."

"How?" Louise said.

"Very much along the lines Mr. Hastings suggested. If this happened the way he laid it out—and there is every reason to believe that it did—then corroboration will not be hard to find. If Lars Heinrick made inquiries about Florence, learned of her vacation, and arranged to be here, too, that can undoubtedly be shown."

"Have you uncovered anything?" Jean said.

"Not yet, but we're just getting started. The point is, if the solution is correct, the evidence must be there."

"But you have nothing to go on?" Joan said.

"Did I say that?" Pinehurst said. "Not at all. I merely said we had not yet run down those particular leads. But as far as having nothing to go on—while Lars Heinrick hasn't confessed, Delmar Hobart has."

The name meant nothing to Louise, but Jean and Joan perked right up.

"Delmar Hobart!"

"The hiker!"

"You mean he was in on it?"

"Not the actual crime," Pinehurst said. "But he was certainly a factor. You see, Delmar Hobart was Lars Heinrick's drug connection."

Jean and Joan's eyes were wide.

"I knew it!" Jean said. "I knew there was something wrong with him."

"And we're the ones who nailed him!" Joan said.

"That's true," Pinehurst said. "Your information did help."

Joan looked positively flattered, but I could see Jean's mind going.

"Wait a minute, wait a minute," Jean said. "If Hobart was the drug connection, and Mrs. McInnerny was asking about drugs . . ." She turned to me accusingly. "And if Mrs. McInnerny overheard your phone call. The one where you learned his name . . ."

Chief Pinehurst bailed me out. "You're right," he said. "That's how she knew. I told Mr. Hastings we'd identified Delmar Hobart as a drug dealer. But I asked him to withhold the fact. You mustn't blame him for not sharing the information. At the time, there was no reason to believe it had anything to do with the case."

Pinehurst turned to me. "However, Mr. Hastings, let me fill you in. When I arrested Lars Heinrick last night, he had a vial on him, which proved to contain cocaine. On the basis of that information, we questioned Delmar Hobart. Who, as I say, has confessed. I'm sure one of the *reasons* he's confessed is we happened to catch him with a considerable quantity of drugs, but the fact is, the man is cooperating. And, according to him, Lars Heinrick purchased cocaine on several occasions. Including the afternoon at Champney Falls."

"So that's what he was doing there," Jean said.

"Absolutely. And his statement tends to corroborate our theory that Lars was following Florence around. According to Delmar Hobart, Lars Heinrick had him come to Champney Falls because he had to be there, and could not wait for him at the inn, even as much as half an hour. Why? Because he was following Florence."

Pinehurst shrugged. "Granted, Delmar Hobart doesn't know that. But it raises the inference, and, taken with everything else, it is corroboration."

"But is it enough to convict?" Louise said. "If he gets off, people will always wonder."

"I can't promise you what a jury will do. But the evidence will be there. Even if a jury fails to find him guilty beyond a reasonable doubt, there will be no doubt in the eyes of the public. That I can promise you."

Florence came around the side of the building with Prince on a leash. Jean and Joan sprang up and ran over to her, ostensibly to offer support, but more likely to relate their thrilling tale of following a drug dealer. Talking animatedly, the three women followed Prince across the lawn.

"Well, I'll be off," Pinehurst said. He gulped the last of his coffee, set down the cup. Gave me a meaningful look. "Just wanted to let you know about the cocaine."

I got it. I had without him underlining it, but it was nice to have the confirmation. Lars' connection with drugs would be established by the vial he was carrying when he was arrested. The cocaine I'd pilfered from his room would disappear.

I watched with satisfaction as Pinehurst got in his car and drove off. No, he hadn't really had to come by this morning. But it was nice to hear him go over it one more time.

Johnny McInnerny appeared, lugging two suitcases from the direction of East Pond. He plodded down to the parking lot, opened his trunk, put them in his car. He slammed the trunk, came back up to the porch.

"I'm checking out," he said to Louise. "Is there anything I need to do?"

"No, just give me the keys."

Johnny passed them over. Like the suitcases, there were two. A sobering fact.

I got up, extended my hand. "Good-bye, Johnny. I'm sorry about anything I may have said last night. About considering you a suspect. It wasn't meant to hurt you, just to fool Lars."

"I know," Johnny said. "You had to get him. I'm glad you did."

He shook my hand, nodded to Louise, turned and plodded off, climbed into his car, and drove away.

Moments later the door banged, and Alice came out on the porch.

"I got through to the camp," she said. "According to his counselor, Tommie hasn't asked for us once. He's signed up for tennis, basketball, baseball, soccer, archery, and riflery, his only problem is choosing, because he wants to do everything. He couldn't talk to me because right now he's in a canoe in the middle of the lake.

He supposedly wrote to us yesterday, so we should have a letter by the time we get home."

"We'd better write to him," I said. "But what can we say? I can't imagine explaining all this in a letter."

"You're leaving today?" Louise said.

I nodded. "As soon as we get packed. I'll stop by the front desk and settle the bill."

I half expected her to say, "Don't bother, there is no charge." I was glad when she didn't. I would have found it embarrassing. And I preferred to remember her as a shrewd businesswoman.

Max came around the corner of the porch, his tail held high. He marched up to us, dropped his hindquarters, sprang up onto the table.

"Max," Louise said, "behave yourself. And in front of the guests."

I reached up, scratched him under the chin.

"No, I think he's entitled. After all, he solved the murder."

"Yes, he did," Louise said. She smiled. "I can still see the look on Lars Heinrick's face."

So could I. Shock, terror, disbelief. The man had to be terribly disconcerted to suddenly have a cat accusing him of a crime.

Which Max wasn't, of course. He hadn't really been in East Pond, and even if he had witnessed the murder, I doubt if he could have picked out the killer.

No, Max was merely doing his Stupid Pet Trick. When I'd helped Lars out of the booth and led him to his chair I'd slipped a sardine in his jacket pocket.

Max had done the rest.

He was a truly remarkable cat. I scratched him behind his ears, and he lay down on the table and began purring.

The chef came out on the porch. Charlie. Louise's husband. As always, he seemed somewhat stiff and unnatural out of the kitchen. He smiled when he saw me petting the cat.

"I understand you're leaving," he said. "I just wanted to say thank you."

"I think it's Max that deserves the thanks," I said. "You might give him a special treat for dinner."

"I will," he said. "But anyway, I'm no good at this sort of thing, but . . . well, here."

He pulled something from behind his back. A large manilla envelope. But he didn't hand it to me, he handed it to Alice.

"Me?" she said. "What is this?"

Alice undid the clasp, opened the envelope. Pulled out a sheaf of papers. As she looked at the top one, her face lit up with a smile.

I leaned across the table to look, though I didn't need to. Alice's reaction told me what they were.

Recipes.